Praise for *The Chosen and the Beautiful*

"Vo's prose is beautifully supple, and the novel shines when she reads *Gatsby* against the grain. . . . A sumptuous, decadent read."
—*The New York Times*

"I love it with the passion of a thousand burning hearts. . . . From the old bones of an American classic, Vo has conjured up something magically alive."
—*The Washington Post*

"A wholly enthralling vision of the American Dream . . . Raise a glass to Nghi Vo, whose name on the spine of a book seems to mean that whatever the pages within hold will be superlative."
—NPR

"Vo has crafted a retelling that, in many ways, surpasses the original. . . . Astonishingly crafted, with luscious prose and appeal for both fans of the original and those who always felt *The Great Gatsby* missed the mark."
—*Kirkus Reviews* (starred review)

"Extraordinary . . . Vo's immersive prose never ceases to captivate. The *Gatsby*-related details and hints of magic will keep readers spellbound from start to finish."
—*Publishers Weekly* (starred review)

"An utterly captivating series of speakeasies, backseat trysts, parties both grand and intimate, and romances both magical and mundane . . . Vo is a remarkable writer whose talent for reviving Fitzgerald's style of prose is reminiscent of Susanna Clarke channeling Jane Austen in *Jonathan Strange & Mr. Norrell*."
—*BookPage* (starred review)

D1051655

"*The Chosen and the Beautiful* finds Jordan fighting for her place in this *Gatsby*-adjacent world as an outsider, a plight that Vo illuminates in heartbreaking specificity." —*Time*

"Beautifully written and magical, *The Chosen and the Beautiful* is destined to become a classic." —*Ms.*

"Soaked in gin and dark magic, *The Chosen and the Beautiful* is one of 2021's must-read novels." —*Bustle*

"Vo creates an extraordinary, multilayered literary experience that both enriches and eclipses the overexposed original." —Shelf Awareness

"Nghi Vo has written us the adaptation of *The Great Gatsby* that we deserve: a sparkling novel of excess and overindulgence told from Jordan Baker's point of view." —*Book Riot*

"Turns Fitzgerald's American classic on its head to present a world recognizable in outline, but brought to new life in imaginative detail." —*The Daily Beast*

"A dazzling reckoning with the fragile and beguiling fantasies we conjure to make sense of the past . . . A mesmerizing, fearless unraveling of a text at the heart of the American literary canon." —*Ancillary Review of Books*

"*The Chosen and the Beautiful* is the perfect reinvention of the classic summer reading list standby." —*The Week*

"Vo's prose is lush and extraordinarily detailed, and so reminiscent of Fitzgerald's writing but somehow even more atmospheric and lyrical." —*The Nerd Daily*

"Offers up a lush glimpse of decadence and corruption, interrogating America's dark history through the eyes of a narrator it is impossible to forget."   —*New York Journal of Books*

"Stellar, captivating, and powerful."
        —Helene Wecker, author of *The Golem and the Jinni*

"A subversive, sexy, atmospheric, sweltering, gin-soaked, hell-haunted vision of Gatsby's New York, with prose that will pull you under."   —Alix E. Harrow, *New York Times* bestselling author of *The Once and Future Witches*

"Nghi Vo subverts and expands the possibilities of an American story, and magic is in the marrow of every sentence."
        —K-Ming Chang, author of *Bestiary* and a National Book Foundation 5 Under 35 Honoree

"Luxurious, thrilling, and sexy, Nghi Vo's debut novel dives into the world of *The Great Gatsby* and wears it like a second skin. A shape-shifter of a book that had me hypnotized from the first pages, *The Chosen and the Beautiful* brings new intensity to a story you thought you knew."   —Adrienne Celt, author of *Invitation to a Bonfire*

"Decadent. Visual. Imaginative. Genius. Not enough words to praise this page-turning novel of sorcery, infernal compacts, and enchanted elixirs in an altogether different 1920s New York."
        —P. Djèlí Clark, winner of the Alex, Locus, and Nebula Awards and author of *Ring Shout*

"A sumptuous novel that tangles with race, magic, sexuality, and class . . . It's bold to play in the realm of *The Great Gatsby*, and Vo's acerbic Jordan Baker is the perfect woman to do it."
        —Erika Swyler, author of *The Book of Speculation*

"This book is Gatsby the way it should have been written—dark, dazzling, and fantastical. . . . Vo has created a perfect response to Fitzgerald in tone, voice, and theme."

—R. F. Kuang, winner of the Astounding
Award and author of *The Poppy War*

"Crisp as paper and delirious as a fever dream, this is a redrawn Gatsby daubed in gold leaf and lip rouge and blood. Nghi Vo gives a freshly imagined Jordan Baker her due, while infusing her glittering New York with a bottomless magical menace that feels both excitingly new and cosmically true to Fitzgerald's original."

—Melissa Albert, *New York Times* bestselling
author of *The Hazel Wood*

"Nghi Vo's perfectly honed prose embodies the intoxicating, knife-sharp dazzle of cruel wealth and hollow people. This book is as sharp and strange as the taste of a licked silver spoon—it's breathtaking."

—Shelley Parker-Chan, author of *She Who Became the Sun*

"The prose is like a bite of caramel that rips out your teeth. It's seething, creamy. It has a bloody taste."

—Hannah Abigail Clarke, author of *The Scapegracers*

➣ ALSO BY NGHI VO ➢

Siren Queen

THE SINGING HILLS CYCLE

The Empress of Salt and Fortune
When the Tiger Came Down the Mountain
Into the Riverlands (forthcoming)

THE
CHOSEN
AND THE
BEAUTIFUL

NGHI VO

A TOM DOHERTY ASSOCIATES BOOK
NEW YORK

This is a work of fiction. All of the characters, organizations, and events portrayed in this novel are either products of the author's imagination or are used fictitiously.

THE CHOSEN AND THE BEAUTIFUL

Copyright © 2021 by Nghi Vo

All rights reserved.

Edited by Ruoxi Chen

A Tordotcom Book
Published by Tom Doherty Associates
120 Broadway
New York, NY 10271

www.tor.com

Tor® is a registered trademark of Macmillan Publishing Group, LLC.

The Library of Congress has cataloged the hardcover edition as follows:

Names: Vo, Nghi, author. | Fitzgerald, F. Scott (Francis Scott), 1896–1940.
　　Great Gatsby.
Title: The chosen and the beautiful / Nghi Vo.
Description: First edition. | New York : Tordotcom, 2021. | A Tom Doherty
　　Associates book.
Identifiers: LCCN 2021008744 (print) | LCCN 2021008745 (ebook) |
　　ISBN 9781250784780 (hardcover) | ISBN 9781250784797 (ebook)
Subjects: LCSH: Asian American women—Fiction. | Gays—Fiction. |
　　Nineteen twenties—Fiction. | GSAFD: Fantasy fiction. | Bildungsromans
Classification: LCC PS3622.O23 C48 2021 (print) | LCC PS3622.O23 (ebook) |
　　DDC 813/.6—dc23
LC record available at https://lccn.loc.gov/2021008744
LC ebook record available at https://lccn.loc.gov/2021008745

ISBN 978-1-250-82012-9 (trade paperback)

Our books may be purchased in bulk for promotional, educational, or business use.
Please contact your local bookseller or the Macmillan Corporate and Premium Sales
Department at 1-800-221-7945, extension 5442, or by email at
MacmillanSpecialMarkets@macmillan.com.

First Tordotcom Paperback Edition: 2022

for Shane

THE
CHOSEN
AND THE
BEAUTIFUL

CHAPTER ONE

The wind came into the house from the Sound, and it blew Daisy and me around her East Egg mansion like puffs of dandelion seeds, like foam, like a pair of young women in white dresses who had no cares to weigh them down.

It was only June, but summer already lay heavy on the ground, threatening to press us softly and heavily towards the parquet floors. We could not stand to go down to the water where the salt air was heavier still, and a long drive into the city felt like an offensive impossibility.

Instead, Daisy cracked open a small charm that she purchased on a whim in Cannes a few short years ago. The charm was made of baked clay in the shape of a woman, and when Daisy broke it to crumbling bits in her fingers, it released the basement smell of fresh kaolin clay mixed with something dark green and herbal. There was a gust of wind of a different kind, and then we were airborne, moving with languid grace along the high ceilings of her house and exclaiming at the strangeness and the secrets we found there. A single flick of our hands or feet sent us skimming through the air, at first adrift and then with surges of speed as we pushed away from the mantels and the columns.

We discovered a rather shocking miniature tableau of Leda and the swan above the bookshelves in the library, and we were so quiet over the heads of a pair of maids that we could flick back their starched white caps before they saw us and shrieked. In the nursery, while Pammy slept, we floated above her like slightly rumpled guardian angels. Daisy reached down to touch her daughter's face with a gentle finger, but when the little girl stirred, Daisy fled, dragging me out of the room with her.

The summer rendered the manor mute that day, and we haunted its silence, moving from place to place before finding ourselves in one of the guest rooms close to the one I was using. The pale green damask wallpaper gave the room a forested look, absorbing everything but the pleasure of being so weightless. I floated on my back, running my fingers along the peak of the window casement and gazing at the bay beyond the glass. It was impossible to imagine how cold the water might be, but I tried, half-napping with my legs dangling down at the knee and one hand resting lightly on my chest. I was half asleep when Daisy spoke up.

"Oh look, Jordan. Do you think it's my color?"

She plucked an enamel pot the size of a Liberty half-dollar from the top of the wardrobe. Lazily curious, I floated closer.

"Who did that belong to?" I wondered out loud.

"What does it matter?" she responded gaily, and she was right, because she and Tom had bought the whole of the manor—from the sprawling grounds down to the beach, the stables, the ghosts, and the history—all for their own.

She opened the enameled pot to reveal a mixture of wax and pigment, a dusty dark no-color until she warmed it with a few hard rubs of her thumb. She spread some of it neatly on first her lower lip and then her upper, and then she hovered upside down over the vanity's mirror to examine her reflection. When I drifted nearer to see the deep rose on her lips, she drew me close and did mine as well.

"Look, we match," she said, tugging me down to gaze at my own face in the mirror, but of course we didn't. She had been a Louisville Fay, with a lineage as close to royalty as the United States would allow, and it showed in her dark blue eyes, her sleek black hair, and the generous width of her smiling mouth. For my part, I was nominally a Louisville Baker, a name with its own distinguished history, but it had always hung oddly on me, adopted from distant Tonkin and with a face that people variously guessed was Chinese, Japanese, Mexican, Venezuelan, or even Persian.

The lipstick looked old-fashioned on her, giving her an antique air, but it brought out the red in my skin, roses instead of tomato, more lively than not. Daisy murmured with pleasure over the difference, and she stuffed the little pot into my pocket, saying of course it was meant to be mine.

She paused with her hand on my hip, both of us hanging upside down in front of the mirror. It was one of Daisy's moments of intense stillness, rare when she was a girl and growing rarer. It gave her pretty face a slackness and an odd hollowness that suggested that anything might have come in to nest behind her eyes.

"I am glad you came when I called you," she said with a slight hiccup. "I don't know *what* I would have done if you hadn't."

"Been prostrate with grief and pined for me, I imagine," I said lightly, and she smiled with relief.

We both looked up when we heard the distant slam of the front door, and then, louder and more insistent, the boom of Tom's voice. There was a briefly startled look on Daisy's face, as if she had forgotten any world where we did not merely drift along the ceiling of her enormous house, and then she took my arm.

"Of course, that's right," she said, pulling me towards the door. "We've arranged to have my cousin to dinner tonight. Come along, my darling, I promise you will find him utterly delightful."

"Well, if you say so, I'm sure he is."

It was Daisy's avocation, setting up her friends and making connections between the members of the right set. She was somewhat famous for it, leaving plenty of variously happy couples and namesake babies in her wake. I had always been a bit of a failure for her, something that I decided was more amusing

than anything else. I did well enough for myself, after all, back
in Louisville and now in the years since I had come to New York.

We came back in the tall sun porch where we had started,
settling on the enormous couch at the center of the room. We
tamed our ruffled hair and smoothed down our dresses just
moments before Tom appeared in the doorway. He was followed,
with a touch of reluctance, by a rangy young man in shirtsleeves,
his jacket thrown over his arm and his quick dark eyes taking in
everything around him with interest.

He entered with an easy smile and a certain dislike for Tom,
which made me like him right away. He gave me a second look,
but didn't stare, and he came to kneel next to Daisy's end of the
couch, paying her the court she liked best. They spoke of the
time they'd passed in Chicago while I was allowed to do what *I*
liked best, which was to watch from a cool distance before I had
to chance an engagement. Tom hovered close by, finally tram-
pling their conversation with a question of Daisy's cousin's occu-
pation and by coincidence giving me his name: Nick Carraway
of the St. Paul Carraways, only son, war hero, and apparently at
loose ends after coming back from overseas.

I remembered vaguely that I had heard of some kind of trouble between him and a girl from St. Paul, a Morgan or a Tulley,
something dishonorable, but you wouldn't know it by the way
he sat as if butter wouldn't melt in his mouth. He looked like a
polite man, though of course you can never tell.

I wondered that Tom couldn't seem to recognize the barbs in
Nick's words to him, barbs that made Daisy's eyes glint a little.
Acid under the good manners, and I liked that quite well. More
interesting by far than the war hero was someone with some
bite to him, and I thought that rather a lot of people might not
know that about Nick.

When he scored another point off Tom, making Daisy's husband snort and declaim, I sat up with a laugh.

"Absolutely!" I said in agreement, giving Nick permission to look at me fully. I smiled at him, levering myself off of the couch and letting him see a little more. I was in my low gray suede heels, giving me a soldier's jaunty carriage; when I rolled my shoulders back to ease the cramp that was forming there, I saw him lower his eyes briefly with a slight smile.

The butler entered with four tall glasses filled with something delicious, and at a murmured word from Daisy, he added two garnet red drops to each tumbler from a rock crystal vial.

"I'm in training," I said with a regretful sigh, but I took my glass anyway, sipping appreciatively. The cocktail was a good one—the Buchanans hadn't ever been ones to stint where it truly counted, and it was no different when it came to the demoniac. The ban on demon's blood had come down just four months before the one on alcohol, and now two years later the good vintages were disappearing from even the better clubs in Manhattan.

Daisy licked her lips like a pleased cat, and even Tom sipped his drink with a kind of somber respect for its quality. Nick drank more cautiously, and I remembered that the Middle West had crashed into Prohibition faster and more readily than the rest of us had. The demoniac was older and richer than what even Aunt Justine kept carefully locked away in the Park Avenue apartment we shared. It stung my lips and warmed my throat until I imagined myself breathing out flickers of candle flame. Legend said it could make tyrants from good men, but it only made me a little mean.

"Drink up," I told Nick. "This isn't St. Paul. You're in New York now, even if you do live in West Egg."

He blinked at me slowly, that slight smile still on his face.

"I do, though I hardly know anyone there."

"*I* do," I said. "And you must. You must know Gatsby."

"Gatsby? *What* Gatsby?" asked Daisy, blinking at me. Her eyes were dilated almost black and she had bitten some of the lipstick off of her lower lip. I was about to tease her for being no better with demon's blood than Nick was when dinner was announced.

Daisy came to take my arm, cutting me off from Nick and Tom as neatly as a sheepdog would, and when she leaned against me, I could smell the bitter almond and candied lemon scent of the demoniac on her breath.

"I need to talk to Nick. Alone, do you understand?" she said, her words hurried and slurred, and I stared at her. She sounded nearly drunk, slightly unsteady on her feet. She never drank to drunkenness that I knew of, save once. The darkness in her eyes and the slight unsteadiness in her step was for something else, and I hastily agreed.

Daisy was a fluttering nervy thing at dinner, snuffing out the candles distractedly as we ate only for the servants to relight them when she wasn't looking. Tom ignored her, but I could see Nick growing more uneasy, his eyes darting between Daisy and me as if thinking there was surely an explanation. There wasn't, any more than there was for anything else, and it was almost a relief when Nick made an innocent comment about civilization that sent Tom barking after one of his particular hobby horses. He shook his head hard, blowing air through his nostrils like one of his own prize polo ponies.

"Civilization's going to pieces," he told us all angrily. "Have you read *The Rise of the Colored Empires* by this man Goddard? It's a fine book, and everybody ought to read it. The idea is if we don't look out, the white race will be—will be utterly submerged. It's all scientific stuff; it's been proved."

"Tom's getting very profound," said Daisy solemnly. "He reads deep books with long words in them."

Nick looked back and forth between them as if he wasn't sure what to make of this, but he relaxed when I winked at him across the table, on the side Tom couldn't see.

"This fellow has worked out the whole thing," Tom said, stabbing a finger into the white tablecloth. "It's up to us, who are the dominant race, to watch out or these other races will have control of things."

"You've got to beat us down, of course," I said dryly, and Nick covered a laugh with his napkin.

Tom arched his neck, glaring at me suspiciously as if unsure what I might mean, and next to me Daisy giggled, just a little hysterical, though this was hardly anything new to us.

"The thing is, Jordan, we Nordics, we've produced all the things that go to make civilization—oh, science and art, and all that. That's what the Manchester Act wants to protect. Do you see?"

There were a dozen things I could have said to that, ranging in order from least cutting to downright murderous, but then the phone rang and the butler came to fetch Tom from the table. Tom went with a kind of confused irritation, and Daisy's mouth opened, and closed again.

Then she dammed up the coming disaster by turning the full force of her Fay blue eyes on Nick. I was used to them after years of acquaintance, but he certainly wasn't. He got a slightly dazed look as she leaned in closer to him. Her voice spiraled higher than it usually went, just a hair shy of shrill, shyer yet of sensible.

"I love to see you at my table, Nick. You remind me of a—of a rose, an absolute rose. Doesn't he?" Daisy turned to me with a flourishing hand gesture, a magician pulling a rose out of a soldier. "An absolute rose?"

He looked nothing like a rose, but I nodded anyway, watching Daisy warily. Her small hand was clenched into a fist next to her half-eaten fish, and I could see the little bruise on the knuckle, the one Tom had given her by grabbing her hand too hard just a day ago.

"Daisy . . ." I said, but she threw her napkin on the table and stalked after Tom without a single excuse, leaving Nick and me alone.

"So you mentioned my neighbor Gatsby," Nick started, but I held up my hand.

"Shush."

My spine and shoulders felt as stiff as wood, my ear strained like piano wire as I listened for something from the next room where the telephone was kept.

"What in the world is happening?" Nick asked, apparently bewildered. Perhaps things were not done like this in St. Paul, or perhaps he was better at playing the innocent than any debutante I had ever met. I didn't much care.

"What happens when a man's girlfriend calls for him while he's at dinner with his wife," I said shortly. "He might have the decency to keep from answering her at mealtimes, don't you think?"

Nick shut up.

Tom and Daisy returned, Tom like a storm cloud and Daisy with her hands fluttering like trapped songbirds. I studied her carefully as she came in. Her color was too high, but her hair hadn't been pulled out of its careful style, and there was no handprint on her face.

"Oh, it couldn't be helped," she cried, her eyes glossy and her cheeks pink. "And I looked outdoors for a minute, and it's very romantic outdoors. There's a bird on the lawn that I think must be a nightingale come over on the Cunard or White Star Line. He's singing away . . . It's romantic, isn't it, Tom?"

Tom muttered something in agreement and then something about his damned horses, and then the phone rang again. This time he stayed in the wreckage of dinner, face brick red and Daisy as bright and brittle as glass. I—and to his credit, Nick—tried to fill the rest of dinner with chatter about the people we both knew (many), and the things we had in common (fairly few).

The phone rang once more as we finished dessert, but then it was silent as we stood from the table. As Tom pointed Nick towards the stable, Daisy took my cool hand in her hot one.

"Remember," she hissed like an oracle from a Gothic, and I nodded.

"Have you seen that new piece from Edgar Wallace that was

meant to be in the *Post* today, Tom?" I asked. "I've not yet, and I was hoping to get to it before I need to sleep tonight."

He hadn't, of course, and we made our way to the library while Nick and Daisy went around to the wide front porch. He looked after them for a moment, and you could almost feel sorry for the baffled look on his face. One got the idea that at some point, something in his marriage had gotten away from him, but damned if he could say what, or if he should miss it, or if he missed it at all.

We settled down on either end of the long couch in the dim ruby light of the library lamps. We had done this a time or two. Daisy couldn't abide the short stories that Tom and I favored, and even the radio gave her a headache. Tom slumped on his end of the couch, and I sat up straight at mine, the *Saturday Evening Post* spread crisply on my lap. I had a good voice for reading out loud. My first tutors at the Willow Street house believed in recitation, and though my voice was higher and softer than Daisy's, it was steady.

I was through one story, and halfway through the next when Tom sighed.

"You're a good girl, Jordan. I'm glad Daisy has you. It's hard for her, with women, you know. She doesn't get on with them. You're different."

"I think she gets along with women just fine," I said, straight-faced.

"She thinks the world of you. So do I. And Nick, well. Dull sort, a bit, but that's a good thing in these irregular days. He's good-looking enough, isn't he?"

I allowed that he was, and Tom nodded as if the matter was decided.

"We'll see you settled before the end of the summer, see if we don't. You know, you're already older than Daisy when she and I tied the knot. Don't know what a pretty girl like you is waiting for, but I'm not a petty tyrant. You can afford to wait for a decent man, with your prospects. Daisy worries, but I know better. You're only waiting for a good match, the best, and what's the matter with that?"

I tried to keep myself from being touched, because it was easy sometimes, when it came to Tom. Brief moments of sympathy and absent-minded kindness did not make a good man, but Tom was also good-looking in a blocky, vital kind of way. Sometimes he forgot that I wasn't a Nordic like he was, and in that forgetting, he could be kind and thoughtful. There are women who will forgive a great deal for a moment of kindness from a handsome man, but Daisy and the other older girls who had taken me under their wings had taught me not to be one of them.

Nick and Daisy came in just as I was finished reading, and I stood as they did.

"Ten o'clock," I said. "Time for this good girl to go to bed."

"Jordan's going to play in the tournament tomorrow," explained Daisy, "over at Westchester."

Nick looked startled, and the penny finally dropped.

"Oh—you're Jordan *Baker*."

I smiled, because I was. He knew my face from the photographs and the sporting magazines. If he was in contact with his gossip-prone Louisville cousins (or more likely, if his mother or aunts were), he might know more than that. Well, I didn't care. It was up to him to decide what he might make of it.

"Wake me at eight, won't you?" I asked, squeezing Daisy's shoulder as I went by.

"If you'll get up," she said with a smile. She looked more normal, less desperate, and I nodded at Nick.

"I will. Good night, Mr. Carraway. See you anon."

"Of course you will," came Daisy's voice, following me up the stairs. "In fact I think I'll arrange a marriage. Come over often, Nick, and I'll sort of—oh—fling you together. You know—lock you up accidentally in linen closets and push you out to sea in a boat, and all that sort of thing."

"Good night," I called back, rolling my eyes. "I haven't heard a word."

As if I needed Daisy's help getting into the closet with a man who looked at me like Nick did. My history in closets was well established from Louisville, and in New York, with its wealth of cars, breakfast nooks, private balconies, and boathouses, I scarcely had to rely on them at all.

I fell asleep immediately, and didn't dream. Daisy woke me up two hours later. She climbed into bed with me as we used to do, and as I rolled over to make room, she curled against my side. The moonlight streamed into my room, silvering her hair and shadowing her eyes.

"Tom's asleep?" I asked groggily.

"Gone," she replied, but there was nothing in her voice that cared for him in the least. Gone, and unlooked for, she might have said. She was still, except for her fingers playing restlessly with the ribbon on my camisole.

"Well?" I asked finally, and her face crumpled.

"I couldn't," she said, her voice small. "Oh Jordan, I couldn't say anything at all, I couldn't make myself say it—"

She sobbed just once, utterly miserable in the way that only a person who is capable of being utterly happy can be, but it had been a long time since she could be utterly happy.

The thought of her happiness struck a chord, and *now* I remembered Jay Gatsby.

CHAPTER TWO

One lazy summer evening in 1910, Daisy Fay sneaked up the stairs during a dinner party to find me. She made it past the extra servants Mrs. Baker hired for the occasion, the squeaking floorboards, and the insubstantial ghost of Anabeth Baker in the hallway, and she didn't stop until she opened the door to my bedroom.

The house on Willow Street sold when I was thirty, and I went back one more time to see it. My room was untouched from the time I was a child, possibly from the time Eliza Baker, fatal fragile zealot, had slept under the lacy pink canopy and pored over her atlas of foreign places. The bed was always too large, soft like a peppermint marshmallow, and the furniture had a kind of bone-like dullness to it that the polished brass chasings could not alleviate. I was not sorry to see it all sold off in one job lot, destined for some other child to dread.

Mrs. Baker had gotten rid of Eliza's atlases before I arrived, so all I had to entertain me were edifying texts about good girls and boys, eating apples, playing in creeks, and obeying their parents. I found, however, that the paper in these books was satisfactorily thick, just begging for sharp scissor blades to sink into the beige card stock. Since no one but me ever looked in the books, I could cut them up as I pleased, starting from the back to make my vandalism less noticeable. Some pages I cut into tiny triangles to hide in the winter boots that sat at the back of my closet, and some I fringed like the dress of a cowgirl from the Old West show I had been taken to see just the year before.

Tonight I was cutting a careful halo around the head of the industrious little girl with the sewing basket when the door creaked open and Daisy peered in. I froze on my bed, scissors guiltily still, and she slipped in like water through a grate, shutting the door behind her.

"Well!" she said in her oddly husky voice. "So *you're* the heathen!"

I shoved the paper and scissors under my pillow, sitting up so my bare legs dangled over the edge of the bed. I wore a ribboned lawn nightgown, but Daisy was well turned out in a short dress of rustling mauve silk. Her neat black boots and dark stockings made me think of the fox kit I had seen in the backyard just a few nights before. Like the fox kit, she was utterly fearless, coming into my room, taking in it and me with an innocent avarice in her large blue eyes. That night she was ten years old, two years older than the age Eliza Baker had guessed I was, just my own age in truth, though it would be a long time before I found that out.

"I was hoping I might see you tonight," she continued. "Mother said that you were no different from the ones who wash our clothes, but you *are* different, aren't you? I can tell, you're not like them at all—you're something *else* . . ."

I wanted to put my hands over my ears to fend off her flood of words. Mrs. Baker was parsimonious with her speech, the judge even more so. I took my education at home with a tutor, and so I had never heard anything like Daisy's chatter before. More to stem her words than from any eagerness on my part, I answered her.

"I was saved from Tonkin," I told her. "Miss Eliza saved me. When I was little."

Her eyes went as large and round as saucers. I saw the white all around them and I thought of a horse running mad. She crossed the small space between us as familiarly as if it were her own room, snatching up my hand in hers. Her hand was hot and soft. She smelled just faintly of citrus, pepper, pine, and musk, her mother's Blenheim Bouquet dabbed modestly behind her well-formed ears. The scent made me pause before pushing her away, but in my imagination, it clung to me.

"Oh *darling*, you must tell me all about Tonkin! I was born in boring old Louisville, and I have never been anywhere at all! I've heard of Tonkin. Papa knows men who trade there, when the French let them, and it sounds *so* much more beautiful and elegant and fine than China. Tell me about it, please!"

"I was very young . . ." I said, but as the excitement drained from her eyes, I felt a surge of desperation, unformed and wordless but no less powerful. I clung more tightly to her hand. I did not want to be alone.

I remembered what Miss Eliza had said about Heaven, where there would be gold in the streets, but no one would care. She was unable to rise from her bed by then, but she whispered about Heaven as if she could see it just beyond the canopy of her bed, touch it if only she could sit up.

"It's gold," I blurted out. "The roofs and the walls and even the roads. At noon, we had to sleep because the sun made it shine so bright it might have blinded us."

"A city of gold?"

If there had been any doubt or animosity in her voice, I would have cried at having been caught in such a lie. I didn't remember Tonkin at all, or at least, I told myself I didn't, but I knew that it had certainly not been leafed with gold.

Instead, there was nothing but pure credulous excitement in her eyes, and she leaned in closer, coming to sit with me on the bed.

"Tell me more," she commanded, and so I did.

Despite being given nothing more than virtuous books to read, I was a child of ferocious imagination. As I told Daisy about flying men who chopped the heads off of screaming maidens, women who rode elephants, and two moons that rose up in the sky, I felt what dry earth must feel when it finally rains. She sat next to me, holding my hand absently and sometimes running her nails over the creases in my palm.

I finally ran out of breath when I told her about the great dancing lions, the ones the priests cut out of thick red paper, so intricate that as the scraps of paper fell away, you could make out round bulging eyes, gaping mouths, and every tight curl on the heavy mane. I paused long enough for Daisy to consider, and she reached under my pillow, drawing out my scissors and my mutilated picture book.

"Show me," she said, and I don't know why I didn't come up with an excuse. I didn't tell her that making a dancing lion was the province of priests, or that I was too tired, too small, or too young to do so.

Instead, I continued my lie, living moment by moment as her blue eyes settled their demanding weight on my hands. Soon, I would have to give it all up, but not yet, not while there existed a fragile bridge of pure trust and wonder between us.

I flipped to a fresh page in the middle of the book, where George and Jane caught fireflies for their sealed jar, and I started to cut. I knew that it would all be over soon, even at that age. I would pull a flimsy, unattractive lion from the paper, and Daisy would know me for the fraud I was.

Only somehow, that didn't happen.

Instead, as I roughed out the lion from the ingratiating smiles of George and Jane, my hands grew more sure, not less, and it seemed as if the light from my little reading lamp grew dimmer. I had seen a lion just once in my life, and it was a toothless and malevolent thing brought to town by a bedraggled circus. Two towns after the Louisville stop, it killed a child acrobat who had wandered too close, and I was deeply unsurprised. In my mind's eye, I saw manes that curled like wisps of steam and at the same time I saw a rufous shock of fur, bitten and half-bald. What I cut from the thick nubby paper was somewhere between the two, as were the four paws delicately tipped with sharp nails, the tail that curved over the beast's back, and the sinuous muscles of the lion's flanks and shoulders.

I was aware of Daisy's breath close to my ear, of the delicate ticking of the ormolu clock on the shelf, the distant chatter of the dinner party below. It all belonged to another country, because as I snipped around the lion's jaws, I could feel its hot breath against my hands. It was weighted with a kind of feline impatience and I cut faster, my cuts growing careless and at the same time more smooth. The blades slid through the paper, parting along some curve that I couldn't see but only felt instead. Once I was certain I had ruined it, but a long scrap curl fell from the figure, and the lion held its shape.

"Oh, how beautiful," Daisy cooed when I held the lion up for her approval.

If it was only that, it would have been enough. But of course, it wasn't.

Pinched between my thin fingers, the paper lion started to shiver as if in a breeze. It wiggled, it danced, and soon enough the four cut paws started to pedal in the air, churning for purchase before arching its rear legs up to scrape at my wrist. It was only paper and smaller than a kitten. It couldn't have hurt me, but the way it moved made me flinch back, certain I would turn my arm and see four thin scrapes all in a row.

Daisy uttered a surprised cry while I bit down on my tongue. We watched as the lion fluttered to the ground, landing with more weight than paper should have had. It hesitated for a moment as if confounded by life in paper as we were, and then it gathered its four paws underneath it, turning several times. Something shifted, and it was more than just card stock and a child's desperate urge to be adored. It was a memory of a murderous lion and a land far away, it was breath and resentment and longing. The hollows I had cut out so quickly were filling up with muscle and hair, and we watched with wonder until we saw that it was also growing.

"Jordan!" Daisy cried, clasping on to my arm. Her sharp nails dug hard into my bare shoulder, but I didn't know what to do any more than she did. We stared at the twisting thing uncoiling beneath our feet, and we could both feel its hot and rancid breath in our face, smell the blood of an acrobat child who had flown over the heads of thousands of people but never slept in a proper bed.

In a panic, I threw my scissors down onto it, and when that did nothing, I slammed the book it came from flat on top of it. That had an effect: it burst into greedy flames, a roar of denial and rage whooshing up from the ground, causing us both to shriek in surprise.

We were perched on my bed now, and I was hanging on to Daisy as if this weren't a mess entirely of my own making. I almost started crying but then Daisy reached over to my bedside table, where Thomasina left me a tall glass of water every night. She picked up the glass and to my eyes, she spilled the water almost by accident over the flames. The orange flames ebbed back down with a high and angry hiss, and dirty gray steam came up in pillowy clouds. Daisy and I had ended up holding hands tightly, our heads bent within inches of each other as we stared down at the smoldering mess that had been a walking, living paper lion.

"Sorry," I muttered, half-tearful, but she gave me a game grin.

"It's all right, it was just fabulous—"

Then the door burst open, Mrs. Baker and Daisy's mother in front with a half-dozen well-dressed adults behind. I reached for something, anything that might have made them believe it wasn't my fault, but Daisy was faster than I was.

She burst into loud shrieking tears, going from silent to a pained and tragic howl in less than a moment. Shoulder to shoulder, I could feel her shaking, and I realized with a kind of silent surprise that she was not faking at all.

There was a roar in the background, and then Mr. Fay was busting into my sugary-pink, smoky room like a bear into a bee-hive. He caught Daisy up in his arms, and she clung to him as tightly as he grabbed on to her. They murmured back and forth in a language I later learned was entirely their own, a cipher of shared blood and beauty, a remnant of some Victorian magery Mr. Fay had learned at Yale.

He bore the quaking Daisy from my room while Mrs. Baker bent down, putting fingers gingerly against the sodden mess of what had been my lion. My terror pulled back to reveal a surprising kind of grief—it had lived and now it was gone.

Mrs. Baker rose, wiping her fingers on one of my handker-chiefs lying by and giving me an impatient angry look. As I said before, she was a woman of few and stingy words. Those words would be thrown like sharp rocks at me in the morning, but for now, she only turned to her guests, shepherding them back to the relief of the sitting rooms and the good port.

Before she left, she turned off my bedside lamp with a hard click, and closed the door after, leaving me in a darkness that purred with fury, that smelled like soggy cotton and burned paper.

CHAPTER THREE

I do not like to make a habit of admitting my mistakes.

When I mentioned Gatsby in Daisy's own house, in front of her own husband, there was nothing in my mind that connected him with Lieutenant Jay Gatsby. That man was fresh out of Camp Taylor with a commission purchased with the very last of his money from Dan Cody and only one pair of decent shoes. The eager young lieutenant had a wondering hungry eye, and the beautiful man in the lavender suit pin-striped in gray had obviously never been hungry a day in his life.

They had the same pale eyes, the same generous and mobile mouth, the same way of carrying their weight as if it were nothing at all, and yet you would never think they were related, let alone the same man.

Of course, the young lieutenant from Camp Taylor still had his soul, and by 1922, Jay Gatsby of West Egg had no such thing.

It was only the year before when the society madcaps went about with a single nail painted slick black, the mark of someone with infernal dealings. It was so fashionable that Maybelline released Chat Noir, its deluxe black nail polish that promised a devilish long-lasting gleam. In the later part of 1921, it seemed as if half of Manhattan's twenty-five-and-under set must have made some kind of infernal pact or another. In 1922, the fad was mostly played out, but a little bit of tackiness was permitted in the very rich.

So Gatsby was a fabulously wealthy man with a harmless

affectation, or perhaps he actually was the one in a million who had sold his soul. No one knew, and that summer, absolutely no one cared when it seemed as if the legendary Canadian pipeline poured good whiskey straight from the solid gold taps of his French facsimile mansion. I was sick of the trend even before it showed up in *McClure's Magazine,* a sure sign that its time was done, but Gatsby wore it well.

At Gatsby's, the clock stood at just five shy of midnight the moment you arrived. Crossing from the main road through the gates of his world, a chill swirled around you, the stars came out, and a moon rose up out of the Sound. It was as round as a golden coin, and so close you could bite it. I had never seen a moon like that before. It was no Mercury dime New York moon, but a harvest moon brought all the way from the wheat fields of North Dakota to shine with sweet benevolence down on the chosen and the beautiful.

Everything was dripping with money and magic, to the point where no one questioned the light that flooded the house from the ballroom and dining rooms to the halls and secluded parlors. The light had a particularly honey-like quality, something like summer in a half-remembered garden, illuminating without glaring and so abundant that you always knew who you were kissing. Some of the guests exclaimed at the magic on display, but I heard the servants marveling at it as well and learned that it was all electricity, the entire house wired at enormous expense to come alive with the flick of a switch.

The lights may have been money, but there was no lack of magic either. In the main hall was a mahogany bar stretching longer than a Ziegfeld Follies kick line, and guests crowded around four and five deep before the brass rail for a taste of . . . well, what was your pleasure? Once I got a tiny scarlet glass filled with something murky white that tasted of cardamom, poppy seed, and honey, the last wine Cleopatra drank before her date with the asp, and Paul Townsend of the Boston Townsends got stinking drunk on something from the nomadic party of great Ubar. These were no dusty bottles salvaged from desert digs; they were fresh from the vintners and brewers themselves, for all that they were long gone dust.

The sky above Gatsby's parties was a deep blue, always clear and just barely garlanded with silky clouds to give it an air of mystery. Once, he had produced a troupe of aerial artistes who did their acts on invisible ladders far above our heads, giving them the appearance of true flight, their sequined costumes flashing tangerine, lemon, and lime from the lights beneath. As we watched, one young woman in chartreuse missed her grip and fell, plummeting towards the flagstones below. Out of the corner of my eye, I saw my friends cover their faces, but I couldn't look away. There was a flash of light the instant she would have struck the ground, and instead of a broken little body, a still-faced man in black held her safe in his arms. There was a stunned look on her face. Her eyes were studded with rhinestone-like tears, and I saw a dark pink mark, mottled blackberry, crawling to cover the side of her neck like a port-wine stain.

He set her down gravely on the ground, and her hand flew to the mark, feeling gingerly for the bones that assuredly had been broken and mended. He took her other hand, and they both bowed to rapturous applause.

"Death doesn't come to Gatsby's" went the rumor, and it might even have been true. Certainly ugliness didn't, and neither did morning or hangovers or hungers that could not be sated. Those things waited for us outside the gates, so whoever wanted to go home?

The first time I ever went to Gatsby's house, I went with Henry Conway's set. I knew his sister from the golfing club where we were both members, and after a match early in May, dinner at L'Aiglon, and drinks at Tatsby, the cry went up that of course we must go to Gatsby's in West Egg.

One girl, some cousin from Atlanta, squeaked that she didn't have an invitation, and Henry Conway gave her an affably sharp look.

"Look, darling, no one *needs* an invitation to go to one of Gatsby's parties. I don't think he's ever sent a single one out."

The girl from Atlanta bit her lip, getting a smudge of inexpertly applied lipstick on her small teeth.

"But then, how do we know we're wanted?"

I forgot who replied to her and how unkind they might have been when they did it, but just a few hours later, just five minutes until midnight, I saw her dancing madly under the harvest moon with some boy from Queens. Her eyes were dilated to bright black shoe buttons and her hands fluttered like sparrows caught on a silvery wire. She came out once or twice after that while I was still passing time with Henry and his crowd, but she disappeared soon after, back to Atlanta, probably, though of course there were the standard rumors of things far stranger.

She was right in the end, and we none of us were wanted, but you never would have guessed it then. The lights that draped the gardens twinkled as if Heaven had come down at Gatsby's command, and the fruit borne in the delicate domestic little orchard by the house was like nothing I ever had before, something smaller than an apple and darker than a plum. When I plucked one down from curiosity, it was so ripe that my fingers bruised it, and licking up the red juice made me dizzy and slightly delirious. For a moment, I saw among the twisted branches a figure that looked like my own, back against a twisted tree and pushing someone down to kneel in the moss, but then I spat and the image was gone.

There was really no need to go picking fruit at Gatsby's mansion. The food on the long white tables—baked ham glazed in sweet apricot, milky clam broth, delicately cut fruit that bloomed like flowers on their celadon platters—were so perfect that you thought it must have been magic rather than the machinery of more than four dozen waitstaff and caterers who made that kind of magic their business.

Gatsby never tried to hide the underpinnings of human work that aided in creating the wonder of his five before midnight world. It would have been gauche. It would have put him with the new money of Astoria, where every meal was whisked to the table by unseen hands and where every fire on the hearth was lit by a snap of the fingers. His servants were more than visible in their crisp black and white, more dignified, more sleekly dressed and more sober than his guests would ever be. For him, as in the hallowed halls of the elite from New York to Chicago to San Francisco, there would always be a human price for his luxury. Otherwise, I could see him musing, what was the point?

What Gatsby's parties were was *easy*. It felt as if every wish you had while within his domain might be granted, and the only rule was that you must be beautiful and witty and bright.

I went first with Henry's set, and then at the end of May with Coral Doughty. I liked going to Gatsby's, the drive along the bridge and through the warmth of the setting sun to emerge into the sweet coolness beyond his gates, but there were other things I liked just as well. There were séances held weekly at St. Regis, a circus of gargoyles in Soho, and of course the delightfully endless round of dinners and soirees to be had if you had some money and just a touch of charm. There was plenty to do that summer, and I had started taking over the odd social responsibility from Aunt Justine as well. She was in no way weakening, she said, but thought it important that I learn to handle my responsibilities as befit my place in her world. We both knew, of course, that my place in her world was tenuous at best and only growing more tenuous the older I became, but she acted as if she could wave that all away with the force of her personality and will.

I was busy, but nevertheless, Gatsby threw a good party, one where I could secret myself in the corner with someone, nursing a drink while they told me what was in their heart.

I was a little crazy after secrets that year. I liked collecting them, and though I seldom told, I did gloat. I was years from who I had been in Louisville, some of those scars healed over to give me a kind of hard polish that made me more mean but less vulnerable. The shades of Louisville were worn away to a few stories that I told to entertain and to disarm. When they asked where I was from, and when the first answer did not satisfy, I asked them where *they* were from; a question they weren't used to and a sincere look spilled all sorts of things between us.

One night in early June, I quickly realized that there were no secrets to be had from the undergrad with whom I had arrived. We were there with his older sister and her husband, and at first, their presence kept the undergrad from being too obnoxious. Then the music started, the first imported California starlet danced out onto the canvas that covered the garden green, and the taps opened. The sister and her husband had a taste for straight gin, and the undergrad was crossing the line from being obnoxious to becoming a serious incident. I sent him to fetch me something with a wedge of lime in it, and under the flickering, foolish lights and the strains of "Sweet Summer June," I slipped away.

I liked being alone in the crowd. It was something that I had grown to find comforting, and I kept a drink in my hand to fend off someone unwelcome bringing me one. There was a famous tenor bullied by his friends to standing on the edge of the fountain, and when he sang the first notes of Parama's solo in *L'Enfer d'Amélie*, the air before his lips shaped itself into sinuous twists of golden light. He sang, and the golden notes came down to dance over the head of a pretty man in a cheap suit. He was a hustler from Queens or from Brooklyn or someplace worse, but with the tenor's grace hanging over him, he was exalted into something else. I watched for a moment until the inevitable happened and someone pushed the tenor into the fountain. The notes went sodden and unhappy before dissipating altogether and then more people were jumping into the fountain, splashing the water as high as the head of the stone nymph who stood at the center.

I wove my way through the crowd, calling to the people I knew, nodding at the people I didn't know as if I did know them, and keeping an eye out for the man himself. By then I remembered him, but Daisy had gone into a funk after that dinner, as she did sometimes. She went quiet and absent from herself, smiling at me in a vague way, as if she were a ghost or I was. In the end, there was nothing for me to do but return to the city. I had not been out to see her since that day, and I thought there might be a chance that I wouldn't see her until the Fourth of July or after.

Still I wanted to look at Gatsby, sort out what kind of disguise he had created that had caused this change. I wanted, as my aunt might have said, to examine the lion's teeth, and of course the best way to do that was to stick my head in the lion's mouth.

So I was, in a lazy and undirected way, looking for Gatsby, and instead I found Nick.

Despite the slightly poleaxed look and the stammering introductions, he would not have stuck out at all if he had not kept asking if Gatsby were about. He learned better after the third or fourth time he asked, when people told him *of course* they had no business with Gatsby. It was one of those people who put the first drink in his hand, but Nick apparently didn't get the hint and only wandered away with it, drinking it faster than he should have.

Nick Carraway was twenty-nine that summer. He had been in the war and killed men, but there was something about the awkward angles of his body in his new white flannel suit, the lost look in his eyes that made me feel oddly soft towards him. I followed him through the crowd, almost at his elbow, eavesdropping as he sought first Gatsby, and then some sort of anchor that would stop him from drowning in the eddies and undertows of Gatsby's entertainments.

Finally, before he could actually embarrass himself—something he was working up to when he took a third cocktail—I dropped my drink behind the hedge and put myself on the stairs in his path. I knew he recognized me. There were a few foreigners in the place, someone's Chinese mistress, a pair of rather beautiful Italian brothers, and a wild gorgeous woman whose dark skin and curly hair proclaimed her an exotic of some kind or another, but I was the only one he had been introduced to.

I spared him the trouble of coming up with a reason to talk to me, instead plucking the drink from his hand. It was a bijou, vermouth and gin flavored with absinthe; a strange choice for Nick if it was a choice he had made at all.

"Thank you." I took a delicate sip. "I was hoping that someone would bring me something."

"I'll bring you anything you want," he said, and I tilted my head at him.

"You ought not say such things to me," I said gravely. "I might ask you for the moon, and what would you do then?"

"Get it for you, of course."

I laughed at that, because something in his voice meant it. He didn't sound like New York at all. The army and foreign travel had rumpled his broad flat northern vowels, but he was still marked out as different from the rest, more subtly than I was, but marked nonetheless. Even then, I knew it wasn't just the place of his birth that set him apart from the crowd, but I could not say what else it might be.

I was just thinking about suggesting we go to the garden maze or perhaps into one of the intimate little rooms in the house when a pair of girls in yellow came down the stairs towards us. I saw them too late to turn, and they came up to us, their cheeks glittering with a dusting of mica and petroleum jelly and their teeth set in identical smiles. I had no problem with Ada, but of course wherever she went May came along, and May was terrible.

"Hullo Jordan," May said sweetly. "So sorry about your match!"

I smiled, because anything else would have been a victory for her. I had lost in the finals, and I mentioned it to Nick, who nodded sympathetically.

"Do you remember us?" Ada said hopefully. "We met you here last month."

"I do remember you," I said. "You've dyed your hair since, haven't you?"

I felt Nick startle slightly. St. Paul still had a deep streak of Protestantism that would see makeup, let alone hair dye, as more than a little morally suspect. He looked closer at Ada, as if to see what degree of fakery he could find in her. He would have found none; Ada and May were on the chorus line at one of the better theaters, and part of their stipend was time at a decent salon.

They asked us to come sit with them, and because it was easier to sit for a few moments and leave than to say no, Nick offered me his arm and we came down the stairs to the veranda. Someone had fished the tenor out of the fountain, and now, drip-drying, he had someone else's plump and pretty wife on his knee as he burbled little amber notes for her. Behind him, still hopeful and a little pathetic, was the hustler from Queens or Brooklyn, but no one was paying any attention to him any longer.

At a table with the girls were three men whose names were deliberately obscured. One wore a black fingernail, but the chips in the finish told me it was only painted on. All three had the self-important air of men who I should know, but I didn't know any of them. They knew me of course, and after the usual pleasantries, I turned to Ada, who was, besides Nick, perhaps the most tolerable of the lot.

"Do you come to these parties often?" I asked. The group's eyes fell on her, allowing me to lay my hand gently over Nick's. There was a minuscule flinch, and then he went still, as if he were afraid my hand were a butterfly he might startle away.

"We were here last month and met you," she reminded me. "But I like to come. There are always so many wonderful people to talk to, so many things to see. Why, just a couple of weeks ago, someone brought a firespeaker from Borneo! She pulled the fire right from the torches and made them dance in wheels and whorls, big as anything. I barely noticed that a spark got on my dress and put a hole straight through the trim until later."

She paused, and then like a bride flourishing her wedding band, she brought out the rest.

"You know, *he* saw? He asked after my name and address, and three days later, a man came from Croirier's with a new evening gown for me!"

Something about fairy gifts and Trojan horses nibbled at the back of my head, something that Daisy's own mother had told us when she walked in on us at play one afternoon. Her eyes were red from crying, and the velvet dressing gown fell half off of her shoulders, and I thought from the way her voice shook that she knew something about the family name of Fay and unlooked-for gifts.

"Did you keep it?" I asked. I wouldn't have been so sanguine about taking gifts from someone like Gatsby, but she gave me an indignant look. Things were different where she came from, apparently, or perhaps she wasn't so very bright.

"Two hundred and sixty-five dollars, gas blue with lavender beads? Of course I did!"

"There's something funny about a fellow that'll do a thing like that," said May. "He doesn't want trouble with anybody."

"Who doesn't?"

Nick's sudden question reminded me of Daisy's *What Gatsby?* That moment, I felt, should have been edged with sable, marked for the disaster it would bring, but of course it wasn't, and I could say many similar things about other moments that were still to come.

May turned to Nick, triumphant under his polite regard.

"Gatsby. Somebody told me—"

She paused and obligingly we all leaned in.

"Somebody told me they thought he killed a man once."

A speculative thrill went through all of us. It was a brush with the underworld, the ones run by the Irish, the Italians, and the Jews in the city and the ones run by the pale-eyed, still-faced gentlemen who all seemed to style themselves princes and dukes of the far reaches of Hell. Both, went the rumor, came to Gatsby's parties, dressed in their best and hiding their natures under hats, gloves, and fine manners. Nick, likely the only one at the table who had actually killed someone, looked reluctantly intrigued. Ada shook her head.

"No, he was a spy during the war."

"For the Germans or the Americans?" asked one of the men I was meant to know.

She shook her head and pursed her lips. She pointed discreetly down, towards other masters, and I saw her other hand stole into her pocket where she was likely rubbing a saint's medal.

"He's no spy, he's one of them," said another man, giving us a significant look. "One of their princes, you know, or the son of such. It was everywhere in Morocco last year."

"No, he must be an American," insisted May. "He was in the American Army during the war. You look at him sometimes when he thinks nobody's looking at him. You can tell right away he's killed a man."

She and Ada shivered dramatically, and I stole a glance at Nick. His mouth was perhaps a trifle stern, but he didn't laugh at her statement. I noticed that our voices had lowered. It wasn't that we were afraid of being overheard, but rather because I wasn't the only one who liked secrets. There was never a secret like Gatsby, and even if he was a public sort of thing, it still intrigued.

Supper was served after that, and poor Nick ended up joining me and the group I had come with. The sister and her husband were drunk and disgustingly in love, and they only had eyes for each other. The undergrad had not been improved by drinking at all, and as the soup course went and the appetizer course arrived, Nick's responses were getting shorter and shorter, and my charming deflections were growing less charming and moving towards some kind of accident with the unused cheese fork.

"Great God, of *course* it doesn't open sideways!" Nick finally cried, and I took that as my hint to pull him away. The undergrad slumped back down with a muttered word I decided not to hear, and when Nick might have said more, I tucked my hand into his arm and started walking.

"Come on, this is getting too polite for me." When he hesitated, I offered, "We can go find Gatsby."

That brought him along.

"What are you looking for him for, anyway?" I asked.

"Well, he invited me. You know. Seemed polite to thank him."

"What? He never did! Show me."

He drew the invitation from his jacket, and I turned it over in my hands. It was good paper, deep red as if dipped in blood, with gold lettering sunk into the card stock. It felt heavy in my hand with all the weight of an imperial summons. It was real, and I doubted more than one or two had ever been printed.

"He *did* invite you," I said, handing it back. The uncertain look was back in his eyes. If he was meant to be the associate of a man who might be a prince in Hell or a German spy, I thought he rather needed to toughen up.

"I didn't think it was so strange," he muttered, just as we passed by a tall and gaunt man with pale eyes and still face talking with Anastasia Polari, the famous silent film beauty. Her eyes were as dark as holes burned in silver nitrate and as hungry as winter, and he held her hand in both of his. There seemed to be either more or less joints in his fingers than there should be. Nick stared, his footsteps slowing, and I pulled him forward, touching my fingertip to his lips.

"Shouldn't stare," I murmured, and he looked at me instead. Long eyelashes, of the kind they say are wasted on a boy, but I never found them wasted. It made him prettier, and gave him an appearance of innocence I doubted he deserved.

For a moment, I thought he might kiss me right there, but I turned and drew him briskly along. I liked the tingle on my skin, the blush and the way I could feel his gaze on the bare back of my neck, the indent of my waist and the sway of my hips. There wasn't much there, but they did sway, and he followed behind. I liked the anticipation as much as the thing itself, and though I hoped Nick wouldn't be one of those, sometimes more.

No Gatsby at the bar or on the veranda. No Gatsby in the music room or the armory or in the private dance that had sprung up in the blue parlor. We ended up in the library, where I had few hopes of finding Gatsby, but where I thought we might be alone for a while.

The library I later heard was a true Gothic miracle. It had burned down sometime in the 1500s, its ashes tilled under the earth. A rather pedestrian apartment block stood there now. Gatsby, they said, resurrected it the way he might resurrect a beloved dead ancestor. As we walked down the cavernous space, our footsteps echoed and the tall stained glass windows flickered with a hot orange light from beyond, a far cry from the cool twinkling stars that lit the party.

There were alcoves set between the shelves, and I had been back there before with Coral Doughty to find that the reading sofa was very comfortable. Nick looked a little sharper when we were alone, as if he had finally figured out what he was for.

"Jordan, wait a minute," he said.

"Are you going to talk to me about your girl in St. Paul?" I asked, raising my eyebrows. It would have surprised me, but I could stand being surprised.

"Shouldn't I?"

"I don't get out of the city much," I said, and slid my fingers down the lapel of his jacket. I didn't touch his skin, not yet, but his breath stuttered.

"Come here," I started to say, and then I had to stifle a yelp when a rumpled gray man sat up from the very sofa that I had had my eye on. He peered around, his eyes enormous behind thick owlish spectacles, and he squinted at us both before looking me up and down. He pointed at the books.

"What do you think?" he demanded.

"About what?" I snapped. I was still blushing, and I hoped it looked like anger.

"The books!"

He had made something of a nest for himself in the little alcove. There was a pile of blankets on the cushion, and a small table close to one side that held a glass of water and the remnants of a sandwich. A pair of slippers peeped out from under the sofa, and he had dragged a lamp over to light the whole affair.

"They're real. They're the real thing. About that. As a matter of fact you needn't bother to ascertain. *I* ascertained."

Something in our faces must have suggested we were in the least interested, because the man rushed to the bookcase and came back brandishing a leather-bound copy of a Renaissance treatise on the machinations of the princes below. It was a gorgeous thing, a volume that I knew Aunt Justine would have coveted, and if it had not made such an obvious gap in the shelves, I might have considered taking it to her.

"See! It is a bona-fide authentic piece of demonologica. He fooled me at first. What thoroughness! What realism! Knew when to stop too—didn't break the seals. But what do you want? What do you expect?"

He showed us the pages that were still shut with old wax and imprinted with the seals of Great Solomon. Terrible things could be learned from the pages underneath those seals, but they were as unbroken as the day they were made.

"Who brought you?" he demanded. "Or did you just come? I was brought. Most people were brought."

"He was *invited*," I said a little spitefully, pointing at Nick, but the man bobbed his head knowingly.

"*I* was brought," he continued. "I've been drunk for about a week now, and I thought it might sober me up to sit in a library."

"Has it?" Nick asked in a tone just a fraction off of mine.

"A little bit, I think. I can't tell yet. I've only been here an hour. Did I tell you about the books? They're real. They're—"

"You told us," I said with mock kindness.

We shook hands with him gravely and went back outdoors.

The dancing had started, and of course it was far too late for anyone who wasn't a good dancer to begin with. Men walked girls much too young for them in awkward circles, and the famous couples competed for the best angles even while keeping in the dimmer reaches of the space in a half-hearted attempt at privacy.

"Should I ask you to dance?" Nick inquired.

"Another time," I said absently, because something had caught my eye. We stood at the base of the steps. In front of us were the garden and all the pleasures that Gatsby had implicitly promised us, but the man himself was not down enjoying them. Instead he stood on the veranda behind us, and he was staring straight at Nick.

"Hey, it's the girls from before," Nick said, pointing towards the stage. Ada and May were doing their baby act, grown women toddling around with big eyes and singing nonsense songs in their high squeaky voices. It was a spectacle all right. Nick had apparently never seen anything like it, because he watched them, allowing Gatsby to watch him, allowing me to watch Gatsby.

I couldn't believe more people weren't watching Gatsby. He stood at the balustrade like an emperor overlooking his kingdom, but in this moment, the *only* thing he had eyes for was

Nick. Everything else was faded for him, all sounds muted. It was almost indecent, and something in me responded to it.

He had the gravitational pull of the sun itself, drawing planets into his orbit even as he summoned up all of New York's smart set for his parties. I couldn't imagine what would happen if he turned that look on someone who saw it, but of course I could. He had looked that way at Daisy, and I knew what had happened to her.

Seeing him then, you knew he would remake the world for the object of his desire, but what a world it would be, and it wasn't as if you could stop him. I knew Gatsby right then for what he was: a predator whose desires were so strong they would swing yours around and put them out of true. I was feeling the reflection of it rather than the thing itself, and I charged myself to remember it as well as the pit of cold wariness that had come to curl in my stomach.

Nick clapped for the girls on the stage, waking me from my reverie. I avoided looking up at Gatsby, and instead took Nick by the arm. Somewhere, he had gotten another finger-bowl of champagne, and his smile was silly and a little puppyish.

"Where shall we go next, Jordan?"

"Right here," I said, sitting him down at a table. I waved away a couple who wanted to join us, and I sat with Nick at the edge of the crowd, clearly visible from the veranda. There was a flushed look to Nick's face, and I stopped myself from reaching to brush the dark hair out of his eyes. I felt strange about it now, as if I was trespassing on territory that Gatsby had claimed with only that one desperate look. It was irritating to say the least, but at least he didn't keep us waiting.

One moment I was collecting a gin rickey for myself, and the next, the man himself was seated at the table with us as if he had been there all along. Up close, he was less handsome, more vital. I could see a faint scar at the point of his chin, old and white against his tanned skin, and his hair, cut so very short, made me think of an army man who had not quite acclimated to life at peace. He had eyes for no one but Nick, and when Nick's head came up from a second finger-bowl of champagne—where was he getting them from?—he gazed at Gatsby with a kind of curious wonder. It might have just been the drinks, but I thought it was more than that. Even I wanted to scoot my chair closer to Gatsby's warmth, touch his bare forearm where it rested on the table, and he wasn't even looking at me.

It was only when Nick met his eyes that Gatsby smiled, and somewhere in the house, the clock chimed midnight.

"Your face is familiar," Gatsby said, his voice low and warm, as if he had no idea who Nick was. "Weren't you in the First Division during the war?"

"Why, yes. I was in the Twenty-Eighth Infantry." Nick spoke automatically, eyes never falling from Gatsby's. His hands, forgotten on the table, twitched as if still seeking a trigger.

I hadn't known Nick's division, but I had heard of the Twenty-Eighth. Everyone had. They had carried away America's first victory in France, and that meant Nick was allowed as only a few other men in the country were to wear the insignia of the Black Lions of Cantigny. I was a little more impressed with him. Every boy who came home was a war hero, but there was apparently something more to this one.

"I was in the Sixteenth until June nineteen-eighteen. I knew I'd seen you somewhere before."

"I would have remembered someone like you," Nick said, attempting a diffidence he obviously did not feel. I couldn't tell whether Gatsby was telling the truth, but Nick was, and I changed the few things I knew about him around a bit in my head.

They talked for a moment about some depressing little villages in France. Gatsby mentioned he had just bought a hydroplane, and was going to try it out in the morning.

"Want to go with me, old sport? Just near the shore along the Sound."

Nick's fingers curled as if they wanted to make a fist but had forgotten how. If he had had his gun there, we would all have been dead.

"What time?"

Gatsby laughed as if Nick's sensible question was delightful.

"Any time that suits you best."

They were staring into each other's eyes, clearly at a standstill in the conversation and not sure where to go next. If I left them like that, perhaps they would simply stare into each other's eyes forever. Then the party would never end, and that would be dreadful.

"Having a gay time now?" I asked, breaking the silence with a smile.

"Much better," Nick admitted, and I felt a pang. He really hadn't been until now, and I hadn't noticed or I hadn't cared to notice.

Nick turned back to Gatsby even as his hand reached over onto mine. I let him have it. I could have used the comfort too if Gatsby was looking at me like that.

"This is an unusual party for me. I haven't even seen the host. I live over there"—he waved vaguely at the invisible hedge in the distance—"and this man Gatsby sent over his chauffeur with an invitation."

Gatsby stared, for a moment at a loss that anyone might not recognize him. He deflated, and in that moment he met my eyes, saw that I was witnessing his embarrassment. All of that charm and for a man who had no idea who he was.

"I'm Gatsby," he said finally.

Nick jumped.

"What!" he exclaimed. "Oh, I beg your pardon."

"I thought you knew, old sport. I'm afraid I'm not a very good host."

He smiled, and just sitting close by, I could feel Gatsby's warmth and earnest belief that of course Nick would forgive him any kind of small sin. In that moment, Nick was open to me too. Nick Carraway, who had gone to war and come home amid some strange family tragedy, who had blown east like an apple seed, and taken root, improbably, in one of the richest neighborhoods on the island. Nick wanted, so deeply, to be known and understood, and it was something that I couldn't give him, even if I wanted to. But Gatsby told you with just his eyes and his smile that he did.

Gatsby's smile was a rare thing, something I have not seen more than four or five times in my life, and it's likely just as well.

A growing certainty came over me that I should let go of Nick's hand before something terrible happened to him and I was pulled along. Before I could, a butler appeared to let Gatsby know that Chicago was calling him on the wire. Gatsby made a face.

"Business, business, business," he sighed.

He rose, gave us both a small bow, and me a second look that held nothing of want and everything of estimation. It was an oddly sexless look, almost bracing after what he had been throwing around before.

"If you want anything just ask for it, old sport," he said to Nick. "Excuse me. I will rejoin you later."

The moment he was gone, Nick turned to me, blinking a little as if one of the girls walking by had slapped him and kept walking. Whatever he had expected, it wasn't that, and to be fair, there was no expecting Gatsby in that kind of form at all.

"Who is he? Do you know?" he demanded.

I shrugged, taking my time and making him wait for it.

"He's just a man named Gatsby."

It was at least the truth. It was better than bringing up any of the rumors we had heard before, whether they were true or not.

"Where is he from, I mean? And what does he do?"

I sighed, because now he was looking at me almost desperately. I liked that, even if it wasn't for me, and I remembered a conversation I had had with the man himself weeks ago. I was rather more drunk than I should have been, and I had somehow found myself talking to him beside the fountain. He stopped me from going in once, but his grin said there had been a chance he would just let me fall in and ruin my dress.

"Now you're started on the subject," I said. "Well, he told me once he was an Oxford man. However, I don't believe it."

"Why not?"

I shrugged.

"I don't know. I just don't believe it."

Lieutenant Gatsby with his one pair of good shoes had never been to Oxford, but we weren't talking about him now. This was another creature entirely. I still doubted him, but, if you understand, in a different way.

"Anyhow, he gives large parties," I said abruptly. There were deeper waters here than I wanted to go swimming in. It was too much to handle for Nick, who I after all had only known for a night, and Gatsby himself, it was clear, was too much trouble for anyone.

"And I like large parties. They're so intimate. At small parties there isn't any privacy." I said it defiantly, daring Nick to bring us back to our host.

Before Nick could answer that, thankfully, a bass drum boomed, and some little man in a tuxedo came up to introduce some music for us. It had apparently been a sensation, and half of the audience laughed in agreement and the other half laughed not to be left out.

The music started, and Nick turned entirely in his seat, looking up with the attention of a dog to his master at the steps where Gatsby now sat. He reclined on the steps, watching over the party not with an emperor's pride but a boy's possession. We were his garden, or his ant farm perhaps. He approved, for the moment, and God only knew what happened when he didn't.

Nick saw, and I did too, how alone Gatsby was. No one came

close. No one leaned their head on his shoulder or took his arm to pull him into a dance. The music was good, the moon was setting. It was after midnight with that tired charm that all parties on the downturn acquire. The fact that a man like him sat alone, no matter the rumors about him, was an unnatural thing. I was used to being alone, and apparently so was Gatsby, but he shouldn't have been, not a man like that, not ever.

There's something wrong with him, I thought, clear as a bell.

I didn't have time to ponder that further when a butler—perhaps the same one as before, perhaps not—appeared next to me.

"Miss Baker?" he inquired. "I beg your pardon, but Mr. Gatsby would like to speak to you alone."

"With me?" I asked, glancing up. He had disappeared from the steps now.

"Yes, madame."

I got up, exchanging a look with Nick. From him, confusion, longing, a little jealousy that was extinguished before he recognized it for what it was. I threw him a casual salute before I went off to follow the butler wherever he would lead me.

CHAPTER FOUR

During the brief time that Nick and I were stepping out together—and afterward, I'm sure—he liked to call me careless. Sometimes he said it with a kind of admiration when I bluffed us past a steel door into an underground gin joint ("Well, that was the password that Arthur Clarence told me last night, wasn't it?"), but towards the end, it was said with a kind of wondering disapproval, as if anyone with any sense would have learned some kind of caution.

He called me careless because he didn't have the words to sort out how jealous he was of my money and my freedom and how very few people in the world could act as I did. I never gave him a real answer because the real answer wasn't one that men got. Men had no idea how careless the women of their set weren't allowed to be. They laughed at how fussy we were about which cars we got into, and they never wondered about the long stretches of bad road between glittering place and glittering place. It was a kind of darkness that could swallow someone whole, and whoever walked back, shoes in her hand, stockings shredded and calling for help from some dingy pay phone, she wouldn't be the same girl who roared off in that unwise Tourister.

There are some kinds of careless that a girl in 1922, if she was rich, if she was pretty, if she was arrogant, could be. I was foreign and orphaned as well, and that added a few more. I might choose to stagger in just past dawn and find Aunt Justine still at the dinner table with her old friends from the suffragette circuit, a demolished plate of baked meats between them and the air thick with the fug of their cigar smoke. There was always a chittering around them, of the imps they had inherited from their Puritan witch ancestresses, and more than one of them trucked in the minor trade of souls that was such big business down in Venezuela and Argentina. They looked like every cartoonist's idea of the ugly suffragette, raucous, crude, and sly, some widows, some spinsters, all with a very certain idea of the place that should be made for them in the world. When I came in in the morning with my stockings hanging down to my ankles and a very respectable bite from Nick at the base of my throat, they laughed and pointed at me, but none of them would ever have troubled themselves to stop me. They had been careless themselves at my age, and they had mostly survived it.

As far as I was concerned, careless when it led to a love bite and some mussed hair was fine. It was another kind of carelessness entirely that sent Daisy around to my house one crystal March day in 1919.

Daisy debuted straight after Armistice in a grand and lovely event that Louisville sorely needed. There were six other girls along with her, and everyone had sighed with relief that things were getting back to normal after all of their sons had been taken away. It would be another few months before their sons came back, missing limbs or carrying a kind of gnawing weight that would eat at them unchecked for the rest of their lives, so the relief was a kind that some of them would never find again.

I was too young to debut with Daisy, and the suspicion had set in, meanwhile, that I never would.

Doors were closing against me that year. Walter Finley was still to come, but I could see patterns developing, growing up around me like the vines around Sleeping Beauty's castle. There were things I could do and things I couldn't, and girls who had been my friends the year before cut me loose. Slowly but surely, I was being left off lists, pruned away as the girls of my class grew up and became gracious ladies.

It was becoming obvious to me and to them that I couldn't follow them into marriage and luncheons and good works. They wouldn't introduce me formally to their brothers and their cousins, and while I had been a delightful pet and mascot, I simply had no place beyond their girlhood days. They knew it instinctively, their mothers knew it definitively, and eventually, I had no choice but to recognize it as well. I existed in a kind of borderland of acceptable and not, sometimes more on one side, sometimes more on another.

During the last year the United States spent in the war, I stopped sleeping at home almost entirely, spending the night with whatever girl I was in love with that week. It was Mrs. Christiansen, Mary Lou Christiansen's mother, who had to take me aside discreetly and tell me that that wasn't something I could do, that I was overstaying my welcome and making people talk.

I was lucky that they were not talking about what I was actually doing, but it was enough to send Daisy to my house the March after her debut. She showed up on my doorstep in her white roadster, with a bright brittle smile and an offer to take me to school.

"I just thought that it's been a while since I saw your dear face," she said, a brown paper bag clutched tight in her hands. "Look, I bought us breakfast!"

She had, from a pastry shop far from where either of us lived. Her usually sleek dark hair looked greasy, and her dress was rumpled and slightly stained. She had been out all night, and I knew the signs well enough to be both concerned and curious.

For the sake of Judge Baker, who was indifferently peering out the window at us, we set off towards the high school, but quickly veered north instead. As soon as we were out of sight of the house, Daisy lit a cigarette and held it between her two long fingers, taking a distracted puff as she drove. When she didn't offer me one, I took it for myself, lighting it with her silver heart-shaped lighter. The pastries were forgotten in the foot well, but their scent, sugary raspberry jam, rose up to mingle with the dried rose petals in Daisy's pale pink cigarettes.

We drove along the river before pulling off in the woods across from Twelve Mile Island.

It was March in Louisville. The clouds hung like swagged sails low over our heads, and I was wishing that I had worn a thicker coat before I let Daisy steal me away.

She parked us on a high bluff above the gray winter water. As if in response to our arrival, it grew choppy and agitated, yellow-white foam topping the waves, the water going darker and less translucent. It didn't stop until Daisy finally smoothed down her hair, taking several deep breaths.

"Jordan, you know people."

"All right," I said more calmly than I felt. "Tell me."

She did. Her mother was in Mobile for the month. There was no one else who would help her. She woke up two days ago to realize that her monthlies hadn't come for two months now, when she had been regular as a clock since she was fourteen.

"And Jean Bisset?" I asked, pronouncing it properly. We had all learned to do so when he came up from New Orleans with his father's business connections and his wide and charming grin. Daisy had claimed him almost by accident. They were mad about each other until they weren't, and right up until a few days ago, it had seemed as if they must be altar-bound.

She shook her head, a narrow little gesture that closed the door on that. It didn't matter if he knew or not, what he felt or not. In these matters, girls were almost always on their own.

"I won't be able to look my father in the eye," Daisy muttered, pressing her hands against her eyes. "This will destroy him."

It wouldn't. She would be fine, in the end. She could go off somewhere, send back postcards of what a delightful time she was having in Waukegan or Columbus or Hartford, and come back with her head mostly held high. However, she might not be Daisy Fay of Louisville again, and she couldn't bear that.

"*Help* me," she said, and I nodded.

This was no time for me to play with her. I thought that if I had told her no, she might have driven us both straight into the water. The Ohio River ran a full thousand miles before it fed its secrets into the Mississippi, and among them, every year, I thought, was a sacrifice of young girls lost and betrayed. Some of those girls had babies inside them, and others had broken hearts or broken heads, but they fed the Mississippi all the same, and I had no interest in being one of them.

"All right," I said. "I know where to go."

The place we were going sold fried fish, taken, the sign insisted, daily from the Ohio River. In summer, the sign would be lit up with charmed fireflies, the large kind that turned the river breaks into a dancing field of stars. Now, though, it was March and all of the fireflies were dead. The charm kept a few still crawling around the edges of the sign, and a few more had kept a trace of their green-gold light, pulsing faintly over the restaurant's name: Fulbright's.

The place was closing as we came in, and a thin girl a few years younger than us stared, hands still on her broom. There was an old man reading a paper in the corner, gumming slowly at a piece of fried fish wrapped in a scrap of paper. Otherwise, the place was empty.

"Are you sure?" hissed Daisy, and I shrugged.

The beaded curtain clacked, and a skinny woman with a blue cloth tied over her hair came out. She took us both in with a cold gaze, so I felt free to study her in turn. She wasn't white, but that was all I could say for sure. Her face was darker than mine, though not by much, and it seemed as if she had not smiled for years. Her mouth was as set as limestone, and there was nothing, she seemed to say, that could erode it away.

"Buy some food," she said to us tersely, and then to the girl with the broom, "Turn over that sign, and get along home before your mama starts to worry."

The old man she left alone, as if he were just another part of the restaurant, like the crackling leather on the stools to the vat of oil that hissed balefully behind the counter. Daisy asked for some pickles, and famished, I ordered a sandwich, the bread oversweet and the fried fish slathered with a lemony egg yolk sauce. The woman busied herself for a moment, wiping needlessly at the counter so she had a moment to watch us. Daisy kept her eyes morosely on her plate, but I watched insolently back. I had a bad habit of staring from the time I was a little girl, but it was fair, I thought, to stare back.

"We didn't come here to eat," Daisy finally said, her hands clenching and unclenching on countertop.

"I know," the woman said scornfully. "But you might take up my time and run all the way home without buying nothing. You can sit for a little."

"You don't want us here any longer than you have to have us," I said, my voice shaking just a little. The food helped, but I was exhausted. I wanted this over with, and she glared at me.

"It's not you with the problem, is it? You look like the Toy girls, and they're too smart for that. Too good too."

I gave her a stony look. I knew of the Toy girls, even if I had never met them. They were the daughters of the laundry owners on Nineteenth Street. I saw them once years ago when Mrs. Baker had some business with their parents. They were as neat as pins, a few years older than me, and as our parents talked about the cleaning job, they elbowed each other and whispered back and forth while staring at me with open curiosity. Then their father left a scorch mark on some Irish linen curtains, and we had no further business with them. Some of the other girls at school would call me Jordan Toy sometimes, but it was a vague sort of insult.

"So you then," she said to Daisy.

"Yes, me," Daisy said in the smallest voice I had ever heard from her. "Please, my father will just *die . . .*"

The woman shrugged.

"Thirty-five dollars," she said, and Daisy flinched.

"I don't have that much, but—"

"How much do you have now?" she asked in irritation. "You didn't come with nothing, did you?"

"No! No, I didn't . . ."

Flustered, Daisy pulled out her pocketbook, spilling ticket stubs and receipts and dried flower petals everywhere. Her fingers were shaking so much that I finally took it from her, pulling out the crisp bills. It was thirty dollars not thirty-five, and the woman shrugged philosophically. She tucked the bills into the same pocket where our food money had gone and nodded.

"All right. Go home. Come back Thursday."

"Oh, but I can't," Daisy protested, and as clearly as looking into a crystal ball, I could see her claiming that she had some party or excursion she simply could not miss. Honestly, the fact that she had spared a full day for this was somewhat exceptional.

"We'll come back for it," I said. "Come *on*, Daisy."

We went back to the car, Daisy fretting the whole time about whether the woman was trustworthy or if anyone had seen us or if it was some kind of fraud, the way so many curatives were. I stifled the urge to smack her, and instead said her name. She turned to me with big scared eyes, and I sighed.

"Daisy, be quiet."

For a miracle, she was, all the way back to the house on Willow Street. I could see the single yellow rectangle of the judge's study; otherwise the house was dark and silent. I started to get out of Daisy's roadster, feeling somehow far more grown-up and more worldly than I had getting into it that morning.

Daisy surprised me by grabbing me from behind in a hug. She was always an affectionate girl, but there was a distance to her little peckish kisses, her embraces. There was no space at all between us in this hug, and for a second, I leaned my head back against hers.

"Don't tell *anyone*," she pleaded, and I decided to pretend she said thank you.

I went upstairs where the ghost of Anabeth Baker stood in the hallway, staring at me balefully as I came up the dim stairs. She no longer terrified me as she had when I was little, watching from darkened doorways, snatching at my ankles from under the bed so that I had to leap to get under the covers every night. She did not like me, but the dislike had turned at least a little more cordial. The air around her was chilly, and I knew not to look too long into her eyes because it could leave me with a queasy feeling that wouldn't fade for hours.

Instead of walking past her this time, however, I stopped to look at her, taking in her old-fashioned dark dress, the smooth pompadour of her hair, and the ring of dark bruises around her neck.

"What was it like for you?" I asked. "Were you careless too?"

Thursday came, and Daisy caught me on the way to school. We hadn't talked since we had gone out to Fulbright's a few days before, but she showed up as if we had arranged it, just a few moments before I would have been on the Blakefield grounds. She smiled to the confused students behind me as I got in, waving at them with the graciousness of a queen.

"You look better," I said, and she laughed.

"Oh, darling, I am simply *terrible*! I haven't slept a wink since last we spoke, and look here . . ."

She lifted her right hand from the gearshift and showed me her fingertips, which were all neatly bandaged save for her thumb.

"I was quite out of my head last night, and I wanted a cup

of tea. It started out just right, but then before I knew it, I was yelping like anything and all of the hot water steaming on the floor, and Mother's ceramic box where she keeps the loose leaf shattered. It was just awful, Jordan . . ."

I stayed quiet, leaning back in my seat and helping myself to one of her cigarettes. I imagined that under her bandages, it would be the pads of her fingertips that were burned. She hadn't just brushed her hand against the side of the copper kettle, she had done something more deliberate.

She shook her head, telling me how her father had scolded her in the morning and given her money to go buy a new ceramic tea box before her mother came home. I let her paint whatever response on me she liked, and as we drove, I looked out over the drab March morning, where the sun was struggling to come out, where people were making their way to school or to work and completely separate from who and what Daisy and I were. We might have been angels drifting through Louisville on some kind of divine mission, invisible in our white roadster.

We pulled up to Fulbright's, which was crowded at this time of day. As we watched, two women in custodial uniforms walked in, still wobbly from their shifts at the nearby Grace of Mary hospital. Beyond the sign of dead fireflies, we could see that the booths were all full, and—

"No, no, absolutely *not*."

Daisy shrank back in her seat, shaking her head and gripping the steering wheel so hard I thought her knuckles would crack straight through her thin skin.

"Jordan! Jordan, no, I just can't . . . Please, please, I can't, I'd rather just go home, I can't. I *can't*."

"Won't, you mean," I snapped, but I slammed out of the roadster, my braids flying behind me.

I used my irritation to propel me through the door into the restaurant, ignoring the stares that I got. I always got stared at when I went out in Louisville. I'd be common as dirt in Chicago, but we weren't in Chicago. I stood as if someone had slid a steel shaft down my spine, and I glared at the little girl sitting at the register. The woman who had talked to us a few nights ago was nowhere to be seen.

"I want a fish sandwich," I said, daring her to make anything of it. I slid my quarter across the counter towards her, and she scraped it up to plunk it into the steel machine.

"Gimme a minute," she said, and she went around back to the kitchen.

The seconds crept past, and I continued staring straight ahead, my face as still as stone, but aware that the back of my neck was as hot as if I had been out of doors all days.

"Hey, which one are you, Angie or Margaret?" came a voice from behind me. Angie and Margaret were the name of the Toy girls, and I ignored it, though later I wondered if I should have claimed one of them. It would have covered my tracks a bit, but as the woman had said, the Toy girls were apparently known to be a little too smart and good to be doing anything like this.

Finally, the girl came back with a paper bag folded neatly at the top. It was stamped with a surprisingly pretty flower design, and she handed it to me diffidently. I took it and stomped out, catching speculative looks out of the corner of my eyes.

I shouldn't have worn my school uniform in, I thought with disgust. *I could have gone around back, but of course Daisy pulled us up around front.*

She was still waiting for me there, ducked down as if her car was at all inconspicuous in that neighborhood.

"Well?" she asked when I got in.

I opened up the bag to pull out my sandwich and also to spill out a jam jar filled with a green mash of herbs and a receipt for a new stove hood. On the back of the receipt were instructions written in a neat rolling hand.

Daisy took the jam jar and the receipt and stuffed them into her bag. I ate my sandwich, and we said no more as she drove.

We went back to Daisy's house, and she sent the cook out for the day with a sweet smile and a fifty-cent piece. Her bandaged fingertips made her clumsy, so I brewed half the noxious sludge at first, in four cups of water as the receipt told us. The air took on a sharp green smell, and there was an odor underneath it that made my stomach twist, an earthy smell, one that brought to mind a garden after a wet winter.

Daisy downed it all at once, lifting her elbow like a soldier. I followed her up the stairs where she lay down in her canopied bed, and where I sat down at her desk to do my homework. I was an indifferent scholar. I got passing grades when I wanted to. School was more about simply going for me, which I had not been allowed to do until Mrs. Baker died.

"What's the point of it all?" Daisy wondered. "What is the point of any of it?"

"If there weren't any point, we wouldn't have done any of this," I said, and my voice was gentle enough that she laughed.

"True."

I finished my math and went on to my geography. Daisy struck a match behind me, lighting a perfumed candle at her windowsill, and the room filled with the scent of lilac. Lying on her back, she drew the smoke to her hands, twisting it between her fingers like a bit of ribbon. If she were a boy, or a much more determined girl, she might have gone on to Yale or even to Oxford for instruction in the aetheric and alchemical arts, but she had been more than ready to be done with school by the time she graduated.

She was already beginning to cramp four hours later when it was time for us to brew the second half of the jam jar. She drank this just as quickly, winced, and then dropped into her bed in a miserable ball, dragging me along with her.

For the next three hours, she drifted in a light sleep, woken from time to time by cramps that racked her entire body.

What if she gave us something too strong? I thought but didn't say. *What if it kills her?*

Daisy was shaking and sweating when she staggered to the bathroom. They had a modern one, thankfully, and she stayed there a long time. From the other side of the door, I heard her crying, quiet sobs that made me pace restlessly beyond. There was nothing I could do for her but wait. The toilet flushed and then flushed again, and I imagined her hand tight on the cord, knuckles white and bandaged fingertips digging into her palm. I was braced to call the doctor, but when she came out, she was pale but steady, her face and hands scrubbed under cold water.

"Come get into bed with me," she said.

There was something exhausted in the air as we lay back down. Everything had changed or maybe only we had.

"If you're still bleeding by tomorrow, you have to go to the doctor," I said suddenly, remembering something that some girl had told me earlier that year. "You *have* to, because—"

"Hush," Daisy said, pressing my head against her shoulder. "It's all fine. It's all fine now."

The smoke hung over our heads, and Daisy drew it into a heart for me, and then a castle and a horse.

"Do you remember when we met?" she murmured dreamily. "Someday, I want you to cut me something grand, far bigger than that lion. Make me a house to live in, and a prince to come save me, and of course so many apple trees to scent the air, and a mountain to put it all on, far, far from here."

"Of course," I said dryly. "No big thing at all."

We both drowsed for a while, not waking up until Mr. Fay knocked on the door, opening it just a crack.

Daisy was cut from his pattern rather than her mother's. He was a lean spare man with hair that was as black as ink, and he had a dreaminess to his eyes as well, as if he were somehow fundamentally unmoored from the world, perpetually startled by its sharp edges and small cruelties.

"Daisy? You sent Cypress away before she could make dinner. I didn't know you were having Jordan over for the evening."

"Sorry, sorry," Daisy yawned, waving her hand sleepily. "There was some tea I wanted to bring to Mother to say sorry for breaking her box, and I wanted to try brewing it myself."

Mr. Fay snorted at his daughter, shaking his head.

"I'll call down to the club and have them send something over."

"Not me, I'm afraid I can't eat anything but moonlight and rose petals tonight, Papa. But do get Jordan something, won't you? She's been looking after me very well, you see."

"Of course. Jordan, will you take a chop and some potatoes?"

"Yes, sir. Thanks much."

He closed the door behind him, leaving us in the evening darkness again, and I closed my eyes. Careful, we had to be so very careful all the time, and the reward was this, lying in the dark as if we were the same girls we had been the week before.

CHAPTER FIVE

A veil dropped down over me as I followed the butler through Gatsby's mansion. It was as sheer as summer-weight chiffon, as light as nothing at all, and it prevented anyone we passed in the halls from seeing me or stopping me. As I walked, I idly wondered if it was simply custom and a healthy sense of self-preservation that prevented people from looking at Gatsby's affairs too closely or if there truly was some kind of charm at work, some little figure in the butler's pocket or the heel of his shoe.

We passed by Mina Lochlear, fresh back from her tour of the Continent, and I saw a pair of men talking avidly under a bust of Antinous in an alcove. One of the men was Denis Rader, the Broadway comedian, and though I didn't know the other young man, I thought they would not have to work very hard at seducing each other. There were no rules at Gatsby's parties, no conventional ones anyway, and I wondered if they would stay like the man in the library had, cut adrift from the world they had come from.

Beneath the shelter of a staircase, there was Senator Barnes Hillcock, with his jacket off and a Maduro Habano cigar in his hand. He was talking with a man who sketched pictures in the air between them with his elongated fingers, and over that man's shoulder, I saw the senator's face grow ruddy and rich with a new ambition that was probably older than the Romans.

Soon we arrived before an elegantly paneled door with a handle made of pure jade. The butler opened it, announced me, and then stepped back with a slight gesture for me to enter. The moment the door shut behind me, I could feel that veil which had surrounded me being whipped away, though I still could not tell whether it was because some charm had been removed or whether Gatsby's eyes were simply that sharp.

"Jordan Baker!" he said with pleasure. "Well, you have grown into a fine-looking girl, haven't you?"

He looked, I decided, as if he had tried out several poses before the butler announced me. The room he had chosen for our meeting was small and intimate with a piano in one rear corner and a cold hearth at the back. I imagined him leaning one elbow on the mantel or staring out the window that looked out over the Sound before simply deciding to wait for me at the center of the room, a smile on his face and his hands stuck in his pockets. Other men might have been awkward about it, but he appeared to be entirely at his ease, content to be gazed at as long as the one doing the gazing was sufficiently awed.

"I have," I agreed, coming farther into the room. "And I might have thought that you would come up with something a little more original. I'm a New Yorker now, and therefore have higher expectations."

There was just enough humor in my voice to keep that smile on his face, and he gestured towards one of the wing-chairs by the fireplace.

"Won't you have a seat, Jordan? Can I pour you something?"

"Whatever you are having, of course."

I had an idea of what was on offer given the rest of the party, but whatever Jay Gatsby was having would be exceptional. He wouldn't allow it to be otherwise, and I watched with interest as he removed a cut-glass stoppered bottle from the delicate drinks cart. The liquid inside was a deep and sticky black, like blackberry syrup. It moved with a languid sluggishness as he poured it into two gold-rimmed thimble glasses. He handed one to me, smiling down at it a little.

"This lot came from Italy. It was actually harder getting it out of Italy than into the States. They had to pack it into a shipment of Malatesta violins, one bottle inside each one. Prato holds those violins sacred, you know, which was funny enough for the purpose they were put to."

He took his seat across from mine, sipping at the drink without taking his eyes away from me.

Demoniac is meant to be drunk straight, a small amount taken for medicine, a larger amount for pleasure. I split the difference because I wasn't with friends, and I held it in my mouth for a moment, letting it go partway to warm vapor before swallowing. It was strong enough that I would have coughed without that precaution, and even then I had to sit up very straight, my eyes focused on a spot on the wall opposite from me as the room gently tilted. It put a pull in my lower belly like falling in love, and I enjoyed it even as I reminded myself it was purely a matter of infernal machinery.

"What happened to the violins?" I asked. I didn't play, but there were musicians on Broadway, not poor ones either, who might have done a little bit of discreet evil for a real Malatesta.

Gatsby shrugged, a slight smile on his face, the glass already empty in his fingertips.

"Smashed, unfortunately. A shame, but the demoniac was worth it, don't you think?"

"Is that a story you often tell to people you want to get on your side?" I asked.

"It is the story I am telling you," he said with a different smile, and that smile tugged at me to suggest that he wouldn't tell just anyone. I was *special*, and the low warmth from the demon's blood in my stomach suggested that it was true.

But I knew that Nick had been special as well, and the stunned, overwhelmed look I remembered in Nick's eyes reminded me again to sit up a little straighter, keeping what was left in the thimble glass rather than drinking it right away.

"Is that meant to convince me to tell you a story as well?"

It was too blunt for him, I could tell. He wanted something agreeable, something sweeter around the edges, but I was never very good at sweet.

"Do you remember me?" he asked instead, looking down at his glass. There was something almost vulnerable in his tone.

I used the opportunity to look him over. By this point in the evening, most men had at least unbuttoned their jackets if not done away with them altogether. He still looked as if he were straight from his dresser, the part in his hair as precise as the cream slash in an expertly made black velvet. His shoes shone as if he had purchased them new for the occasion, and the patent leather echoed only poorly the glossy black nail on his ring finger.

It was on the tip of my tongue to say that I didn't remember him, not in the least, but then he looked up at me. It spun me a little, because it felt as if he were letting me see all the way to the center of him, that empty room, and it wasn't empty because there was nothing to fill it with. No, there was a mansion full of things and people waiting to fill it, and a legion of demons, likely, standing by to do the same.

It was empty because he had refused to fill it, held off, barred the door. It was too easy to see how someone might stumble into such a place and be lost forever. A person could never fill that place. It would take a story.

The door snapped closed, and the look that Gatsby gave me was alarmed. I had seen too much, more than he intended; that wasn't the way it was supposed to go. I turned back to my glass, taking another tiny sip to give us both time to recover.

"Jordan, I need your help."

Whatever I had anticipated from him, it was not that. My eyes felt too big in the dimness of the room, as if they were gobbling up all the light that they could to form an image of him. It wasn't easy, the demoniac in my blood told me. There was too much to him, something bigger than a person should be, as if I could not see every part of him at once.

"Of course you do," I said pertly, and he smiled as if I had said something genuinely amusing.

"Will you talk to Nick for me? Will you tell him about me?"

"I don't know anything about you," I said. "And I like him. Why should I?"

His smile got a little harder before it relaxed into something more rueful. That looked enough like the truth that I blinked.

"Because I am a romantic. I always have been."

"That's not an answer."

"It is," he insisted. "I need to speak to Nick. I need him . . . to know who I am, who I really am."

"You spoke to him on your own just fine earlier," I protested, but he shook his head.

"No, of course I didn't," he said. "We were at a party, we spoke of the war, and his head was getting turned every few moments by some distraction or another."

I wondered for a moment if he remembered the same conversation I did. I learned later that it was entirely possible that he didn't.

"I don't like to involve myself with other people's love affairs," I lied.

"It's not like that," he said hastily, but the guilt that flashed over his face told me otherwise. "Look. I want to be fair to you. What do you like, what do—"

"No!" I said, glaring at him. "We are not doing that, do you hear me? No bargains, please, not for this. I'm just fine as I am, thank you."

The corner of his mouth kicked up in a little smile.

"I could find something you wanted. I could *give* you something you wanted. I'm good at that. I'm the best."

I tossed the rest of the demoniac down because I didn't want to look at him being right, because he probably was. I hadn't even reached the bottom of learning what I wanted, and even if he couldn't give those things to me, maybe I liked that he wanted to try.

I licked my lips, ready to stand up and storm out in high drama, but then he was crouched down by the arm of my chair, looking up at me with those pretty eyes and absolutely no hint of Hell in him at all.

"Please, Jordan?"

That hint of vulnerability again, and I sighed, because even then I knew I liked it too much. He was older than I was, more important in every way that the world cared about, and the fact that he had to say please to me sat in my heart like a warming ember.

"You're the only one that can do this, you know," he murmured. "There's no one else I could ask, no one else I could count on."

He reached for my hand, but I moved it quickly away from him. I didn't know why, maybe the demoniac. It was self-destruction in a pretty bottle, but there was something else and other about Jay Gatsby.

He looked faintly offended, but before he could capitalize on that, I nodded.

"Fine," I said. "There are things that I don't share, but I don't suppose that Nick Carraway is one of them."

Gatsby smiled, no artifice or seduction in it, but only relief. I gasped when he took my hand in both of his, squeezing tightly before letting go. No, I did not like it much at all.

"Someday, I'll dance at your wedding," he promised, and that hurt was smoothed over enough that I could laugh.

"As if anyone would be good enough for me," I said lightly. "Shall I tell him that you hung the moon or that you defeated the Huns single-handedly at the Rhône?"

He hesitated, and I could see then what sort of creature he

was. He wanted me to tell Nick just that, but in the end, he shook his head.

"You remember me from before I shipped out, don't you? When I was with—"

"Yes."

"Tell him about me then."

That touched me unexpectedly. If he wanted Nick to know about who he was before, when he still had a soul, when he was only an ambitious young man who loved someone he couldn't have, well, that was romance, wasn't it? I had seen little enough of it in my life that I smiled a bit wistfully at him.

"All right. Now may I return to my world?"

"Of course, Miss Baker."

He rose smoothly to his feet to give me a hand out of my chair and drew me to the door. Senator Hillcock was passing by, as neat as a doctor's case full of morphine vials and scalpels, and he gave Gatsby a formal nod. Gatsby, smiling, touched two fingers to his temple in a brief salute.

"Honestly, these new money types," he said.

It would have made some sense if Gatsby had released me to the crowd then, but he didn't. Instead, he kept me by his side, my hand tucked firmly in his arm, and back in the living glamour of his natural setting, something shifted in him again.

He was my friend now, squiring me through the halls, taking care to steer me around the pile of debs at the foot of the grand stairway, and smiling just for me. Gatsby wasn't showing me off, nor was he trying to impress me. Instead, when he leaned in closer to murmur something scandalous about that admiral or to tell me that a certain redhead's dress would look much lovelier on me, I realized it was something otherwise.

You and I are made out of the same stuff, he seemed to be saying. *Won't we have fun?*

I knew it was a white lie at best, but as we passed through his golden halls, the strains of music drifting up from the garden and smell of money in the air, I realized that he might not think it was.

My God, he thinks he's sincere, I thought with wonder, and perhaps in that moment, I warmed to him just a little more. It was just a tiny crack in my defenses, but it was really all that was necessary.

He gestured in the air with long-fingered hands, an excitement in his voice for the brilliant new innovations of his house, for how big the world after the war could be. It was as if he was inviting me into his world, wanting to share all its pleasures with me.

And with Nick, of course, but as I watched his hands tracing gleaming patterns in front of us and the shape of his lips around his grandiose words, I decided that if I were asked properly, I would not mind sharing so very much.

The party was winding down into a graceless mess, something that had always irritated me. People are at their worst in transition, moving from one life to another. All of Gatsby's beautiful people were being revealed for the sloppy, irritable, wayward, and human creatures they really were. There was a fight going on in the drive, not even magic could get everyone into the same coats and shoes they had when they first showed up, and the light suddenly seemed to reveal all manner of blemishes where before it had hid them.

In the crowded front hall, I was pressed against Gatsby by the common crush, and courteously, he put his arm around me to keep me from falling. The sudden push of our bodies together made me blush, and something in his gaze heated at that.

"Why, you're lovely, Miss Baker," he said softly, and I could tell in his surprise that he meant it.

"I am," I said with a smile, and that won one in return from him.

Then Gatsby went stiff, something impatient on his face. I thought for a moment he had remembered himself, but then I followed his eyes and saw a pair of those tall men in dark suits approaching, expectant in their stance and their stride if not in their still faces.

"I'm afraid you'll have to forgive me," he said shortly, stepping away from me.

It didn't look like a scene that he cared to have observed or that I cared to witness, and right about then, anyway, the ones I came with, thankfully minus the undergrad, started waving at me from the porch. Before I could grudgingly go to them, however, I nearly walked straight into Nick, who had been standing so close that I was surprised I hadn't seen him. I wondered if there was something stiff about the way he looked at me; he had obviously seen my good-bye with Gatsby. I wavered between impatient and fond, and settled on intrigue instead.

I went up on tiptoe because he was surprisingly tall, and put my hand on his shoulder to steady myself.

"I've just heard the most amazing thing," I whispered. "How long were we in there?"

He shivered a little with my breath so close to his ear, and his arm went around my waist as I had hoped it would.

"Why, about an hour."

Of course it had been. The showoff.

"It was—simply amazing," I murmured. "But I swore I wouldn't say any more and here I am tantalizing you."

He looked dubious, but I could tell that wouldn't last. He had come to Gatsby's party, he had eaten the food, he had fallen under Gatsby's spell. It was already too late.

I told him to come find me when he liked. I was in the phone book under Aunt Justine, Mrs. Sigourney Howard. I thought he might, provided Gatsby didn't snap him up like something good to eat. Nick didn't strike me as the sort to make a good mistress, living off another man's money and light in some little Park Avenue apartment, but he might flirt with the experience of it before running back to Minnesota.

The grand glass doors with the late night behind them were a perfect mirror of the room. In their reflection, I saw Nick's hungry eyes on me as I walked away, and I could see as well the moment they turned from me towards Gatsby too.

CHAPTER SIX

And then? The whole thing slipped my mind.

At a distance, it might have seemed as if my entire summer was occupied with time at Daisy's and a rather remarkable party at Gatsby's. However, it was a crowded summer, and it was not until later, when I could thread the steps to disaster together like glass beads on a string, that those times stood out at all.

The undergrad that I had attended that particular party with disappeared, and since his family was a good one, there was a slight commotion over it. He wasn't seen again after that night, and there were some dark rumors before his sister told everyone he had gone to study abroad. No one believed it, but then, we were not required to. I took up one of Aunt Justine's causes, campaigning against the dress trade down in the garment district. Young girls would rent out their bodies for ten minutes, an hour, or a day, and though there were charms to prevent pregnancy, injury, and disease, more than one girl opened her eyes to find herself in trouble with some group or other, whether it was the law, one of the organized crime factions, or some duped man who had been entranced by canny eyes in a fresh young face.

The dress girls, or vêtes, as they were called after the French Caribbean tradition, were mostly white, mostly too young, and variously clever. Under Aunt Justine's instruction, I posted bail, took accounts, wrote determined letters, and mainly just came to the conclusion that if I were in their position, I would be a fair amount more clever than they were about who got to sit behind their faces. It took me around the city from the precincts to the courthouse to the poorhouses, and though I was never terribly diligent about it the good I did piled up willy-nilly like a careless mound of coins close to the laundry bin.

When the good work got to be too tedious, there were plenty of people to see. New York in the summer was a playful kind of purgatory. The men sent their wives and the kids to the shore or the countryside, and then they sent for their pretty girls and boys who could bear the heat. Despite the lack of actual children, there was a childish, carnival air to the still summer months, of a breeze that would carry a hint of saltwater taffy and the soft shrill cry of a carousel carillon.

The summer of 1922 came with a whoosh of hot dry air. Upstate the fires had begun, and they wouldn't stop until the autumn rains came. Sometimes, the ash that blew down from the Catskills tumbled over the city, large fat black flakes settling down on our shoulders to mar crisp white linen beyond repair. In the city, we started out the summer irritable and indolent, and we only grew worse as time went on.

I lost sight of Nick for a few weeks after Gatsby's party. I wondered in an absent kind of way if Gatsby had gotten him or if perhaps he had lapsed into that genteel kind of obscurity that affected so many who came to the city from the Middle West. They came East looking for some kind of excitement they thought they lacked, and then they shut themselves up in stuffy rooms like they had never left home.

I thought about calling over at Daisy's, to see when he might be around, but Daisy, restless and rootless, had blown down to Atlantic City for a short while. One night, while Tom was out with his girl, she wandered into the Toybox Casino and won a hundred dollars in a single bored moment at the tables. She was in the papers the next day for standing high up on the green baize table and casting chips to the less lucky below her. Her mouth was opened in a smile, and for a short moment, captured forever in inky, blotchy tabloid newsprint, she was a goddess.

So no Daisy, and I figured that that meant no Nick, until one evening when I was leaving the Bijoux with Nan Harper, a handsome girl who was more than a little stuck on herself. The show had been a good one, and after bidding her a pleasant good-bye, I scanned the street for a cab. I was distracted or else Nick would never have been able to come up to me.

"Where can I take you?" he asked, his voice welcoming and soft.

"Oh!" I said, looking him up and down and back again, and instead of telling him that I was rather looking forward to going to bed, I had him take us to the Lyric, a speakeasy built straight underneath a subway station that didn't strictly exist. You had to get on the subway at Wall Street, take it across the river to the Henry Street station, and then ride back again. If you did this at least twice, you might find that on the return trip, there would be a station stop that hadn't been there the first time around, the Columbia Street station. It took three trips back and forth before the train paused at the Columbia Street station for us, and I tugged him onto the platform by his tie, careful not to get my heel caught in the gap. I pulled him across the platform and partway down the tunnel, making him nervous as we heard the distant rumble of another train.

I ignored it, rapping twice on what looked like a service door, and when it opened, we were met by a burst of laughter and a blast of tinny horns. The Lyric was popular that year, setting a trend for more secretive speakeasies. They tipped out to the NYPD just as the more open clubs did, but the fun was in pretending that they didn't. That added element of danger helped make up for the Lyric's obscurity, and that summer, it was doing a brisk business, people crammed in cheek to jowl even when they weren't on the imported dance floor.

At the bar, I ordered us two corpse revivers before turning

back to Nick, who was gazing around at the warm red brick, the tapestries on the walls, and the curved ceiling over us from which sprouted, mushroom-like, orange Tiffany lights. The velvet booths weren't as full as they would have been on a weekend, but it was still a notable assemblage. From where I stood, I could see a few hungry young lawyers from the district attorney's office, a silver-haired Russian plutocrat with two Ziegfeld girls on his arms, and Donna Brunswick, less popular than she had been but still dressed to the nines in what might have been real gold snakeskin.

"Quite a place," he said, and I grinned.

"You thought I was just mad over subways?"

"I admit I'm not sure quite what to expect."

"From me?"

Nick's eyes flickered to one side briefly, a little as if he were looking for the exits.

"From New York, maybe," he said, and I took his hand, kissing his palm before I gave it back.

"Well, don't worry," I said. "I can show you around."

He liked the corpse reviver well enough that he had two others, and by then he was carefree enough to come dance with me. He was more graceful than I thought he would be, and after the first few turns, he was confident enough to enjoy himself without the standard protestations of inexpertise.

By the end, he was closer to me than he intended to be, and warm and flushed, I pulled us into one of the more humble booths towards the back. The high sides blocked out most of the sound, and I came to sit on the same side with him, tucking myself neatly under his arm. Whatever he wore, it smelled good, fresh and a little unrefined, but that seemed to suit me right this moment.

"I don't get you," he said, not moving away from me. He rested his warm cheek on the top of my head, folding his hand over mine where it curled around my drink, a sidecar this time.

"What's not to get?" I asked gaily. "I play golf. I go to parties. I like you."

"*Do* you?" he asked, so surprised and earnest that I laughed.

"*Yes,* I do. Otherwise I wouldn't be making the time. Do you like me?"

"Well, I don't know you."

"Oh, what does that have to do with liking me?"

I thought he might kiss me then, but instead he pulled away, looking slightly abashed.

"I don't know you," he said, "but I think I would like to."

I took a sip of my drink to buy some time because that wasn't a line I heard very often. I wasn't sure I liked it, but with Nick's eyes on me, I decided I did.

"I think I might let you get to know me," I said, and he smiled with real pleasure.

In the end, we stayed at the Lyric for a few hours, and then we were both hungry so we stopped for a short while at a restaurant for a shared plate of corned beef hash and eggs. Nick told me a little about the war, nothing dark at all, but the day the sun came up silver instead of gold over Cantigny, the peeping of chicks inside an abandoned helmet. I wasn't much of a soldier's girl, but I liked listening to him, more solemn than I usually was over our meal.

After that, there were only a handful of hours left before Nick needed to be back at his work, which made me laugh because it had been some time since I had been with anyone who needed to worry about something like that.

"Don't go back to West Egg," I said. "Come home with me. You may have your own room. I promise I won't even climb into bed with you and keep you up."

It looked like he might attempt to be chivalrous about it and insist on going home, so I scooted close to him on the bench seat, taking him by his shirt and planting a little kiss right behind his ear.

"Don't make me ask again," I murmured. "I'll be cross with you."

"Can't have that," he said with a faint smile, but when he tried to hold me close for a kiss of his own, I retreated ladylike back to my side of the car. I liked that he only sighed after it a little, and then he turned the car north on Park Avenue towards home, where Aunt Justine's friends were just now breaking things up.

"Ah, that's a nice one for you, Jordan," cried Mrs. Crenshaw, who had after all killed her husband and replaced him with a soldier even prettier than Nick. Her imp, held by a delicate Tiffany chain dangling from her wrist, hissed speculatively at us, and I tugged my skirt out of the way. It was the delicate silk overlaid with sheer chiffon, and I was hoping to wear it to the party on Governors Island the next Saturday.

"Goodness, it's been a while since we've seen you with a lad, my dear," said Mrs. Baddicock sternly. "Do make sure he minds his place."

"Of course," I said, and left him there while I rang for Lara, Aunt Justine's girl of all work. She shook out the guest room and even managed to locate a pair of striped pajamas that had belonged to the late Mr. Sigourney Howard. I took them from her and went to find Nick, who was having a nightcap with my aunt.

I paused at the doorway, amused at how they looked like a cartoon about flaming youth and severe age. Nick was looking quite debauched with his eyes glassy and his tie undone, while Aunt Justine, who had likely been drinking more than we had, gave him a cool look with her spine perfectly straight and her hair swept back in immaculate silver wings. He was trying to thank her for letting him stay, and she was telling him that it had nothing to do with her.

"Nick," I said. "I'm being ever so domestic. I have some pajamas for you here."

He mumbled something to my aunt and followed me to the room, where he took the striped pajamas from me with an awkward nod of thanks.

"I think your aunt hates me," he said, sitting down on the edge of the newly turned bed.

"She might. I would say she doesn't know you well enough to hate you yet. She probably only disapproves of you and dislikes you."

"Wouldn't that bother you?" he asked, and I smiled.

"It used to, when I was very young. Now it seems so much less important."

"And what is important to you in your great old age?"

I let him take me by the hand and draw me to stand between his legs. He was of course older than I was, but in the soft light from the green-shaded lamp, he looked only my age or perhaps even younger. His hands rested lightly on the curve of my waist as he looked up to me. He was almost painfully in earnest and so very sincere.

I leaned down to cup his face in my hands, kissing his forehead gently. He was going to get even less sleep than we had thought.

"Being clever. Knowing things. Knowing myself best of all."

"Miss Baker, I don't think you're always a very nice girl," he said, reaching up to cover my hands with his. There was a teasing note to his voice, as well something that might turn into genuine affection someday.

For some reason, it made me draw back, my hands falling away from his like water. Being liked like that felt like a little too much in that moment. I would have to go back to my room for a while, among my own safe and familiar things, to mull it over before I decided if it was all right or not.

"I'm not a nice girl at all," I said with a wink. "I'm better."

I closed the door behind me when I went, and it felt like there were bubbles in my chest and a champagne sweetness. My face was warm, and it had nothing to do with the drinks we had had or the heat that seeped into the apartment through the cracks, giving the whole building a kind of damp sogginess that made the walls swelter in the summer.

Oh I like him, I thought, a little giddy.

I passed by my aunt's study on my way to my own bedroom. Her light was still on; she had taken on the restless habit of sleeping away the heat of the day. I poked my head in to say goodnight, but ever unsentimental, she only shook hers.

"I hope you know what you are doing," she said mildly.

"Of course I do," I said with confidence.

I slept a few hours in my own bed, dreaming of a train full of people whose faces had been rubbed away by an enormous gum eraser. I awoke just before eight to the sound of Aunt Justine finally going to bed. I thought about rolling over and going back to sleep, but then I remembered Nick all on his lonesome in the guest room.

Barefoot, I padded down the hall and opened the door to find him still asleep, and as silently as I knew how, I crept in to look at him. He slept on his belly, all pushed over to one side of the large bed with one arm hanging down so that his fingertips grazed the floor. There was something quaintly old-fashioned about him in my great-uncle's striped cotton pajamas, and with a slight smile, I slipped between the sheets with him. I wanted to look at him more closely, perhaps to touch his face while it was so loose and relaxed, but his eyes opened before I could do so.

For a moment, there was a perfect blankness to him, like the first page in a school notebook. He had no idea who I was, where he was, or what I meant. Then his mouth smiled, and slowly the rest of him came along.

"Good morning," Nick said quietly, reaching out to cover my hand with his where it lay on the pillow. "Am I so late that I might as well stay in bed?"

"I'm afraid not," I said. "But you are early enough to run down the street for breakfast if you hurry."

"And if I don't hurry?"

In response, I propped myself up on one elbow and bent down to kiss him, my other hand tangled in his short hair. I kissed his eyelids, his cheeks, the edge of his jaw, and the corners of his mouth before swinging my legs over the edge of the bed.

"Well, Lara will probably do you up some toast and eggs when she does mine, but you do have to get dressed for that. My aunt does not tolerate slovenliness from men at her table."

I started to stand up, but Nick had come up behind me, wrapping his arms around me from behind. I tensed for a moment, but he only wanted to nuzzle at the back of my neck.

"I think I made a good start in getting to know you yesterday. When can I continue the process?"

I was glad that I was facing away from him, because it wouldn't do to let him see how very pleased I was over that.

"I'm playing a match in East Hills Friday afternoon," I said. "You can come and cheer me on after work if you like."

"I would. And would you like to come to my house after that? It wouldn't be far from East Hills to West Egg."

"I'll be spending the night at the Tysons' unfortunately. I rather promised Chrissy I would."

"Ah. Can't disappoint Chrissy. I'll come and bring you a lemonade, how's that?"

"Perfect. Now get a move on if you want that toast and eggs. You dawdled so long you'll have to leave straightaway after."

Aunt Justine once gave me some advice when I was newly come to New York. If I was going to be passing anything more than time in public with a man, I should always find out what happened when he heard *no*, whether it was from me, a taxi driver, a waiter, or his employer.

"You may decide what to do after that," she said, "but most times, your course of action will be clear."

Nick passed that bar when plenty of other people hadn't, and at breakfast, he was valiantly charming with Aunt Justine, who had come out to take his measure. She had never had that much time for men, so Nick ended up chattering like a jaybird while she examined him like an exhibit in a museum and I watched them both with a fond amusement.

"He's not quite all there, is he, dear?" she asked after he left. "Something missing in the eyes."

"What he's got is fine for me. It's probably just for summer, anyway."

"Are you sure?"

No, I wasn't. I was different, as Walter Finley and Louisville had so emphatically pointed out, but Nick was too. I wasn't really interested in making a go of it with anyone, no matter what Tom and Daisy were pushing, but part of that disinterest came from the place of a rather arrogant person realizing that she *couldn't*. There was nothing as uninteresting as something I couldn't have.

Nick, however. Nick was saying that I might have him, and I could see something in the tricky mess of that, somewhere where we might meet and pass a summer or a year or five years or fifty. That was a tricky kind of ground, especially with the miscegenation laws that were applied like uneven powder all over the country, but there was talk that even that might change. White women had only gotten the vote two years ago, and no one knew what might happen in the time to come.

Of course I only thought about this in a vague and daylight way. I hadn't gotten as far as I had by looking ahead to any kind of future. I was grounded firmly in the present, never looking much further than the next two weeks or so. I would show my sky-blue planner to people who wanted to make plans further out, shaking my head mournfully.

"Can't do it, I'm afraid. I can't see that far."

The future had never looked further away that summer. There was too much of the present built up in front of it, the entire city and its surrounding tributaries reaching up towards the hot blue sky. Who had time for the future in a summer like that one?

CHAPTER SEVEN

One rainy night in late summer of 1917, Judge Baker caught me sneaking in through the back door. The lights were off, and he was drinking alone in the kitchen. I think he meant to catch me and scold me, but by then he was too far gone to do much besides shake a thick finger at me. Finally, he shook his head, rising unsteadily from the kitchen chair and retreating up to his room. He paused in the doorway, the hanging judge who would never give a Black man ten when he could give him twenty.

"I forgive you," he said, his words thick. "For Eliza. I forgive you. I don't blame you."

He nodded magnanimously, and I wondered what he would make of the fact that I never blamed myself for Eliza Baker's death, nor felt as if I needed one moment of forgiveness for it. I attended church every Sunday, and when I was meant to be thinking of pious things, I sat in our front pew and pretended I was balancing teacups on my chin, head up and uncaring about the eyes that bored into the back of my skull. That kind of defensive pride left very little room for guilt, so I didn't trouble myself with it.

There were eight pictures of Eliza Baker secreted through the house, hidden from view in places like Mrs. Baker's vanity and under the judge's desk blotter. In those pictures, she was a round-faced girl with enormous dark eyes and an Edwardian pompadour of gracious height. She had the tensile strength of spun steel, hard enough to bear her parents' fury when she converted, sharp enough to make her way to the exotic shores she had always dreamed of, and she didn't return to Louisville until the French and Chinese made living in Tonkin a misery. Unlike most, she could leave, and when she did, she took me with her all the way back to her home on Willow Street.

"You were my very favorite," she told me in my earliest memories. "Just the very best baby. I could not leave you, I could not bear it."

Favorite among what, I should have asked, but I never did.

She died less than a year after her return, and I stood between her parents at the funeral. It was a grim and Presbyterian thing, my first outing in Louisville society. The heavens poured rain from a leaden sky, and through the deluge, Mrs. Baker grasped my hand tight in hers, her black plumed hat drooping to either side of her tightly closed face.

The relief of having her only daughter home from foreign shores crystallized into despair when Eliza fell ill, and then after Eliza died, something shattered in Mrs. Baker. She went on until she couldn't any longer, and then she died, all broken-hearted after failing to fashion me into any kind of satisfying echo of Eliza.

The judge stood by Mrs. Baker's gravestone for long hours after the funeral while I sat anxiously in the car. I saw his shape, like a gravestone itself on the hill, and it wasn't until the shadows grew long and deep that he finally came to the car and we were allowed to go home.

What a broken, brittle people, I thought, discreetly studying his face out of the corner of my eye, and I promised myself I would never be so easy to shatter.

It was like a set of dominoes that Eliza had set into motion with her thin and graceful hand. Anabeth Baker, the hallway ghost with her bruised throat and her desperate angry mouth, spoke of a chain of disaster going back even further, and I decided to be grateful for the most recent generation of Bakers, who seemed inclined to die of broken hearts, worn-out souls, and pleurisy.

With Mrs. Baker gone, I was allowed to attend the local high school, and it was a relief from the oppressive dolor of the house where I lived. Whenever I came home to a stillness in the house that absorbed sound and air like a sponge, I knew to pack up a bag and make my way to a friend's house.

I at last had friends, and that was, whether she meant it or not, Daisy's doing. I had a hint of it the night we met, but she needed to talk like other people needed to eat or to breathe. At some point, she realized that it didn't matter at all what she said, and so she turned into a bubble of fashionable bon mots, non sequiturs, and giddy dizzy excitement. She could drown a delta city with her words, and I was swept up in it, tossed like a broken stalk of flowers into her tide and carried along so neatly that her friends seemed to think that I had always been there.

I was the youngest girl of the set, the baby. When we posed for the society photographers, before those photographers went off to the war, at least, they pushed me to the front with their hands over my shoulders or their arms slung around my waist. The older girls cooed over me, telling me I must remain exactly that small and that sweet.

I smiled wide with my white sharp teeth, and I learned to laugh like the clink of champagne flutes, but even then I never had much interest in sweetness. Eliza Baker was as sweet as candied almonds, and see where it got her. Daisy, as pretty as she was, was never sweet either, though she sparkled so bright it was easy to think she was. It was easy to think that Daisy was many things.

Helen Archer never cared much for sweetness either, and that was why I ended up in the back of the closet with her at the Botleys' smash in the summer of 1917. The two Botley boys were going to war and Louisville society turned out to see them off.

They left, Thomas and Sandy, but it was only Thomas who came back. I saw him years later in New York, and I knew at once that whoever it was who came back with Thomas's face, it was not him. It came to me that it must be Sandy instead, and I crossed to the other side of the street so there would be no awkwardness when he saw that I knew.

That day in July, there were still two bold Botley boys, however, and they looked very fine in their uniforms and their officer's bars. The girls were mad for both of them, and they seemed a little mad themselves, sneaking behind the pool house with every girl who would go as the adults pretended not to see.

Curious, I went behind the pool house with Thomas, older, kinder, and more thoughtful than Sandy. He was dashing, with hair like pale gold, and there was an excitement in kissing him, though it came more from his nervy fear about being sent overseas than for his good looks. I kissed some of that fear off of him, and I thought there was a kind of pleasant bitterness to it, like dark chocolate or good tea. It was interesting, but I could never develop a taste for sorrow, so when he started to slide his hand under my lilac frock I pushed him away and ran back into the house.

My cheeks were flushed, and my eyes too bright, like I had bitten an electric wire and now it lit me up. I thought I had better go inside and hide for a little while until I was more composed. The party was on the back lawn, and the Botley house, even with all the windows thrown open, was humid and still. Looking for a quiet place to lie down for a quarter hour, I instead found Botley Sr.'s treasured map room, and there, paging through the maps in their enormous racks, was Helen.

She was two years older than me, unfashionable, but the Archers were so wealthy that she became a kind of fashion all on her own. She pulled her spectacles out of their tortoiseshell case, and when I came in still overwarm from the kisses and the sticky weather outside, she slid them down her nose to peer at me.

"Come here," she said at last. "Mr. Botley has a very fine map of Tonkin."

Helen had a fortune and a kind of roundness to her that made me think of Christmas ornaments and buns dusted with large sugar crystals. Her dark thick brows were as straight as the trolley rail, and I saw that her nails were bitten down to the quick where she traced the rivers of Tonkin, hovering but too respectful to touch.

I didn't care much about the map, but I suddenly wanted very much to stand by her as she spoke of mountains and city centers. It was as if kissing Thomas had laid me open to a world where anyone might be kissed, and standing next to Helen as she recited the names of those foreign cities, I became aware that she had a mouth as well.

At some point, she realized I was looking at her instead of the map, and her words trailed off. With a confidence I had never had before, I reached up to cup the side of her warm neck with my hand. For just a moment, it was enough to feel her pulse under my palm and to feel the way my touch made her swallow hard.

It might have come to no more than that, but then we both heard the door slam somewhere, and a bubble of unwelcome voices echoing through the halls of the house. The voices were young and light, tumbling like a tide towards us, and I acted without thinking.

I seized Helen's hand and pulled her with me into the narrow closet close by. We fought for space with the mop and broom and with each other as well until we got the door closed behind us. Then her hand clasped mine hard, and we didn't even have to lean towards one another before we were kissing.

We didn't fit each other, but the small space made it seem as if we did, and there was enough room at least to touch each other's faces, to make an utter ruin of our carefully set hair. Her fingers ended up in my mouth somehow, and she half-shrieked, half-giggled when I bit. It was hellishly hot and sodden in the closet, and I felt as if I would surely melt when I pressed my cheek to hers or when my hands slid up her bare wrists.

Somehow, we were not caught, and eventually, we came out of the closet holding hands and with our eyes gleaming. We just looked like girls who had taken a turn with the Botley boys behind the pool house, so that was all right, and when the party adjourned for the night, I went home to the Archers' house with Helen.

After that, I became the most elegant kind of vagabond. I stayed almost three weeks with the Archers, who thought I was the most clever thing. Then when Helen and I fell out, I was only a few days at home before I finagled an invitation for a visit with the Featherstones, where Alicia Featherstone and I enjoyed almost a month together before I decided I could not stand her snoring. Under the auspice of his sister Paulette, I passed some time with Victor Reed before he was old enough to enlist, and he was a better kisser than Thomas, though less thoughtful than Alicia had been.

Being a guest suited me. I ate with the family and slept in the same beds with the girls I liked best, and as I went along, I was turning into a marvelous mimic. I copied the Featherstones' polished manners, the Banners' Mid-Atlantic accent, and the Wilkins' easy command of those they deemed their social inferiors, which was to say, everyone.

I learned the trick of simply assuming I was welcome wherever I went, and for the most part, I was. I was clever enough to know that it was my exotic looks and faintly tragic history that made me such an attractive curiosity, and I was not yet clever enough to mind when they prodded at my differences for a conversation piece at dinner.

I was staying with the Fays for the week when Daisy was set to meet with a few dashing young officers from Camp Taylor. By that point, we were all well and tired of doing that, but her father was old friends with the commandant there, so of course she had to, and since she was, I had to as well.

She dressed me in a soft cream dress that smelled faintly of lavender, and she put on a rather dreamy blue thing that floated around her like mist from the Ohio River.

"Should I have the headache or should you?" I asked her as she pinned her dark hair back, and she smiled at me in the mirror.

"Oh, I will, certainly," she drawled. "You can put me to bed, and after it gets dark, we can run off to see about Barbara Blake and that cousin of hers from Virginia."

I descended in Daisy's wake into a parlor full of officers and we set about the surprisingly difficult and tedious work of being just the right kind of charmed without giving out the impression that we wanted to do more than sit and converse. Mrs. Fay told us that the right kind of welcoming was "parlor and no farther," and that was occasionally a fine line to tread.

Daisy had to be as bubbly as champagne, and I was allowed to be quieter and mysterious, and that was how I knew that I saw Jay Gatsby first. He hung back from the others, stood up by the window like a toy soldier while the others scattered around the Fays' formal parlor. He looked, I thought from my hard straight-backed chair, a bit like a man awed in church, gazing around at the Persian carpets that were meant to be walked on, the brass table that came all the way from Turkey, the lofting windows that recalled the Fays' French ancestors. His quick eyes darted over me as well, and I thought with some wry distaste of him cataloging me as some Oriental handmaiden, brought to beautify the place like the stained glass rose window and the elephant foot umbrella stand.

He didn't even dare look at Daisy until she called out to him, saying something silly about not being shy.

Then he looked at her, and everything in the room just . . . stopped.

"Oh," Daisy said, her voice small, and I could almost feel the breath catch in her throat as her hands fell into her lap. She looked dazed, and when I followed her gaze to the young lieutenant at the window, I could see why.

You weren't meant to look at people the way that Lieutenant Gatsby looked at Daisy Fay. You couldn't peel your skin back and show them how your heart had gone up in flames, how nothing that had come before mattered and nothing that came afterward mattered as long as you had what you wanted.

In that one still moment, it was as if Daisy had, all unknowing, taken Jay Gatsby's heart for her own, and he would spend the rest of his life trying to get it back.

"Oh, ha, my—my goodness," she stammered with a charming laugh. "Aren't you just the thing. Why, you make me think of that song, what was it, Jordan, 'Poor Butterfly'? Why, I could not get that song out of my head, isn't that silly, everyone, why don't we just have a chorus now . . ."

Somehow, she got the whole room obediently singing the song with her, and the strange moment passed, though somehow, I think it never did.

She did fabricate a headache after that, but she pushed a slip of paper into Lieutenant Gatsby's hand on his way out, and that night, she didn't go out to meet Barbara Blake's cousin at all, even if he was educated in Paris and heir to a steel mill.

I did, however, and I was having my first taste of absinthe on the hidden dock on Twelve Mile Island when someone cried out to look out over the river.

It was like the moon had settled on the water, casting shards of light on the broken waves. A man and a woman sat in a rowboat, no lantern on the prow, but a white glow charting their figures, the shape of the man's profile, the softness of the woman's arms as she reached for him. The darkness and the distance made it impossible to see who it was, even when they stood and kissed like something out of the old Shawnee stories about doomed

lovers and descended stars, and all along the shore, the mischie-
vous girls and dangerous boys of Louisville were silenced.

Someone tried to call to them, breaking the spell, and the
man turned slightly, pulling the woman's face against his shoulder to comfort her or to hide her. A shadow passed over the face
of the moon, and they were gone, another strange night before
the war came.

In the morning, Daisy and I were both decently back in her
bed, and I thought I could still detect a shimmer of starlight in
the corner of her mouth, tangled in the hair at her nape.

Daisy and her lieutenant were the great secret of the summer,
one that I was thrilled to be included in. I covered for Daisy, I
watched them with bated breath because it was all terribly romantic, wasn't it, and when he finally left for Europe with the others,
Daisy wasn't seen for days, locked in her bedroom and refusing
food and comfort.

She had come out in fall, when there was Red Cross and relief
work to do, and then not long after that, her aunt in Baltimore
grew sickly, and she went with her mother to look after her and
to see Baltimore. Daisy and I drifted apart, somewhat, after that,
and we would have drifted even further if it wasn't for the thing
I helped her with a few years later. That year, however, enshrined
her in my heart as something gleaming and shining, something
whose touch was almost holy and whose heart could call down
light.

I was a little bereft after Daisy went to Baltimore, but I found
my feet quickly when I realized that the excuse of war work
could keep me out for long hours rolling bandages and preparing
care packages. I spent the war years hopping houses and hopping
beds, restless in my own way and strangely comforted by the un-
ease that soaked into everything we did. The world was on fire,
but we could only smell the smoke.

Daisy wouldn't have come to some of the places I wanted to
go then, anyway, and as the war hung over everything and my

position in Louisville became stranger and even less sure, there were a *lot* of places I wanted to go and things I wanted to do.

Daisy had the world in her hands, but she was never what you would call worldly. Her pleasures were domestic, her disasters, similar. They always had been.

Then the war ended, everything changed, and nothing changed, and I was still, frustratingly enough, nothing more than myself.

The judge was in a long and dignified decline. He was simply seen less and less often in town, and then less and less often at home. It drove his clerks to distraction, and at home sometimes I would enter a room and think I was quite alone until I smelled the scent of his tobacco, carried in a little embroidered pouch in his pocket, and heard his customary grumbling cough.

He had good days and bad ones. On the good days, he was nearly solid again, rattling his silverware against the china, handing the servants their pay and venturing up the street for a bit of ham and mustard on rye, what he liked to speak of as his only indulgence. (It wasn't. There were also the gambling slips to be paid off after he died as well as the annuity of a beautiful young girl just a few years older than me who lived on Toussaint Avenue.)

On the bad days, there was a hollowness to his eyes, and his body took on a shapeless colorless quality. It was as if he was testing out his next role as a ghost, choosing a look that was positively medieval over his own modern appearance. On the bad days, he lurked in the corner of the eye, full of a kind of dull menace. Two servants quit when they saw him drift rapidly towards them in the upper hallway, and he broke one poor girl's neck when he startled her and she fell down the stairs.

He revived, briefly, for Daisy's wedding. She married Tom nine months after Armistice, the shadow of her bad March not even touching her hems. She woke Louisville to a ringing of bells and glamour, life returned, and even the judge had to heed it.

Before I let myself get swept away by Walter Finley, I remembered the judge seated at a table of town luminaries, nodding and looking gravely pleased, even if he was put out by the fact that Daisy had insisted on an integrated jazz band for at least a portion of the reception. The war was over, and the world was breaking down the doors even in Louisville.

The judge left early, and I left late with Walter. Walter was from St. Louis, staying with his Fenton cousins in Louisville, and he was related to Daisy through some rather tortuous chain of blood. After the war, he lost a great deal of the tiresome dignity and restraint that he had been bred to, and so was banished from St. Louis until he could remember some of it again.

"Who knows if I want to go back," he said to me very late that night. "Or who knows who I might bring back with me."

"I'm not someone who gets brought along," I told him, even if it was something of a lie. He laughed, his head resting on my discarded dress, which we had rolled up to make a pillow. We were stretched on the parlor floor of the mother-in-law unit behind my house, and somewhere faintly in the distance, we could hear the music from Daisy's reception playing on, even if she had left hours ago.

"Not even if I'm the one bringing you?" he asked, and he kept me from answering by kissing my throat just right.

I was less careful than I should have been that night, and for the next three weeks, while being gay and lovely for Walter, I was something of a nervous wreck. I kept reminding myself that there was always Fulbright's, that if Daisy could bear a thing I could, but it is different, isn't it, when it's your body, your future, your reputation, and your mistake.

In the end, my luck held, it was nothing at all, and of course by then, Walter had worked his way through his post-war wildness. We were through. I liked him better than I had let on, even to myself, and I came home at dawn three weeks after Daisy's wedding, my throat hoarse from arguing, and my eyes and nose aching from the tears I refused to cry.

I crept into a house that was finally empty of guests, but it wasn't until dead Anabeth met me on the stairs that I realized something was wrong.

Anabeth had recognized right away that I was no real Baker. When I first came to live on Willow Street, she had kept me up and crying in terror at all hours, but as I grew, and especially when I started having my monthlies, I crossed some river in her mostly-gone mind, and she gentled, no longer waiting for me in the corner of my room or coming upon me while I was having my evening bath.

Now, though, she stood on the stairway as she never had before, and the temperature dropped so fast I could see my breath for a brief moment. I froze, ready to run, but she pointed down towards the side hallway, where the only room was the judge's study.

I followed her pointing finger, aware the whole time of her eyes on the back of my neck. I opened the door, and for a moment I was actually relieved to see the judge sitting at the desk, the only light from the single lamp in the corner.

Then he looked up at me, nothing living in his eyes, and I became aware of the pair of feet peeking out from behind the desk, all that was visible of the judge after he had fallen from a fast and fatal stroke.

I stared to scream, but the ghost, not putting down his pen, pointed at me. His eyes, like Anabeth's, were shaded dark, completely without light or anything like human emotion.

"No," he said, in a voice that seemed to come from a great distance over a silver wire. "You were taught better."

I had been. I closed the door gently behind me, and went to the front room, turning on every light as I did so. I went to the phone, and with a voice that I was convinced would never shake again, I started to make the necessary calls, to the Coy Funeral Parlor, which had been burying Bakers since before the Civil War, and to First Grace Presbyterian, where the judge and I attended only sporadically without Mrs. Baker to force us.

Then it was time to take Mrs. Baker's little leather-bound

book from its spot by the phone, and to call the family. I did well enough until I came to one I hardly knew. It was the judge's aunt, listed only as Mrs. Sigourney Howard.

I introduced myself, explained what had happened, accepted her condolences and well wishes as I had already done two dozen times that morning, and then she paused, the distance between Louisville and New York crackling along the wire.

"My dear, you needn't be so strong. We're family. Tell me how you are."

It wouldn't have hit with any force on a regular day, but that morning, the rain coming down hard, my heart more broken than I wanted to admit, and a new ghost in the house, it pried something open in me that had always been shut before. The tears escaped, and I gasped at the pain of it before I started sobbing, sitting on the ground with the telephone cord stretched to its full extent.

"I don't want to be here anymore," I cried, and I meant Louisville, the house on Willow Street, my own tattered reputation, with the dead and without Daisy.

"Why, then you must come stay with me," she said, as if it was the most natural thing in the world, and I sobbed harder. She made it sound easy, and for a miracle, just that once, it was.

The judge's funeral, respectable but sparsely attended, was held five days later, and two days after that, I was on my way home to New York with Mrs. Sigourney Howard, who graciously permitted me to call her my own Aunt Justine.

We departed from St. Louis, her in the black she had kept on after her husband died, and me in the fashionable black frock that was part of my new mourning set.

"Six months at the outside," she told me sternly. "It isn't appropriate for a young thing like you to be stuck in mourning too long."

On the train, in our private compartment, she gave me my first drop of real demoniac, making my eyes water and my throat ache. All I had had before were fakes made from cherry liqueur mixed with a queasy amount of goat blood, only good for making young debs sick off of hayrides and at church socials. Demoniac was still legal then, and something of an old man's tipple still, a remnant from an age more alchemical than mustard gas.

When I had gotten over the discomfort of those first few moments, a sense of peace spilled over me, warm like I had never been warm before and more easy in the world and in my skin than I had ever been. I glanced out the train window to see a shimmer of bright gold traveling over the flat blue Middle Western sky.

Out my window, for just a moment, I saw a pair of Black farmers on either end of a broad fallow field. One lifted his hand and a burn line spread out to the right and left of him, glowing red, moving fast and leaving black rich earth behind it. The line of fire raced towards the other man, the one closer to the tracks, and I glimpsed a smile on his face as he held up his hands and the fire went suddenly cold and white in front of him. It was land magic, earth magic of a kind you never saw in the city, and with the demoniac whispering in my belly and my blood, I lost all of my city reserve and educated pretension to stare in awe and pleasure and wonder at the sight of it.

CHAPTER EIGHT

As it turned out, Nick and I were possessed of a basic incompatibility that we both gamely ignored in order to spend time with one another. He did well in New York, where charming ex-soldiers were de rigueur, and where his Middle Western good looks contrasted nicely with mine. He liked being shocked by the extravagances of the city, but he was not ready for the people that came with the wonder, who lived shoulder to shoulder with wonder and thus grew immune to it.

Also, Daisy's cousin or not, he was of another class entirely, unable to comprehend how very *little* money meant once you had a certain amount of it. I brought him one weekend up to Warwick, where the Dancy siblings, Margaret and Highland, were throwing their annual midsummer crush. I borrowed Max Peabody's car for the weekend because Nick's wasn't fit to be seen, and I drove us up on Friday so we'd have the full two nights.

It was a good weekend, with Nick and me stealing off quick moments on the hidden beach, before breakfast in one of the dining alcoves, and yes, just once, in a little closet that smelled of fresh detergent and pallid violets. I saw a bit less of him than I might have preferred, because he took up with some men he recognized from his time in the city. He turned out to be popular with them, sitting up late on the veranda and talking business, politics, and women late into the night. I was slightly put out, but I could hardly blame him for making the most of things.

It rained on Friday night, and as it happened I had forgotten to put the top up on Max's car. He arrived with Carol Linney on his arm, crossing the crowded breakfast room to playfully scold me for my mistake. Max was a big bluff thing, avuncular even at the age of twenty-one, and he told me that he would have to put me to work drying off the seats and polishing the chrome to say sorry.

"Well, *someone's* going to have to do that, but it certainly won't be me," I told him. "I had someone else do the parking for me, and they must have left the top down. I am dreadfully sorry for it, Max, and of course I'll pay to have it taken care of, if you like . . ."

He didn't care at all, of course, more interested in telling us all about his recent trip to Thessaloniki than anything like cleaning a car. Nick's gaze roved between us as if he was watching a tennis match, and before bed, he caught up with me in the greenhouse, where I had gone to catch my breath from the events of the day.

"You lied to him," he said, and for a moment, I had no idea who he was talking about.

"Who, Max? What does it matter?"

"You should have told him the truth," Nick said doggedly, and I snorted.

"Why? I offered to have it cleaned up. What more should I have done?"

Nick frowned, brows drawing together in disapproval.

"It was dishonest."

"Show me someone who cares, and I'll come clean," I offered. We both knew that Max and Carol had disappeared with the Timberly twins and Prescott Lind to smoke hashish on the upper veranda. They wouldn't be caring about anything for hours.

Nick shook his head.

"It's still not right."

"Probably not. Are you going to let it bother you all weekend?"

He watched me pluck a velvety white flower from its stalk and tuck it behind my ear. He was keeping some distance between us as if slightly wary of me.

"Let me guess, your girl in Jersey City wouldn't do such a thing."

He jumped, and my estimation of him lowered a bit. I didn't mind the girl much, but I did mind his assumption that I didn't know.

"What do you know about—"

"Not her name, and I don't care to," I lied. Of course I did. Mrs. Crenshaw's imp was a fifteenth century antique and incredibly reliable.

"All I know, Nick, is that if you want honest and impeccable, you ought to go back to your girl in Jersey City, though maybe you should tell her about me and Miss Minnesota and let her make her own judgment."

"Jordan . . ."

He sounded like he wanted to keep talking about this, but I shook my head. I took the flower from my ear and tucked it behind his. With his complexion, it looked better on him anyway.

"I don't care," I said impatiently. "And if you do, fine. But if you want someone to talk to about morality it isn't going to be me. I was rather hoping to go walking down by the willows."

We had a room, but the Dancys had had some summer mage whisk up will-o-wisps to light the bowers created by the drooping willow branches, and there was really only one reason to go down there. Nick wavered, and I decided I was pleased when he offered me his arm and we slipped out of the greenhouse.

He was a perfect gentleman, stopping and going like the most well-mannered Tennessee walking horse. I laid him out under the willow and we had gotten each other half-undressed before I stopped, mostly to see what he would do.

"I'm not easy," I warned him. "I may be exactly this stubborn forever, or I might change my mind at any moment. What do you think of that?"

"I hope you change your mind, but I like it when you're

stubborn," he replied, and I laughed at him, kissing him because while I wasn't easy, I realized he was.

"Jordan," he said, half-desperate, and I laughed again, got back to it.

By the time we drove home, questions of dishonesty were forgotten, and we never bothered to speak of it again, not when there were so many other exciting things to speak of.

I lured him to my favorite dance clubs and speakeasies, introduced him to actors and radicals and gin babies. It was a pleasure to see everything through his wide eyes, and unlike so many other men, he never turned around and gave that instruction back to me as if I should be grateful. He was the grateful one, and he followed where I led; it was one of my favorite things about him. But I couldn't take Nick everywhere.

Even when he showed up wearing a cologne that I didn't recognize and with an extremely livid bite mark that I only found when opening his shirt, he was lukewarm on going to the Cendrillon.

Of course I could have just dragged him along as I had to the Lyric, but doing the same at the Cendrillon had been disastrous for me a time or two. Instead I described it to him, and watched with fascination as a cloud of confusion, fear, and longing came across his face. It settled into a kind of stony wariness, and he sat back from me, shaking his head.

"I don't know why—I'm not like that."

I tilted my head to one side, examining him with a careful eye. We were having a nightcap at my place just past four in the morning. He was getting used to late nights, and making himself presentable in other people's bathrooms, but now he looked more nervous than he had in a few weeks.

"You're not?" I asked, and he shook his head hard.

"No. Absolutely not. I don't go to that kind of place."

"I am, and I do," I offered, and Nick gave me a little smile that understood more than he let on.

"I know you are and that you do. You're different. It's different for women."

"Not at the Cendrillon," I said, but he took my hand, not looking at me.

"I'm not like that," he said, his voice shaking just a little. "Please?"

"I'm not the one who decides that," I said as gently as I knew how. I cupped my hand over the back of his head, ruffling his hair slightly with my fingertips. I kissed him on the ear.

"All right. Never mind. But that's where I'm going on Saturday."

There were a dozen and one ways that the Cendrillon got away with being what it was. It was on the border between Cathedral Heights and Harlem, it paid off everyone from the local patrol-men up to the commissioner, and the owners, a pair of spare older men whose suits were worth more than most of my closet put together, were easily three times as paranoid as any place like the Lyric or Roberson's.

At the Lyric, only the method for getting there was hidden. At the Cendrillon, unless you wore the right flower on your per-son, unless you knew the password, and unless you had a look the doorman liked, you would simply be at a rather shabby theater that rotated through a complement of dull comedians, inexpert tumblers, and bad tenors. I once passed a sulky night at one of their shows when I'd forgotten that I should have been wearing a white gardenia instead of a spray of baby's breath on my lapel. There were apparently some people from the neighborhood who honestly thought it was just a sad little theater.

Some serious magic—some infernal, some subterranean French, some American swamp medicine—made it so that the Cendrillon was overlaid by the ramshackle theater. You didn't go up into a loft or down into a basement. It was the same space, and when the magic ebbed just a little bit, sometimes you could see one from the other, quickly and more like déjà vu than anything as solid as a mirage.

I found out about the Cendrillon when I first came to New York, and it had taken me four months to get up the courage to go. I had to find Margot Van Der Veen, and then I had to go into that cautious dance of hints, looks, and shared references that told her I was the right kind of safe. In Louisville, I had crashed through the world like a cannonball, but here, I could see that that wouldn't serve. There would be a time for crashing through the veils and birch wood screens, but it couldn't happen when I was seventeen and so achingly new and strange.

The first time I went, I was in a shimmering black beaded dress that was rather too old for me and too soaked in Scandinavian gloom for words. I wore a red rosebud pinned to my dress, and I'd stolen Aunt Justine's sparkling diamond earrings to complete the picture. I shook a little, thinking that this was when everything was going to change. I had escaped Louisville, come to New York, and everything would be different.

I gave the password in my most unaccented voice, conspiring to look bored when the man looked me over and opened the door. If I didn't pass muster, I wondered if I was prepared to spend the next hour or so watching the Amazing Ming juggle plates in the scanty dusty theater or to walk out in defeat. There were already a few people in the seats who looked excited by the prospect and I was certain that if I had to sit with them, I would simply perish.

The man at the door nodded me in, and the moment I stepped past the threshold, I felt as if I were falling, not plummeting down a rabbit hole, but instead that gut-clenching rush of missing the very last steep stair in the basement. My foot came down, and I looked down into an elegant ballroom of veiled mirrored walls, a long bar of rosewood and brass, and an integrated orchestra that were, to a man, playing blindfolded.

I felt a rush of heat and pleasure when I looked down at all the people below me and knew, rather than suspected or hoped, that they were like me. Of course they weren't, but that single moment left me speechless and almost in tears before a party of young men arrived behind me and pushed me out of the way to descend the stairs and join the fun.

That shove broke me out of my spell somewhat, but even four years later, I felt a trace of that old wonder as I came through the door with a showy pink peony tucked behind my ear, wearing my emerald green silk slip dress with its dancing fringe of copper beads. I had come with plenty of energy to spare that night, and as the band struck up the first song, I found myself in the arms of a fat Black girl in a white tuxedo, the satin of her lapels gleaming like stars in the soft light. She had long eyelashes that curled up like angel wings, and when she pressed her round cheek against mine, she made my heart beat faster. She was light on her feet, but I wondered if she had mistaken me for someone else because she passed me on at the end of "Broadway Baby."

After the girl in the tuxedo came Maurice Wilder, who struck a strange and exciting chord in me by being the most handsome boy in a flaming red dress.

"Tacky," I teased him, liking the blush that came up on his narrow face when I did, and he pulled me close to hide his face in my hair. Someone should have told him to wear a slip, because I could feel every inch of him through the gossamer fabric, but I was glad that no one had told him yet. He let me pull him behind one of the vast Boston ferns to kiss him, but I let him go when he wouldn't let me do more.

Like every halfway fashionable thing, I had a tab at the Cendrillon. Mine was under the name Miss Shanghai, something I absolutely did not choose for myself, but it still got me delicious drinks in Venetian glassware. I was wearing green that night, and fortunately they had a good absinthe, straight from their supplier on the Gulf. I leaned against the bar to watch the bartender set the drink up for me, from the thick glass tumbler just barely tinted to enhance the green of the drink to the slotted spoon where a little sugar cat crouched, its face, paws, and tail lightly singed brown. The bartender balanced the spoon in the notch on the tumbler's edge, and then holding the cloudy bottle high so that the arc was elegant and narrow, poured the green alcohol over the cat. When the sugar dissolved entirely and the tumbler was three-fourths of the way full, the bartender slid the glass towards me, and I smiled, taking the spoon to mix my drink and find myself a seat.

People make such a fuss about home. Daisy talked in raptures about Louisville and Chicago, while Nick, when he had a few, could be quite a pain about Minnesota snow and the pale faces and gleaming eyes seen from the car in the cornfields. I listened, but I never cared all that much.

Despite that, the Cendrillon was one of my homes, and I could perch on the high stools by the ruby-glass mirror and sip my drink, my legs crossed so that if someone I wanted walked by, I could tap them easily on the thigh and make them look at me.

Without windows, the Cendrillon had an underground feel. It kept things cooler in the summer months, but it was New York in one of the hottest years on record. We were in a roiling boil, and I only kept cool by filling an old perfume atomizer with water and spritzing myself liberally as the night went on. I added a few drops of actual perfume to the mix, so not long into the evening, I was lightly drenched in citron, but still a little cooler and a little more alert than the other people there.

"Why, Jordan Baker!"

I was already smiling as I turned because it was Miriam Howe, and everyone loved Miriam Howe. She was tall and lean with the far-seeing eyes of some fabulous savannah cat, and when she draped herself around you, it was better than wearing mink, not that anyone could think of mink in New York in the summertime.

That night, she was glamorous in a lilac silk sack dress that left her long throat and her soft white arms bare. Around her neck was a fortune in perfectly matched pink pearls, and the moment I saw them, I wanted to put my mouth to them and her skin underneath.

The band slowed down for "Lavender Blue Moon," and I put my arm around her waist to lead her onto the floor. She let me lead, and we swayed together, more in time with the massive fans above our head than with the saxophone.

"Are you here with Nan again?" asked Miriam.

"No, Nan went off to Athens for the summer. Who knows who I'll be when she gets back."

Miriam gave me a slightly calculated smile, twin to the one I gave her.

"And you," I said. "Still trying to get a ring out of Perry Sloane?"

"Oh *darling*, where have *you* been? Perry found God."

"Scandalous," I said with a grin, and so we were clear.

Miriam was a good dancer, at least as good as I was and likely better, so we stayed on the dance floor for a while. We were attractive together, and I liked the look of my body next to hers as we twirled past the tall mirrors. The last song was fast enough to make us both sweat, and when she threw her arm over my shoulder, we slipped against each other in the most intriguing way.

"Get me a ginger water, won't you?" she asked. "I'll find us a spot in back."

I elbowed my way to the bar to get Miriam's ginger water and to get a caipirinha for myself. I sipped at my drink diligently as I went to find Miriam, but by the time I got to the back, I could see that someone else had found her first.

His back was to me, and past his shoulder, I caught Miriam's face, chagrined, nervous, and maybe a little hypnotized. Then the man turned around, and I could see that it was Jay Gatsby, sharp as a razor blade in a pale gray suit, buttons undone and the color high on his cheeks.

"There you are, Miss Baker. Miss Howe and I were just talking about you."

One thing I liked about Miriam, she was never one to let grass grow under her feet. She was around Gatsby in a heartbeat, and she even made it look natural. She plucked the ginger water from my hand as she went by, gave me a significant look, and then was gone. At a loss for what to do, I took a slow sip of my drink, watching Gatsby over the edge of my glass. There was a bubble around us, as if the crowd could be ordered as nicely as his clothes or his shoes.

"Are they afraid of you or did you do something?" I asked, and he grinned.

"Does it matter? Come here."

"I don't have to," I told him, gripping my drink a little tighter. He looked surprised.

"Of course you don't. It was a request."

No, it really wasn't, I thought.

"Then make a request," I said, staying right where I was. Around us, the other patrons were oblivious, not even watching us out of the corner of their eyes to report elsewhere later. He had done something, and the only comfort was that he hadn't done more.

He looked at me for a moment, blank-eyed, and then he smiled. His eyes got soft, and so did his mouth, and it came to me that he had such a *beautiful* mouth. It was something I liked on men and women, a beautiful mouth that might kiss me or whisper secrets in my ear or open and let me kiss them . . .

I realized that I was flushed all over, and I just barely managed to stop my drink from tumbling from my hand. I swallowed, took a better hold of the glass, and gave him a look to tell him I knew exactly what he was doing.

"Jordan, will you please come with me?"

"Yes," I sighed. Sometimes, the only excuse for doing something stupid is knowing that you are doing it and being willing to accept the consequences.

He put his hand at the small of my back to press me forward

and I went, just barely stopping myself from leaning against him. Just because I liked how he felt, just because it was intriguing and appealing and delicious was no reason to reward him for this display.

The back rooms at the Cendrillon are numerous, dim and cool, clad in brick and boned with bare rafters. Jacquard couches that were quite big enough to fit two or three, Pashmin rugs and delicately embroidered lampshades mostly hid the fact that they were in reality something a great deal like cells. Gatsby handed me the key to the room he had found for us and then spread himself out on one end of the couch, watching me through half-lidded eyes.

He was good to look at, so I looked, and I saw the dark love bites that peppered his throat, the disorder of his clothes and the looseness of his limbs. His mouth was almost as red as what I painted on, and I bet that if I touched him there, he would flinch.

"Does Nick know you're here?" I asked, and he shot me a bemused look.

"Of course he doesn't. He wouldn't want to hear about a place like this."

I could still feel Nick pressed against my shoulder, hear that soft *please*, and I shrugged.

"You could bring him. He'd come for *you*."

Gatsby smiled disarmingly.

"Oh he won't do anything for me," he said. "Nick thinks I'm a social climber. Very Minnesota of him. He can't forgive people for their origins, and at the same time, he won't forgive people for trying to overcome them."

"Is that what you're doing?" I asked, finally relenting to come and sit next to him. I kept some space between us—it wouldn't do to get overly familiar with him, but there was something there that told me he wasn't a hazard to me, not tonight.

"You haven't spoken to him," he said, reaching for the hem of my dress. He toyed with the fringe there for a moment. "Have you decided against me?"

"I haven't decided anything," I said a little sharply. "I've been busy."

"With Nick?"

"You don't own him," I said stubbornly, and he blinked as if something had snapped into focus.

"I don't want to own him any more than I want to own the Sound," he protested, and I gave him a sideways look.

"Would you mind awfully owning the Sound?"

The bright grin was unexpected in this place, like a knife cutting through an opium fog.

"No, I would probably like that. All right, shall we lay our cards on the table, Miss Baker?"

"I would if I were playing cards. That's just you."

He sat up, leaning towards me and with the sensuality he had been wearing set aside. He didn't seem to know what to do with me, which face worked best, which tone would melt me. Now Gatsby looked at me, a little blank, a little curious, and to my surprise, a little desperate.

"I need Nick," he said quietly. "I need him to get Daisy."

I stared at him, because of all places to hear Daisy's name, the Cendrillon wasn't one of them. She might dance with a girl to cause a scene, but anything else made her feel funny. I would have taken it more personally if I didn't suspect she felt that way about boys too, once the kissing and petting turned to something else.

"What's this to do with Daisy?"

"Oh, Jordan, I love her," he said, and I burst out laughing.

"You knew her for—"

I had suspected he was fast and strong. I didn't realize how much so until he had taken me by the shoulders and dragged me up to my feet. I had been hauled around enough to know that I didn't like it, but staring up into his eyes, I forgot all about how

I had been taught to strip shins and break foot bones. I could barely feel any strain in his hands or his body, and my feet still touched the ground, but it was a close thing.

I knew that there was something empty in him before, but now I could see that it wasn't empty all the time. Now there was a monstrous want there, remorseless and relentless, and it made my stomach turn that it thought itself love.

"I *love* her, Miss Baker," he said, his face close to mine. "I have never loved anyone else. And I know that she loves me. She has since we first met."

Unwillingly I remembered a cry that sounded as if it had been dug up from Daisy's body, as if she had stretched out on the ground and someone had driven a spade deep into her. I remembered the smell of crème de menthe and how I still couldn't bear to drink it after that evening.

The night before her wedding, Daisy taught me that after the world ended, you still had to get up in the morning, and the things that you ruined would still be there, needing to be fixed. When I looked at famous Jay Gatsby, soul gone and some terrible engine he called love driving him now, I could see that for him, the world was always ending. For him, it was all a wreck and a ruin, and he had no idea why the rest of us weren't screaming.

I didn't look away, and I didn't fight him, because I had some idea how terribly stupid such a thing might be. The only way to deal with a thing that terrifying was to not be afraid, or at least, to make sure that it didn't think you were.

"I remember," I said, which was only the truth. I remembered a lot of things. "Now put me down."

He blinked and let go of me. He was either surprised at himself or he thought he was. All that mattered to me was that he pulled back.

"Miss Baker, I do not like to repeat myself, but I think I will have to ask again."

"Yes, I'll sing your praises the next time I see Nick."

"It might not be enough. I want him to bring her to West Egg."

"You're . . . asking Nick to bring his own cousin to you like some pretty baby off of Broadway?"

"No!" He looked genuinely shocked at that, looking at me as if unsure what kind of serpent he had brought to his bosom. This was a look I actually got a lot.

"Then what?"

"I want him to bring Daisy to his house in West Egg. I can be there. I can meet her, talk to her. Remind her."

I gave him a long look.

"It actually made more sense when I thought you wanted her served up like a bit of cold lapin."

"Don't be disgusting."

"Oh really? Whose cock were you sucking before you spotted me and Miriam Howe?"

"Some expensive boy from Amherst, what does *that* matter?"

And I could see that to him, it didn't. I marveled at that a little, and he took my hand. This time he was careful about it, holding it like something too fragile.

"Look, Miss Baker. *Jordan*. I need your help. Have him bring her to West Egg."

I didn't tell him I could do it, because I wasn't sure I wanted to. Gatsby was like a storm blowing up far out to sea, and soon enough he would crash to the land. Whether he struck marshland or a coastal city was still uncertain but I was beginning to realize how little control I had over all of this.

"What if I say no?"

His eyes darkened, and his mouth firmed at that. This was something that he had considered, and he was angry with me for even bringing it up.

"Then I hope you are prepared to run, Miss Baker," he said, obviously sorry that I had to go ruining his polite intimidation.

"I'm not," I said, trying to sound bored. "Fine. I'll tell Nick. Happy?"

"I will be." He hesitated. I wondered if he was getting some inkling that his grand romance was involving an awful lot of underhanded threats.

"This isn't real," he said abruptly. "What I have said here with you. It's not real."

"It feels real to me," I responded, and he gave me the most charming and oblivious smile. This was never a man who could tell me to run. This was in fact someone that Daisy might have been in love with, someone she really would cheat on Tom for. He looked boyish, endearingly regretful. It was enough to give me whiplash.

"I'm so sorry you got the wrong idea," Gatsby said, reaching over to tuck a strand of hair behind my ear. "But you will tell Nick?"

"Of course I will," I said, and I must have sounded forgiving or chipper enough to make him beam.

He took my hands in his, kissing them in grand style.

"Thank you again, you're an absolute darling, Jordan Baker."

What Jordan Baker was was alarmed, overly warm, and intensely ill at ease. I was back in the main hall of the Cendrillon, and though Miriam was long gone, clever thing, Maurice Wilder had just gotten his heart broken over something, so I dragged him into one of the rear booths, hanging on to a fold of his dress and letting him drape half over me. I held on to him and drank something light and fizzy to clear my mind, but there was really no clearing it of something like Jay Gatsby. I kissed Maurice all over his face and shoulders, but in the end I couldn't sustain it.

He sat up, cupping his sharp chin in his hand, sighing.

"Bit of a wash for both of us, isn't it?" he asked.

"Yes, I suppose it is."

I rolled my cool glass over his shoulder, making him shiver a little.

"Well, Jordan, should I see you home? I think I'm about done for."

"No, I—yes, actually. That would be ever so good if you came by car."

I would go home, I decided, but I wasn't there to stay.

No, in the morning, I had to take the train out to East Egg to see Daisy.

CHAPTER NINE

I didn't end up going to sleep when I got home after all, and I made myself some very strong Turkish coffee to compensate. The harshness of the drink made me feel as if I was vibrating two inches beyond the barrier of my skin, and I knew my mouth would taste dark and a little gritty all day, but that was fine.

I ended up on the first train to East Egg, and in a plain cotton dress in Oxford blue, I curled up next to a window to watch the world go by. The tall buildings of Manhattan gave way to smaller residences, marble and glass to brick and wood, and I felt something in me ease up slightly, as if relieved to see more of the watercolor blue sky.

With a slightly superstitious air, I crossed my fingers as the train surged through Willets Point in Queens, where all the city's ash came to rest. Even this early in the morning, fine light white sediment billowed up from the ground in a feathery fury, curling up into the air like some kind of secret. Wind cut the tallest and broadest heaps with intricate desert-like ridges, making me think of the far-off deserts of the Sahara or the Atacama, and watching over all of this was a perfectly horrid, perfectly tacky billboard of some long-defunct spectacle maker, two great eyes staring down with lurid interest over what went on below.

Down among the ashes, their faces and hands turned gray and grimy with the refuse of New York, I could see the men who lived and worked in the ash. It was their lot to shovel the ash that came in. It was a titanic struggle that I imagined they could only cope with by realizing that they were after an impossible goal and therefore were free to ignore it. Their shapes flickered among the little shanties that they had put together, made from spare pieces of wood and the odd bit of cast-off wealth of the city. From my spot on the train, as we pulled into the station for a brief and pointless stop, I could see them plodding with a kind of dull and frustrated purpose among the ash heaps, armed with shovels and clothed in grime. I imagined their lungs were protected in their youth by keeping their mouths shut tight. Then as they grew older themselves, more prone to voice their opinions, more eager to make sure that the world did not go one second longer without their words than it absolutely had to, the ash won over, sliding over their skin and then into their open mouths.

As we pulled away, I saw an unlikely woman with flaming red hair dressed in lemon yellow. She came out of a garage door, a cigarette between two stiff fingers, and a dark fingerprint smudging of ash already on her skirt. She watched after the train with something I could only term a contemptuous longing, and I swore for a moment that our eyes met.

I forgot all about her when we pulled into the station stop at Lilac Hill, still a mile away from Daisy's house. I thought about ringing her to send a car for me, but I summoned up a cab instead. Lilac Hill was a little more stiff-necked about such things than we were in the city. It took almost twenty minutes before I could find a cab that would take me, and when I did, I tipped the driver, a silver-haired Black man, as extravagantly as I could.

I should have called, I thought, as I made my way up the broad front steps. *I don't even know if she's in.*

The Buchanans' butler, at least, did not look surprised to see me, and he had one of the men take my small bag to the guest room I customarily used before escorting me to the blue and ivory solar that was generally kept for Daisy's use.

The room's tall windows were open to the Sound, and I looked out over the water. From where I stood, I realized with some discomfort that I could easily see Gatsby's mansion, the white walls gleaming even across the misty distance, the glittering gold beach and the pier that stretched out from it.

He stands on that pier, I thought suddenly. *He stands there, and he looks across the water, and he looks across the years to when she was his and when she will be his.*

I was startled from my strange thoughts by a crash, followed by an outraged shriek. I flew to the door, throwing it open just as the butler appeared again with an icy glass of limeade and a small plate of water crackers and cucumber slices. He wasn't a big man, but he wore his importance like a barred gate, and there was no getting around him.

"Madame will be with you shortly," he told me, his face serene. "In the meantime, I have brought you some refreshments. Would you care for some reading materials?"

"Just the *Post*," I said reluctantly, and I sat back down. I had no doubt that if I tried to leave the solar again that he would be there like magic, hemming me in.

He brought me the *Post*, and I thumbed through it impatiently until Daisy made an appearance, blowing in like a gale from some wild place. She moved so lightly, her color so high, that I had to glance down to make sure that her kid slippers touched the ground.

"Oh Jordan, what a delight, what a wonder!" she cried, reaching for me. "I had thought you had quite forsaken me! Now that Tom has thrown me over, I must look to my real friends, mustn't I?"

I was usually quite immune to Daisy's flights of fancy, but this one made me blink twice. Before she appeared, I had heard a great stomping and slamming, followed by an inarticulate shout of the kind I associated with football matches.

"Thrown you over . . . ?"

Her hands fluttered like shot birds, her mouth red and smiling. She couldn't be bothered to tell me the details, so she told me the very heart of it instead.

"Oh he *will* go out with that girl this evening. He doesn't care. He doesn't care about me."

This then was why Daisy kept me. Unlike her other friends, I didn't tell her that it would be all right or swear vengeance or offer her a way to be so beautiful he would never turn from her again. It wouldn't be all right, there was precious little vengeance a woman like Daisy might have against her man, and she was already so beautiful. Instead, I offered her something else.

"Listen," I said, looking around. "Take me someplace safe. Someplace you trust."

Her eyes shone, and she took my hand.

"Oh, an adventure? Jordan, you dear, you always know what I need."

"Maybe," I said.

She took me out in her midnight-blue roadster, tearing around the hills of East Egg as if they had personally offended her. We went past the paddock where Tom's ponies grazed, through a small copse of trees where Daisy told me the last witch of Long Island had been hung, and then we stopped at the high and sandy dunes on the undeveloped side of the peninsula. She parked us overlooking the water, nothing in view but blue and the encroaching creep of Briarwood Island, and then she slumped over, her head on my shoulder and both her hands playing with one of mine.

"So what's the crisis, darling?" she asked, her voice conspiratorial. "Have you fallen in love with Nick after all? I had so many plans to bring you two together, but you both keep on in the city as if there's anything there."

"There's nothing but sand and sea here," I said. "Daisy . . . Gatsby wants you."

She went still, her head a weight on my shoulder, her hands suddenly squeezing mine tight before letting go. She didn't move.

"Oh?" she asked. Her voice sounded as well-balanced as a throwing knife, but she had no target at the moment, only me in her car with her, overlooking the glittering water.

"Yes . . . look."

I told her all of it, starting from the night I had met Nick at Gatsby's party, through to what had happened last night at the Cendrillon. I spared nothing, not the love bites on Nick's throat or how Gatsby had looked after his expensive Amherst boy. I might have been telling her a fairy tale, none of it real enough to reach her where she was huddled against my side.

I came to a stop, because the story had run out for the moment, and I prodded her so she would finally sit up. She did so reluctantly, and to my shock, my complete and utter shock, her eyes were full of tears.

"My God, my God," she said in a fascinated whisper. "He *loves* me."

"I don't know if he does," I said. "There was . . . I don't *know*, Daisy."

"He does," she said, her hand tightening into small fists. "He does, he does."

Over the Sound, dark clouds were forming, and a cold breeze chilled the sweat on my bare arms. An ache came to rest between my eyes and through my temples as the clouds rolled like a croupier's dice.

"Daisy . . ."

"Tell me again," she demanded, turning to me. The Sound and the sky had gone to match her eyes, and I told her again.

The words sank into her, and as I finished, fat drops of water fell on us, wide-spaced and hard, leaving us speckled rather than soaked in our light dresses.

When she finally looked away from me, I fell back against the seat, wisps of my hair stuck to my face from the falling water. Almost as an afterthought, Daisy raised the roadster's roof and lit us both cigarettes. We smoked together in silence, and her hand covered mine, possessively and almost afraid.

It'll be fine, I thought to myself. I remembered the last time she had held my hand like that, and it had been fine then too.

CHAPTER TEN

Daisy married Tom just nine months after the Armistice, three months after Fulbright's, and just three years before I came looking for her at her home in East Egg. It had been a rainy June, but that Sunday morning, the sun came out to burn away the clouds as if it could not resist the soon-to-be Mrs. Thomas Buchanan.

Daisy's wedding was a wonder, and it drew people from all over the state and beyond. There were Carlyles from Fulton County, Parrishes from Upton, and of course plenty of Tom's people from Chicago: the Weltys, the Anselms, the Evanston Palmers, and the Tollands. Daisy's side of the aisle was hardly lacking either, with Phelpses, Moons, and Petries, and a scattering of relatives from farther afield. The Carraways, distant and distinguished, sent along a representative despite suffering some small tragedy earlier that year, and the Millays from Wisconsin provided Daisy with a flower girl in the form of a tiny cousin who was like a rosebud come to life.

The wedding took place at Church of the Nazarene, where we had both attended since we were little girls, and the entire place bloomed with blue hyacinth, perfume that made me feel almost drunk as I walked in. Hyacinth starts to die the moment it is cut, I told Walter Finley much later that night; they had had the florists there and setting up the arrangements at four in the morning to make sure that they didn't go brown and limp before the processional.

Tom wore sharp black, Daisy floated in white, and the brides-maids were in blue voile that made us look a bit like the hya-cinth, though perhaps a little more sturdy. I was partnered with Peter Woolsey, a friend of Tom's from college. He was built like a wall someone dressed up in decent tie and tails, and before the wedding, Tom's mother charged me with making sure he didn't drink himself silly and make a rude toast. I did my duty and kept him on champagne until the reception started, and after that, everyone was drinking and making rude toasts, so I gave up and joined in.

The stars danced overhead for Daisy's wedding, and I found myself with Walter, fresh back from the war, and sporting a rather dashing black sling for his wounded arm. It didn't keep him from the dance floor, and when he kissed me at one in the morning, I started to laugh as if I had never been kissed before.

It would be a few hours yet before the mother-in-law unit be-hind my house would be occupied by out-of-town guests, so I took him back there. I liked Walter for his pretty eyes and his generous mouth, for the way he swung me around the dance floor and was so bitingly polite to Audrey Lister that she barely knew she had been insulted. I liked him a great deal, but I also wanted to keep my mind off of what had happened just twenty-four hours before.

Daisy had made me a bridesmaid on account, I suspected, of what I had done for her in March, and I was the only one who was at her house the day before the wedding, when the letter came. We had been making up the garlands that we would carry the next day, hardy daisies and carnations twined into long ropes, wound with long strings of glass beads to make them shine. We coiled them up like snakes in the Fays' ice box, and I stayed for lunch while Verna Wilcox and Amity Peters went home.

I curled up for a nap on the sun porch, and when I awoke it was dusk. I wondered if I could catch a ride home rather than walking or perhaps if the Fays might not mind my staying the night and going home for my dress and shoes in the morning.

As I was thinking things over in the late afternoon light, Mrs. Fay came in, dressed for an outing in her violet walking dress. She was sharp where her husband and daughter were all curves, and while Mr. Fay, I thought, found me to be a charming novelty, she had no such patience.

"The Columbus cousins are arriving in half an hour and expect to be taken to dinner," she said, speaking as clipped as she might to a servant. "*Do* something about Daisy."

"Do what about Daisy?" I asked, but she was already turning.

"As if anything can be done about that girl," she said to herself, and then I was left alone.

The lower level of the Buchanan house was a riot of tulle, paper flowers, extra invitations, and luggage for the honeymoon trip. Daisy had wanted an Old World tour, but Tom had won out with the South Seas, and so her luggage was loaded up with light dresses, shoes with blindingly intricate leather cutwork, and cunning straw hats decorated with bands of pure silk ribbon.

I dodged around the dress dummy that had stood in the parlor for six weeks, sized exactly like Daisy and used for her dress fittings when she was too tired to bear the dressmaker's pins, and climbed the stairs. When I knocked lightly on the door, the only response I got was a deep sob, and so I entered anyway.

Daisy was sprawled on her bed, flat as a playing card, facedown, her head cradled in one hand while the other clung to a completely empty bottle of Sauternes. I had enough experience with the stuff to know that it was sickly sweet going down and burned like fire if it came back up. I closed the door after me, and she didn't even realize I was there until I pried the bottle from her hand and set it aside.

When I placed it on her windowsill, she rolled over to her side to look at me, her limbs as careless as that of a marionette whose strings had given way.

"'Gratulate me," she muttered. "Never had a drink before, but oh how I do enjoy it."

"Daisy, what's the matter?" I asked uneasily. She hadn't a reputation for drinking, but I figured she did it in private company, with those she trusted more than the rest. Now though, I could see she wasn't lying. Her face was slack and her eyes slitted, too careless of her looks to be anything but honest. I had never seen her like that before, and I felt as if some cold finger were numbering the bumps of my spine.

In answer, she reached into the wastebasket by her bed, and to my surprise she pulled out a string of creamy white pearls, graded so that the smallest was the size of a pill bug and the largest the size of the ball of my thumb. Tom had presented her with the pearls just seven weeks ago, and she had worn them at the announcement dinner. They were a little too pale for her coloring, washing her out, but something about the light made them look ruddy in her hand.

"Here, dearest," she said, taking my hand and folding the pearls into it. "Take 'em downstairs and give 'em back to whoever they belong to. Tell 'em all Daisy's change' her mine. Say: 'Daisy's change' her mine!'"

She met my eyes when she said it, pleading with me and making me think of March. Somehow, I got the idea that this wasn't something I could fix with the right connections. I could see a thin sheet of onionskin paper in her hand, crumpled so only the ends emerged from her fist. I pocketed the pearls because I didn't know what else to do with them, and I tore my eyes away from the letter because I could tell that Daisy would not suffer to have it taken from her.

I sat on the bed next to her, rubbing her back for a moment, trying to think. My mind spun like a whipped top, and I was distracted by how she curled up against my hip, still crying with a helpless and burnt-out sound that tore at me.

"It's the bridal dinner tonight," I told her. "Don't you want to go, Daisy?"

She shook her head, crying into the coverlet. She looked so small, as if she wished the world would go away and leave her be. She was Daisy Fay, soon to be Buchanan, however, and that wasn't going to happen.

"Daisy," I said, almost begging. "Please. Please get up. People want to see you."

I sounded like a little idiot, but the truth was I was frightened. Daisy's tears were like a deluge, flowing in sheets down her face, and I thought of the fact that if they were allowed to do so, those tears would drown exactly one person, and that was Daisy herself.

Maybe that wouldn't be so bad. Maybe if she breaks enough, something true will come out.

The thought shocked me with its gibbous nature. I didn't know how to deal with it, so I stuffed it in the same pocket as the pearls, and put it out of my mind.

It became very clear, very quickly that there was no way that we could get her ready for dinner in half an hour. Her face was a blotchy red mess, her eyes swollen from tears, and somehow in the middle of it, she had raked long scratches into her thin arms, not breaking skin but leaving raised red welts on both wrists.

At some point, Daisy stumbled to her feet, pawing at my pocket for the pearls.

"I'll go tell them myself," she swore. "If you won't take them I will. I'll take them to the . . . I'll . . . I'll . . ."

A confused look came over her face. She shook her head.

"I have to go to the bridal dinner," she said in surprise. "Oh God, I need to go, I don't . . ."

Her hand was still in my pocket where the pearls were. I didn't know what she thought then, if she needed to go as Tom Buchanan's fiancée or as someone else entirely. I didn't trust it either way, and after a moment, I could tell that she didn't either.

"Jordan . . ."

"Bathroom," I said, as firmly as I could. "We need to get you under some cold water."

She stumbled a little as I dragged her into the hallway, but she was pliant as a doll as I filled the tub with cold water, removed her frock and her underthings, and helped her get into it.

"Oh Jordan, cold! You beastly little thing, why is it so cold?"

"It'll help," I told her. "Nina Martin told me that cold could sober you up quicker than anything."

She gingerly sank into the water until she was covered up to the chin, and slowly, by degrees, she relaxed until her head was tilted against the curved edge of the tub. Her left hand, the one she would be offering to Tom tomorrow, was clenched into a fist and pressed against her heart. As she relaxed, tears started to flow down her face, slowly at first, and then more quickly.

She went from looking like the funeral mask of some great queen to looking like a blotchy tomato as she sobbed, eyes screwed tight, and her closed fist striking her chest several times like a mourner from ancient Greece.

I grabbed her fist to stop her from doing herself harm and spoiling her décolletage for the gown she was wearing tomorrow. She gave up easily, and I realized that she had had the letter clenched in her fist. I pulled it away from her trembling fingers, opening it up, but it tore at once, the ink all run together into an unreadable mess. The ink was of a particularly cheap kind, I noted, and when it ran, instead of a deep blue black, it went a kind of scabby reddish brown.

I chucked the ruined letter into the wastebasket close by. No use keeping that or trying to iron it out. Instead, I sat on the edge of the tub and poured cup after cup of cold water over Daisy's head. She looked calmer with every moment that passed, even if her eyes were swollen almost shut. I folded a cloth soaked with cold water and she pressed it to her eyes, murmuring at the relief, but when she finally stepped out of the tub, steady, and almost blue with cold, we both knew she wasn't going anywhere.

"Fifteen minutes," hissed Mrs. Fay from beyond the door, and Daisy's shoulders heaved twice.

"I can't, can I?" she muttered, her voice hoarse.

Before I could answer, she was throwing up, just barely making it to the toilet in time. She was racked with the spasms of her body giving up the alcohol it wasn't used to consuming, and when she looked up, I could see all the hollows of her face, how corpselike she could look when the light inside her was flickering.

"No, you really can't," I said, and when she was empty, I hauled her back to her own room, where she ended up on her knees by the bed, like a child in prayer.

"Jordan, Jordan, fix this for me," she implored. "Get me ready for my bridal dinner, I have to go, Jordan. The cousins have come from Columbus, and Tom will be ever so disappointed if I don't."

"I'm going to go make your apologies," I told her, though the last thing I wanted to do was to face Mrs. Fay, who already thought I rather ruined the other matched blond bridesmaids.

"No, no, wait, here . . ."

She tipped over a basket from under the bed, covering the floor with the detritus of several years. I could see cards from her graduation, hagstones strung on bits of ribbon, tangles of crochet thread, packets of needles, and more, and then she withdrew a pair of large steel shears, slapping them into my hand.

I bit my lip, but Daisy was already moving again, going to her nightstand and breaking a fragile frame that had a picture of her from high school. In it, her face seemed much rounder and the artificial color tinted on the apples of her cheeks and her lips gave her a fevered glow.

"Here, use this," she said. "I know you can."

I didn't know. Ever since the night we had met, I hadn't even wanted to cut out valentines. It seemed like too much to add to everything I already had going on, and at night, sometimes I dreamed of paper dolls coming alive to push me shouting towards a great pair of snapping scissors.

"Daisy . . ."

She clasped her photo to my hand. Her eyes sat in cavernous

hollows, and there were unhealthy lavender smudges to her skin that made me pull back a little. She didn't let me go, however, her hands on my wrists.

"Of course you can," she said, and even without her beauty and charm, I nodded jerkily and took a firmer grip on the photograph and the shears. Daisy was beautiful, and Daisy was charming, but her beauty and charm were cheap, offered to everyone who came near, from the maid to President Wilson the time he came to Louisville on the campaign trail. This was a rare thing, and as far as I knew, she had only offered it to me.

I started to cut, the sharp shears snicking through the thick dry paper like they were hungry.

The judge once told me that there was a class at Yale called the Paper Cutter Cults of Indochina. It was taught by a leathery strip of a man who called his Cambodian maid his wife when he thought he could get away with it, and the only time the class was ever full was when he presented the section on paper wives of the Lac Dragon Kings. Depending on the lecture, paper cutting was effigy magic, ancestor worship, and another sign of the barbarity of the region, where paper was given the same accord as human life, given rights, given property.

The judge did not tell me that paper cutting had never been duplicated in the West, as of 1922, or it might have made me more nervous to try what we did next.

I sat on the floor with Daisy draped over my back like a heavy mink, one finger rubbing nervously up and down my bare arm. It was too hot, too close, and it felt like she was going to wear a raw patch on my arm, but it didn't matter. I was too intent on shearing increasingly small bits from the paper.

Mrs. Fay rapped on the door, making Daisy flinch against my back.

"Just another few minutes, I'm just trying to make myself beautiful!" Daisy trilled, and that won us a little more time.

I didn't actually trace around the Daisy in the picture. Instead, working free-handed, I snipped a figure that approximated Daisy's own out of the card stock. With Daisy whispering encouragement in my ear, with my eyes half-closed and a kind of instinct guiding me that I usually preferred to ignore, I cut out her entire figure, her bob, her neat hands, her love of the water, and her quick clever dancing. I made sure to cut out her narrow hips, her full lips, the way Christmas lights sparkled in her eyes as soon as the first of December rolled around, and how summer left her nearly stunned with sweat and exhaustion.

Daisy's soft voice in my ear sent shivers down my spine. She told me how good and clever I was, how absolutely sweet it was that I was doing this for her. She had absolute faith in me, she knew I could do it, so of course I could do it. With Daisy's certainty, there was no room for my own doubt, so I simply packed it into a box and left it by the door for some other unfortunate person to pick up.

A few moments later, the scissors fell from my numb hands and I slouched back against her dresser. My fresh new bangs were plastered to my forehead with sweat, and I was grateful I had lost my thick braids for the occasion. My breath came hard, and at first, I could only stare at the violet-dyed slippers in front of me. They contained the feet of a whole new Daisy who hummed slightly, swinging her hips a little to see her hems swirl.

"Oh no," I murmured, because it was very much a high-school Daisy. There was something slightly unformed about her, rounded and a little pallid. It was a difference of two years, perhaps even three, and it was obvious to me that this Daisy was someone else.

Daisy herself, however, only hummed with satisfaction as she circled the newcomer, reaching over to lift her chin and fluff her hair a little bit.

"Oh well done, Jordan," she said. "Except for the hand, of course."

I had gotten too hasty close to the end. With a single snip of the shears, I'd sliced away the three smallest fingers from her right hand. Daisy took her double's hand in hers, inspecting the clean slice thoughtfully. Her double stood quiescent, smiling a little. I could smell something chemical about her, something that spoke of darkrooms and pigments that gave her cheeks their plumpness and their gleam. She had Daisy's coloring at least, and not that of the silvery photograph, so that was fine.

"Oh, here, I have it . . ."

Daisy stuffed the fingers of a fine pair of white silk gloves with scraps of fringe torn off her bedspread. When the gloves were on, Daisy's double looked all right, and Daisy stepped up to her, taking the pearls I had been holding in my pocket and threading them around her double's thin neck.

"All right, you," she said. "You're made for going out to dinner, for being utterly charming in the best possible way, for making sure that everyone *loves* you, and then for coming back here, all right? Have you got that?"

To my discomfort, the paper double's eyes flickered to me. I was sitting slumped on the floor, hot and sweaty and as done as I ever had been. I felt I had already done my part, and I did not want to be involved any further. I waved at her, nodding.

"What she said."

Just then, Mrs. Fay knocked again, hard enough that it suggested that it was the last courtesy we were going to get. Daisy slid herself flat behind the door, opening it with her lip bitten hard between her pearl-like teeth.

"There you are at last, Daisy," her mother said. "Don't think you can give yourself airs because you'll be gone tomorrow . . ."

Mrs. Fay's lips trembled a little upon seeing Daisy's frock. I had thought it was silly that Daisy might go out in something she probably gave away after high school, but Mrs. Fay nodded.

"All right. You were always a sentimental little thing. Jordan?"

I jumped.

"Yes, Mrs. Fay?"

"Of course we'll have Wilfred see you home . . ."

For the first time, the Daisy made of paper spoke.

"Oh no, Mama, Jordan *must* stay! She's taking care of securing some of my laces on my dress before tomorrow . . ."

Wordlessly, because hearing the Daisy made of paper speak took my breath away, I held up the shears still in my hand. I don't know what kind of strange little goblin-like creature I appeared to be, on the floor, drenched in sweat and working a pair of scissors, but it was good enough for Mrs. Fay, who threw her hands up in the air.

"Fine, fine, you'll be running your own household soon enough. Jordan, if you want something to eat, just go down to the kitchen. They'll take care of you. Now come *along*, Daisy. You know that your aunt Opal has never been able to abide lateness . . ."

The door shut behind them, and Daisy bent over, knees buckling, a knuckle between her teeth. We were both frozen until we heard the telltale squeak of heels on the carpeted grand stairs, and then she burst into panicked laughter.

"Oh my God," she said over and over again, and I crawled to where she lay still naked on the floor, legs out flat and her hands crossed over her breast as if she were prepared for burial. Kneeling by her side, I took her hands in mine, wincing at how cold they were, and how I could see a little crescent of blue at the base of each of her nails.

"It's all right, Daisy," I said. "Come on, it's all right. She'll do fine, no one will be the wiser."

"I don't care about that," she said, shaking her head, and I nearly bit my tongue in half to keep myself from asking why on earth I had done it, then? The answer came to me while she was still sobbing: because there was something in me that *wanted* to do it, and I felt far too young and new to pursue that. I shoved it to the back of my mind and locked in the closet I kept for such things as Eliza Baker, vague memories of a slow river I had never seen, and how I felt after Janie Greenway broke my heart.

She finally stilled, lying on the ground by the door like a

corpse. The minutes ticked by on her ormolu clock, and slowly, her hands warmed in mine. Her face lost its vaguely blue tint, but her fingers kept it. She was bad at the cold; it was a miracle she had lasted in Chicago as long as she had.

"Why won't you ask me what the matter is?" she asked finally.

"Because you'll tell me in your own time, or you won't," I said. It would do no good to show her how afraid I was for her. Instead I smiled to take some of the sting out of my words, and she let go of my hands to touch my cheek. I flinched a little from her chilly fingers, but she pressed them to my face, cooing at how warm I was.

"It's from Jay," she said. "From Camp Taylor. *You* remember."

I swallowed. I did. I remembered pale eyes. I remembered a hand that reached out to touch Daisy as if he barely believed he could be worthy of her. I remembered how the heat of that summer two years ago put a haze over both of them, as if I were seeing something strange and a little otherworldly, something I wasn't meant to be seeing.

"He's back. He lives. He wants me."

My heart shivered at that. It was like all the stories we had been told in the movie palaces were trembling just outside the door. I saw a single packed bag, an arrival to some distant bus station where Daisy's heels would clack against the concrete, slowly at first and then running to meet—

She sat up slowly, moving from the tense muscles of her core, not using her hands to push herself along. There was something eerie about it, something unseeing in her eyes.

"Come here, darling," she murmured. "Hold me for a little while. I feel ever so chilled for June. It *is* June, isn't it? It's so strange. Why, it seems like just yesterday it was Christmas and Mother had those splendid little gold and silver ornaments out for the tree. I wonder if she would be angry if I asked her to send them to Chicago to me next year. Why, I'll be a married lady then, won't I, with my own house along the lake, oh maybe even a little bump to house a dear little baby for Tom and me . . ."

She shaped her aimless hands over her flat stomach, and we both shivered a little.

"Daisy . . ." I said, because perhaps part of me wasn't ready to give up on the fantasy of her and Gatsby. "You said you changed your mind . . ."

"And then I changed it back," she said, her voice brutally practical. "After all, all of the relatives have descended, haven't they? All the hotels are full, and the hyacinth are coming at the very crack of dawn. Can't disappoint, darling, never can . . . and that is all that Jay Gatsby will do."

For a moment, just a moment there, she had sounded like Mrs. Fay, but then she burst into tears, so hard that I had to help her to the bathroom. She was sick again, but there was nothing to throw up anymore. She was just retching until the blue veins of her face stood out in vivid relief. Her face was a porcelain dish with cracks through it, showing the unglazed portion inside.

I emptied the bath, and ran merely cool water in it this time, but this time instead of getting in when I told her to, she grabbed me by the hand.

"Get in with me," she urged. "I'll be so lonely if you don't. I'll drown if you don't."

After a moment of hesitation, I stripped and followed her into the water, yelping a little as the cool seeped into my skin and as we made the tub overflow. The water sloshed onto the blue tiles, and I leaned back into her arms, her legs on either side of mine, my head back on her shoulder.

She played with me fitfully like she would a doll, her hands light and fretful, me holding my breath because this was too much. This was Daisy, the flower of Louisville. While my brain buzzed like a paper nest of hornets, she sang to me, her voice low and rolling out the words of "Loch Lomond" as if it were a dark blue ribbon pulled out of her hair.

"Daisy," I murmured, "what are you going to do?"

My voice was small and childish in the echo of the bathroom.

She was only two years older than me, but it felt as if somehow, she had sprinted far ahead. I thought that it must have been love that changed her, that gave her a faraway look in her eye, the soft and hollow tone to her voice. She felt almost unspeakably grown up then, nothing like the girl who had begged me to go into Fulbright's for her. I wondered how she had done it, or if it had come down upon her all at once, like some kind of sacrament that I had forgotten to take.

"Why, darling, I am going to get married tomorrow, of course," she said, her voice slow and slurred. Her hand came over mine, closing tightly around my fingers. I was something she could touch, something she could hang on to. I wasn't going anywhere.

When the water grew unpleasantly tepid, we dried off and went looking for her mother's demoniac, kept in a cut-crystal bottle no larger than her hand. I was wary of the stuff, but Daisy took a sip and then a second one. When she caught her breath, she dabbed a few drops on her fingertips and spread them over her eyelids and under her eyes. Almost immediately, her color returned and her swollen eyes went back to normal. She winked at me, first one blue eye and then the other.

"See? That's a trick that Victoria Powell taught me. Can't tell that I've been crying at all, can you?"

"No, Daisy," I said. I stuck with the Talisker whiskey her father preferred, getting myself warm and just a little numb, because I had an idea about what was coming next.

The bridal party came back sometime past one, loud, boozy, and happy. They had to roll Mr. Fay to bed, but Mrs. Fay stayed up to get everyone settled, showing the Columbus relatives to their beds and making sure that everyone had the toothbrushes, pajamas, and pillows necessary to maintain a civilized sleep.

"Well, Jordan, I'm sure we've kept you too long," she said, giving me a sharp look. "It really was too bad of Daisy to keep you at the mending."

"Anything for Daisy," I said with a slight smile. She could

tell that I had been at her husband's whiskey, but as I had said, *anything for Daisy.*

I walked down the porch steps and down the sidewalk as if I were running along home, but then I doubled back and slipped into the overgrown yard where Daisy was waiting for me under the dogwoods. As I watched, she stripped off her dress, hanging it from a handy branch and turning to face me in her white silk slip.

"All right," she said, and I scooped up some pebbles in my hand.

The small stones rattled against Daisy's window, and a moment later, the lace curtains twitched aside. I got a glimpse of her round face, and her bright smile. Then the curtains closed, and a few moments later, she was tripping across the lawn towards me. I took her hand and led her deeper into the dogwoods.

"How did it go?" I asked, my tongue and throat still slightly numb from the whiskey.

"Good, oh so good!" she bubbled. "Everyone was ever so kind, and we all looked as if we had stepped out of the pages of some beautiful novel. Tom squired me around to speak to all of his people, and Cousin Sandy from Columbus was ever so charmed—"

Her words cut off as Daisy rose behind her, the spade caked with earth swung high in her hands and then down hard against her double's skull. There was a crack like some great earthenware jug splitting in two, dark wine spilling out, and in the torrent were lost sweet sparkling gems, there and gone again.

Daisy's double fell to the ground with the first blow. She didn't cry because her mouth ended up in the sod, and Daisy struck her again and again. There was a smoldering smell, something a little like old blood and a little like freesia perfume, and then dim embers ate up her frock, hungrily devouring her. In all paper was fire, and the whiskey sloshed uneasily in me. I was ready to be sick, but then there would have been no one to watch

Daisy, hitting her paper double with the spade and then when the flames would have risen up, digging into the nearby garden patch to throw fresh earth over her.

At some point, I landed on my rear in the bushes. I wasn't ill, but my eyes felt too dry and too hot. With my arms around me, I could only hear the refrain *I shall live with this the rest of my life and God, is that a long time.*

Finally, the shovel fell out of Daisy's hands and the only thing left of the poor paper girl was a smoking pile of earth and ash, something for the Fays' gardener to fix when he rose the next morning and wondered what in the name of Heaven had happened on his nice lawn.

By the light of the nearly full moon, Daisy was streaked with earth and sweat, her leg bleeding from where she had gashed herself with the sharp spade, triumphant. She had never looked saner as she stared down at her work. She reached down, picking through the mush for the pearls that were stained but somehow unbroken. For safekeeping, she fastened them around her own throat before turning to me.

Daisy lifted my hand to her lips, kissing it almost gallantly, and then she went to put her frock on over all that mess. The slip was a loss, and the dress might be too, but it would likely get her back into the house without any questions.

"You're an absolute doll, my Jordan," she said. "Are you sure you won't take a ride home?"

"N-no," I said. I managed to stop my teeth from chattering because she was so calm and cool. Perhaps I should have tried the demoniac after all. "I'll walk."

She kissed my hand again before pulling back.

"All right, dear. Remember, back here at seven, bright and early. Mother insisted on that beastly veil, and it will take you and the other girls to get it on me."

"Of course."

I went out of the yard, walking down the street with my shadow cast in front of me by the yellow-eyed streetlamps. There was no wind at all on that hot June night, and out of the corner of my eye, I saw prowling lions and the figures of young girls rattling in the shadows, thin enough that when they turned sideways, they would cease to be visible at all.

CHAPTER ELEVEN

Nick appeared uncharacteristically late for lunch that next Sunday, hair ruffled and a summery red flush on his cheeks. The only reason he was wearing his jacket was because going without at the Plaza tea-garden was simply not done. He slid into the chair opposite from me with a muttered apology, and I excused him because I was probably going to ruin his summer.

"Gatsby?" I asked, and he looked down, nodding.

"He brought me into the city," he said, and I waved him away.

"Darling, you must know by now that I do not care."

He looked uncertain about that, but he took my hand gratefully when I offered it. I had chosen a discreet spot in the tea-garden for our meeting, one sheltered by tall Boston ferns, almost invisible from the main room. It gave everything an Eden-like green glow, and barring the gentle clink of silverware on china, the murmur of the other patrons, and the distant wail of the automobiles motoring by, it was a private kind of place.

Risking a quick look around, I brought his hand up to my lips for a quiet kiss, but before he could smile too much at me, I shook his head.

"Business before pleasure, I'm afraid. Let me tell you a story, and at the end, you shall tell me how it ends."

"Is this a game?" he asked with a slight and willing smile.

"Of course it is, dear heart," I lied. "Now shush and listen."

I told him three stories.

The first was set in October of 1917, the time I had come

walking down the road and seen, all unlooked for, Daisy with her arms around a dashing soldier, someone so poor and so un-refined that there was no way to predict the creature he would become. It had taken a war to change him, or a murder, or a deal with the devil, but whatever he was in October of 1917, he looked at Daisy as if she were his heart left his chest, as if he didn't care where she went so long as he could follow.

"He looked at her," I told Nick, "like every girl longs to be looked at."

"Do you?" Nick asked, but I waved him away impatiently.

"I haven't the time for that kind of nonsense," I said, sidestep-ping the question, and then I went on to tell him about what had happened the night before Daisy's wedding, though of course I gave him the version that Daisy wanted told, the one where she wept and then was ready to join the bridal dinner in half an hour. I could see that Nick believed an eighteen-year-old new drunk, heartbroken and half-mad, could pull herself together inside of half an hour, and it told me that he didn't know his cousin very well. Some girls could do it. I could likely do it, though I pre-ferred to make sure that I was never in such a situation in the first place. Daisy wasn't good for that sort of thing. She could only lash out, quick and potentially deadly, but for anything that required a sustained effort, she was at a loss.

Neither Daisy nor Gatsby asked me to tell him the third story.

"They honeymooned in Hawaii for three months, and then they returned to Santa Barbara just after Christmas. By that time, I was living with Aunt Justine, and she could never bear a New York winter. We were out in Santa Barbara too, so she could catch up with her California friends, and all by chance, we were at the same hotel where Daisy and Tom were staying.

"You never saw a girl so in love, or I hadn't, anyway. She would sit on the beach with him by the hour, his head on her legs, pet-ting his face as if he were the dearest thing. She never liked to let him out of her sight, and I thought they were on their way to becoming one of those couples joined at the hip and the lip."

"Jealous?" Nick asked, and I gave him my best withering glance.

"Never of Tom," I said. "Aunt Justine wanted to go on to Colorado after Santa Barbara, so we left, and I had it by way of *Denver Post* that Tom had been in a wretched smashup, his car against a wagon on the Ventura Road. They named him, and they named Pilar Velazquez as well."

"Who's—"

"The girl who worked at that hotel where he and Daisy were staying."

Nick shifted, looking uncomfortable.

"Surely he was just taking her home?"

I gave him a long look, and he colored, shaking his head.

"I sound like a fool, don't I?"

"Of all the people in the world to defend without question, I should think that Tom would not be very high on that list," I said archly.

"You're . . . likely right about that."

"I am. About nine months after that, in April, little Pammy was born. Then they were off to France for a year, and then it was back to Chicago to set up housekeeping close by Tom's people. And that . . . didn't last, though I don't know the details of it."

I frowned at that, and Nick chucked me lightly under the chin.

"Though not for want of digging?"

I smiled at him, wrinkling my nose.

"You're getting to know me a little better. I never heard much about it, except from Daisy. She never drank like she did that night again, you know, and Chicago's a hard-drinking town. I know they were planning to stay and then suddenly came East. I know that Tom doesn't want to go back, but Daisy maybe does. But they've settled in the East now, and they're as snug as oysters in a bucket. Or at least, they were until you showed up."

"Me?"

"Yes. You and Gatsby."

He went as pale as paper at that statement, and I made a face, reaching over to squeeze his hand.

"No, not like that. Gatsby's in love with Daisy. He wants you to invite her over to your house so he can meet her there."

Nick's face took on a wondering look.

"He wants to . . . have an affair with my cousin at my house? *My* house?"

"Oh . . . Oh no. No one wants to have an affair there. No. He wants you to bring her over so he can meet her there. Since you're right next door, you know? He wants it to be . . . I don't know. Some kind of *beautiful happenstance*. A chance meeting where they meet each other through luck and fate."

"Luck and fate that he asked us to set up."

I lifted my champagne glass to him in acknowledgment.

He convinced me to go for a ride in a victoria around Central Park before I returned home to prepare for dinner with Aunt Justine. I would have said no, but after lunch and the morning I knew he must have had with Gatsby, I was feeling closer to him. The privacy of the covered carriage driving through the shady paths of Central Park was more appealing than I had ever found it to be before.

Settled in the curve of his arm, I tipped us a drop each of demoniac from the crystal bottle in my purse. He licked his droplet off my finger, making me giggle a little. He was handsome when he wasn't going on about his Middle Western manners and morals. I pulled down the voile curtain that separated us from the driver, and twitched open his collar, where I found what I thought I would, a dark bite mark from a wide mouth.

"Jordan . . ."

"You must know by now I don't mind," I said.

"Maybe I do."

"If you mind, then you ought not do it," I said smartly, and then I hesitated. "You . . . do *want* to, right? He isn't . . ."

Nick colored to the tips of his ears. I knew that he probably wouldn't tell me one way or another. I sighed, petting his soft, dark hair.

"Never mind," I said. "You're a dear. I don't care about that."

"Do you care about anything?"

It wasn't an accusation, but an actual question. I hesitated, and he took my hand, kissing the palm gently. It sent a shiver through me, and I pressed closer to him. Even in the heat, he felt good, and I buried my face in the crook of his neck, pretending at a shyness I never had.

"I care about a lot of things," I said. "How much fun I have. What people think about me. My aunt. Daisy."

I hesitated.

"You." It wasn't exactly true, not the way I suspected he wanted it to be, but it wasn't *not* true either.

He smiled as if the sun had come out, and it made me swallow hard, blushing a little.

"Anyway, Daisy ought to have something in her life," I said, looking away. "*Will* you arrange the meeting?"

"Does she want to see Gatsby?"

Of course she did. The moment I had told her he existed, the moment she knew he wanted her, she had been ready to fly to him. The only thing that stopped her was the fact that Gatsby wanted things done just so, fitting into some story that made me wary and intrigued Daisy.

"She's not to know about it," I said, sidestepping neatly. "Gatsby doesn't want her to know. You're just supposed to invite her to tea."

Nick made an agreeable noise, and as the victoria made its way through the shadows of the lowering sun, I curled a little closer to him, letting him cup my face and lean down to kiss me. In that moment, I knew that he had put all thoughts of Daisy and Gatsby and the rest of the world aside.

I reached up to ruffle my fingers through his hair, making him laugh a little.

"You're going to make me look a wreck when we get out," he murmured.

"Good. I want you utterly ruined, completely wrecked."

I kissed him harder until I could feel him rouse, his hips shifting a little as his kisses became more urgent.

"No marks," I murmured in his ear. "I don't have the benefit of high collars like you do."

In response, he slid the scanty strap of my dress aside slightly, and I felt the nip of his teeth against the humid skin there. I clung to him as he put a discreet but credible bite on my skin, and then just as the victoria pulled out of the trees and onto the busier thoroughfare alongside Sixty-Fifth Street, I pushed him away, sitting up straight with my knees together, almost trapping his hand between my thighs before he pulled back.

Nick grinned at me, looking quite debauched with his hair sticking up in all directions and his mouth red, and I decided that perhaps I did love him after all.

"Wicked thing," he said with some delight.

"Of course," I replied, pleased.

CHAPTER TWELVE

Dinner with Aunt Justine that night was a late affair at Christine's with some of her friends. I affected a rather bored air whenever I was around them, women much older than me who occasionally said the odd deeply unfortunate thing about my race, but truth be told, I liked their company. I liked their independence, their wealth, the fact that they were so well-fed and poison-tipped, and they never cared who knew it.

In some ways, it was a version of the role I had played in Louisville to the older girls, pet and doll and charmer. In other ways, it was like being set adrift in a sea where I couldn't drown, where all the monsters lurking in the depths rather liked me and wouldn't upset my little craft.

After a rather good dinner of jellied chicken bouillon and a spectacular crown of lamb, the ladies lit cigars or their delicate hashish cigarettes according to their preference and got down to the real business of the day, which turned out to be the holy march that was setting up in Washington, DC, in just a few weeks.

"It really is too very bad that everyone couldn't keep their eyes up front and their hands to themselves," said Mrs. Crenshaw. "I tell you, if you had not had the foreigners campaigning for the vote and devils putting their fingers into politicians' pockets . . . well, the fun might never have stopped."

"I never thought it would last," said Mrs. Wentworth, thumping her horse-head cane on the carpeted floor. She was a formidable woman who glared about her as if we were going to fight about it. "Demons, foreigners, one's as bad as the other. By all rights, they should have been pushed back the first time we tried to quell the Chinese, begging your pardon, young Jordan."

"Accepted, since I'm not Chinese," I said with a light laugh, but Aunt Justine frowned.

"Really, Beulah," she said. "I don't see the Chinese or the demons making as much trouble as your average young hawk on the hill. I'm still not convinced the march needs my time or my dollars."

They were talking not just about the demons, I knew, but also about the soulless, though where they thought they could push them back *to* was unclear.

The number of people who had actually sold their souls, I learned much later, was far less than what it was made out to be that summer. They were discerning, the men in dark suits who came through Jay Gatsby's door. They liked power, they liked promise. The newspapers made it sound as if we were drowning in an infernal tide, and of course everyone knew someone who knew someone else who had done it. The temperance marchers, out their target after Prohibition passed, came after the damned, and there had been meetings, marches, the whole song and dance.

I thought of what my aunt's friends would make of Gatsby and his palace in West Egg. They had seen greater excesses at the fin de siècle, however, and they had also seen how that ended. As in, they might like to have their good time, but they also might have wanted to get well clear before the shooting started.

After dinner, I kissed Aunt Justine good-bye and asked her to have Lara pack up some of my good dresses and my nicer shoes and send them on to East Egg, care of the Buchanans.

"You're getting along well with Daisy this summer," she said.

"I am. She's been a dear, having me stay before my matches and all."

"And her man, is he behaving himself?"

I rolled my eyes.

"Of course not, Aunt Justine. But you know the type. A new girl every time he looks about and finds his arm free."

"Well, that's a shame for Daisy, then. She ought to keep him in better line."

I thought sometimes that my aunt forgot about how big men were, how much space and air they could take up. Even Nick did it sometimes, though he made up for it at other times by being little more than a shadow at the back of the clubs and in overfull booths. Tom was like a hulking stone that some great hand had set down in the world, and it was the responsibility of others to move around him.

That was too much to drag out on a Sunday night, so I only agreed, said my farewells, and gratefully took my aunt's offer of the car and driver.

I dozed on the way over the bridge, not waking up until the first stars were coming out and the air was finally beginning to think of cooling down. Before I rang the bell, I looked out across the Sound to see that Gatsby's place was lit up again, so bright that it shone a jagged path of light across the waves towards me. I wondered for a moment if it was possible to cross the Sound on that broken path, and at the same time, I realized that while I couldn't, there was a better than average chance that Daisy might.

The butler opened the door for me with some slight resignation, and I was headed up to my usual room when I met Tom coming down the stairs. He was pulling on a pair of driving gloves with a distracted look. He gave me a rather befuddled look as we drew even on the steps.

"She call you already?"

"No, I'm just here to take advantage of your hospitality and your excellent food," I said jauntily. "Why, should Daisy have called me?"

Tom sighed, dragging all ten fingers through his hair.

"She needs some sympathy," he said, making a face. "I'm *apparently* being brutish again."

"Oh, I see."

He frowned when I didn't immediately defend him to himself.

"Talk to her, make her see sense," he said, a begging note in his voice. "You *know* how she gets."

"Of course I do, Tom," I said, sidestepping him. "Will you be back for breakfast?"

"No, some business is keeping me in the city," he said. "Thank you, Jordan. You're a star."

I was, even if he had no reason at all to thank me. He went downstairs, and I went up, tired enough that I just wanted to strip out of my clothes and climb between my borrowed sheets.

Not so different from Louisville after all, I mused, and instead of going to bed, I continued on to Daisy's suite, where I could see her shadow moving back and forth through the light from under the door. I tapped lightly on the door, and I was answered by a low wail.

"Oh do go away, I don't want to see you," she cried.

"I think you might," I said, and she opened the door almost immediately, flying into my arms with a flutter of silk sleeves. In her hand-painted robe, she looked a bit like a magpie, the long bars of blue, black, and white calling to mind a rustle of feathers and the fan-spread of an elegant tail.

I let her hang on to me for a few moments, and then I pushed her back, bringing her back towards the light and turning her face this way and that by her chin.

"Do I just look too awful?" she asked, hiccupping slightly and offering me a nervous smile through her tears. "It's not so bad, is it?"

I made a show of peering at her face, and then her throat and her shoulders. She was half out of her robe like a snowdrop unsheathed after the winter, fragile and more than a little raw. There was a small drinks cart where a small bottle of demoniac perched, and I shook a few drops onto my fingers, spreading them neatly over her eyelids and under her eyes. She freshened up right away, and I licked the demoniac from my fingers before I nodded.

"You look just fine, darling, just beautiful, I promise. And I saw that Tom is on his way out, so that will suit us very well."

"Oh! Have you had word yet?"

I grinned, letting her take my hands in a surprisingly tight grip.

"I met with Nick today, the dear thing. He says that he will call to invite you to his place soon, and you can happen to meet Gatsby there."

"Oh but why?" she asked. "I could fly into his arms. I could do it right now, just get up on the widow's walk and take wing, float to him across the Sound . . ."

I took a firm hold on her arm, because after all, there was a chance that she might have tried it. She had that edge to her that was revealed sometimes, when things got strange or hard.

There was a part of me that wanted to let her go. After all, it would all have been the same in the end. Even if I refused to let her fly, we could take her roadster south in East Egg, north in West Egg, and then we would be there. Outside, the rain pattered gently onto the concrete, onto the grass and the earth. I imagined her dashing from the roadster, the wings of her robe flaring behind her as her hair took on the raindrops like dew. She would ring the doorbell, and for some reason, he would answer it. They would look at each other, reach for each other, crashing together in a way that could have set the entire world deaf if they could only hear it.

I remembered Jay Gatsby's request at the Cendrillon, however. I remembered the intent look in his eyes, his refusal to take any kind of shortcut, to act in any way like a sensible man, and I took a firmer hold on Daisy.

"He won't want that," I said with a helpless shrug, and the laugh she gave me was brittle with humor.

"I can't be expected to wait," she said. "Why dear, how deadly dull and proper!"

She was worn out after her fight with Tom, however, and I convinced her to come with me to her solar for a glass of champagne. We sent back down to the drowsy kitchen for a plate of crackers and cold salmon smothered with cream and dill, and we dragged the sofa to the windows, where the thunder had come to join the rain. One particularly powerful stroke lit up the world from Daisy's lawn to West Egg and to the city beyond it. In that flash of brighter than bright light, I saw Gatsby's mansion across the Sound, still lit up boldly against the summer darkness that draped down on top of us.

I thought of how the party-goers must be shrieking in the rain, how the gentlemen's fine suits would be ruined, how the sleeting water would plaster silk dresses to their wearers' bodies. Then it came to me that, no, there was no party at Gatsby's tonight. The place buzzed with light, but that light wasn't shining for anyone besides Gatsby, if he cared at all. It burned without illuminating or warming, and all of that emptiness made me a little ill, a little dizzy.

Daisy stared into the rain, crushing a cracker into crumbs. After a moment, she picked up a strip of fleshy pink salmon with her fingertips, rolling it into a tight little bundle before setting it on a cracker and giving it to me. The salty richness of the fish and the buttery crispness of the cracker grounded me a little, and so I made one for her.

Sometime after one, we both heard a thin wailing echo through the house behind us.

"A ghost," Daisy said without interest.

"No," I said, tilting my head. "That's Pammy. Listen, you can hear her nurse singing to her."

"I never wanted her. Tom may keep her after this. He gave me a diamond bracelet for her when the doctors told us she would live. I'll give it back to him, and her as well."

This was all uttered without rancor, but also without the

thoughtlessness that accompanied so many of Daisy's pro-
nouncements. She said things, they lit up gold in the air, and
then they fell to nothing like so much cigarette ash. This wasn't
something that floated around inside her head and then out
her mouth. This was something she had put away somewhere
dark, where the light wouldn't fade it, where no one could talk
her out of it.

I didn't say anything, taking her hand in mine, and we watched
the storm roll over the Sound.

CHAPTER THIRTEEN

Nick, good boy, called the next morning, and Daisy took his call on the ivory-white phone in her bedroom, half-dressed and me with my chin on her shoulder listening close. He didn't seem to notice how high and tight her voice was when she greeted him with her customary gaiety, passing a few easy words until he got to business.

"Listen, Daisy, I was thinking you might come over to my place this Saturday, around about three for tea."

"Oh three for tea, that sounds splendid to me," she caroled, the telephone cord wound strangling tight around her fingers. "How wonderful. Of course I will cancel my brunch with the Boston Prestons to be there. It shall be the very delight of my summer season!"

Nick laughed dutifully at that.

"Don't bring Tom," he said, his voice a little different.

"What?"

"Don't bring Tom," he repeated. "That is, it would be rather . . ."

"Who is 'Tom'?" she asked, letting him off the hook.

She hung up and turned to me with a rather pitying glance.

"He's not very good at this, is he?"

"I don't know that I want him to be," I retorted, and she reached out to pinch my cheek lightly.

"So you want to be the one to do all the sneaking about? How selfish, my dear!"

It rained for the rest of the week, giving us what felt like a delivery of fall in the heat of the summer. In Daisy's mansion in East Egg, we had somehow become unmoored from the mainland. Tom, in a high sulk, was still off in the city, likely with his girl from Willets Point or one from some other such exotic place. We were all alone in the house, the servants coming and going with a dignified hush that was more pointed than silence could be.

We smoked on the porch, we ate dinner at midnight, and we went through Daisy's yearbook from Louisville, guessing where everyone else had ended up. The answer was largely Louisville, and looking at the blur of black-and-white faces in the yearbook pages, I felt a kind of pride in how far away I had gotten, even if it was through no special effort of my own.

When Saturday rolled around, I woke up at a thundering and rainy dawn to find that Daisy had not slept at all. Her suite looked as if a modiste's shop had grown too full and simply split apart at the seams, throwing vast drifts of silk and cotton and beads and lace on every spare surface. Still in my robe, I dodged Valerie, Daisy's maid, as she ran out in tears, a bright red handprint on her face.

"A little early to be beating the help, isn't it?" I asked, and Daisy spun towards me, her eyes red and her pearly white teeth bared.

"It won't do, Jordan," she insisted. "It won't. I haven't a single thing to wear here. I shall have to go to New York to find something new, and there simply isn't the time for that, but I can't be seen in this last season tat . . ."

I took the gray silk frock out of her hands before she could ruin it, and then I made her sit down at her dressing table. When Valerie, cringing but dry-eyed, returned, I sent her for a little bit of beef glanced at the skillet, and a glass of orange juice.

"With champagne, of course?" she asked hopefully, and I nodded. She wouldn't get through this drunk, but I doubted she would get through this entirely sober either.

When Daisy had gotten some barely singed beef in her and had a refreshing drink, we sifted through the ruins of her closet to find a rather unassuming little Worth number, a pale violet decorated with the softest, dreamiest cream fringe. It made her blue eyes even bluer, and when matched with a pair of satin shoes with elegant wooden heels stained to match, she calmed enough to let Valerie set her hair.

"My darling, what are you wearing?"

I raised an eyebrow.

"I hadn't thought I was coming."

"Well, of course you are, if only to make sure that poor Nick doesn't feel like a third wheel."

"So you'll have a pair of them."

In truth, I didn't mind. Like a cat with that fatal old flaw, I wanted to see how this all turned out. In addition to that, I hadn't seen Nick all week. I wasn't sure he even knew I was in East Egg, and I suddenly wanted to see him again, his game smile, the easy way he held his body after a few drinks.

My clothes had caught up with me by then, and I had a dusky absinthe-colored dress that orbited low on my hips and bloomed with an embroidery of vines around my throat and my hems. I borrowed from Daisy a pair of gold satin shoes and a flower pin wrought in gold for my hair, and after that we were late. Daisy was too nervous to drive, so we roused Ferdie, the chauffeur, and a little while later, we were zipping along the road to West Egg.

The day when Daisy met Jay Gatsby again should have been beautiful, the same kind of day on which she had been married, or at least a crisp and dying summer day like the one where she had met the handsome young soldier. Instead silvery clouds hung overhead like wet rags out to dry, and when we stepped out of the car in front of Nick's humble little place, we could both smell the rain, paused for the moment, but by no means gone. Back in Louisville, that high wet smell coupled with the uncomfortable prickling heat meant that a twister was on the way, crossing the flat cropland with a destructive fury that was out to ruin lives.

We were in the East, however, and we had other ways to ruin our lives.

Nick's house was a strange thing, little more than a gardener's cottage on a sliver of lawn that had nevertheless been neatly mowed. To one side was the house of a steel magnate, currently on holiday in France until certain scandals died away, and beyond Nick's place on the other side was the looming estate of Jay Gatsby. There was something diminished about it during the day, I thought, as if even magic must sleep sometime.

We came out of the car to see Nick crossing the lawn to greet us. He was well turned out in a lovely gray suit, but there was a slightly harassed and hunted air about him, something papered over with relief when he saw us. He greeted us both with hugs, and Daisy hung on for a moment longer than was proper, ticking her fingers along his buttons.

"Why, dear Nick, are you in love with me, and that was why I needed to come alone?"

I had almost forgotten that Daisy was meant to be the unknowing lamb in this scene. She grinned flirtatiously up at Nick, who tactfully pried her off of him, trading a glance with me. I suddenly couldn't tell if I was meant to be in a conspiracy with him or with her, but I was rather grateful when he walked ahead of us to show us into his home. I never knew I was the jealous type before. Usually, things ended before I ever got to that point.

I had been to Nick's house a time or two. It was dark and narrow, but his maid kept it as trim as a Navy ship berth, the floors scrubbed within an inch of their lives, the doorknobs and windows gleaming. I caught a glimpse of her narrow and nervous face peeping at us from down the hall. I imagined we must be the strangest creatures to her, moving so lightly through the house that she must consider in some way her own.

We came to the small living room, where I was briefly stunned with the profusion of flowers set on nearly every flat surface. Even Daisy, who had something of a mania for sunflowers, looked around in surprise. It was as if someone had emptied out a greenhouse and jammed it into Nick's small parlor. The air was hung with the heavy scents of jacaranda and jasmine, so thickly dizzying that I thought there must be some magic keeping them young and fresh.

What a ridiculous thing, I thought, a little light-headed. *Nick doesn't have the money for this . . .*

I saw Nick open his mouth and then close it again. He looked around, as if it might be possible for someone to hide under the divan or among the blossoms.

"Well, that's funny," he muttered.

"What is?" asked Daisy, batting her eyes.

Before he could answer, there was a rap at the door, and Nick excused himself to see to it.

Daisy gave me a baffled look, and all I could do was shrug.

Then there was a step in the hallway, and when Jay Gatsby actually appeared, we both gave him an appalled look.

I don't know what Daisy had built up in her head, but I know that the picture I had come up with was beautiful. It was probably wrong, and like the wallpaper that had gassed all those people in London, probably poisonous, but it was beautiful.

Gatsby was sodden from the light rain that had started to fall again, the dark spots showing clearly on his pale suit. He looked, I thought, like nothing so much as a cat who had endured a wetting in the garden, and now only cared about getting inside.

Daisy sat stock still, her hands twitching as he stalked by her to take a patently false pose at the mantel.

Seated with my feet together in the spindly needlepoint chair by the window, I didn't dare move or make a sound, but Daisy trilled an unsteady laugh.

"I certainly am *awfully* glad to see you again," she said, her words knocking against each other like marbles. She kept looking between me and Gatsby, as if hoping that I could at least somehow start to explain this disaster, or perhaps thinking that this was some kind of terrible joke I was playing on her.

Nick entered just as Gatsby uttered a diffident "We've met before," making Daisy's hands flutter a little in dismay. Nick and I exchanged a glance and tiny bewildered shrugs. *This* was why I preferred large parties to small ones. You couldn't get away with being this unbearably odd at a large party, or if you did, no one would ever have cared. Now we were all trapped by the gravity of Jay Gatsby, locked in with fervent blooms of white flowers as if we were in some kind of fond memory box.

There was a restless quality about him, and suddenly I felt as if I were in a cage with something large, afraid, and hungry. I sat very still and straight in my chair as his eyes passed over me, my hands folded nicely in my lap. He looked at me more than he looked at Daisy; every time his eyes came to her, they seemed to skip, as if after years of not seeing her, he had to become accustomed to her brightness again. Daisy kept trying to meet his eyes, but I could see that her hands were fisted on her knees. She had no idea how to move things forward. Neither did Nick or I.

Some of Gatsby's restless fidgeting sent the small clock on Nick's mantelplace plummeting towards the floor. I cringed, anticipating the crash, but Gatsby caught it again, an indolent show of athleticism that another man would have taken care to point out. Instead he held the clock in his hands for a moment, muttering an apology.

Nick, acting out of instinct, I think, put his hand on Gatsby's shoulder.

"It's only an old clock," he started, but Gatsby shook him off with a furious look and left the room entirely.

I caught the stricken expression on Nick's face, and he trailed after Gatsby, dodging his servant as she came in with the tea. Something about her utterly impassive air struck me as hilarious, and I laughed, shaking my head. When the door shut behind her as well, I crossed over to Daisy, who was sitting as still as a statue, pale under her powder, not even laughing in that helpless way she had.

"All right, Daisy, do you want to leave?" I asked, but she shook her head.

"Of course not. That's *Jay Gatsby*. That's really him."

"At least it used to be," I said. "I don't know what he is now."

Daisy looked up at me, a calm in her eyes that didn't reach the slightly manic smile on her lips. She had used a shade of lipstick to match her violet dress, tender and delicate and bruised. It looked unlucky to me, and when she smiled up at me, she looked ever so slightly monstrous.

"I want to find out," she insisted, and then we both heard a step at the door. I hurried back to my seat, but I needn't have worried.

Gatsby blew in like a barley seed on a storm wind, his hair rumpled, his eyes wide but sure. I saw that he had his left hand clasped loosely in a fist so that the black nail didn't show. This time, he didn't spare me a glimpse as he came in, going down on both knees at Daisy's side, setting his free hand on her waist.

Daisy shrank back a bit at this sudden close contact. She was used to being courted from a distance. He started to talk to her, his voice low and urgent. I couldn't make out what he was saying, but Daisy's face softened, her lips parted, and her hand came up, faltering and then stronger to touch Gatsby's short dark hair.

I got up as quietly as I could, making my way out the door and shutting it behind me. Just as it closed, Daisy burst out in a bright peal of laughter, delighted and breathy with an edge of tears. I went looking for Nick.

He wasn't in the bedroom just off the main hallway. I looked around curiously because we hadn't spent any time there. It was close and dim, just big enough for a wardrobe and a bed with an iron headboard. Everything was old rather than antique. The bed was unmade, and as I passed by, I touched the dent in the pillow, the sleeping pills that sat on the windowsill next to his head along with a bottle of brandy.

In his wardrobe, there was a packet of unopened letters stuck in a dusty pair of shoes. I pulled them out, noted that they were from Minnesota, and put them back with a slight smile. I half-hoped that Nick would come in, because there was some part of me that was strangely curious about his bed and what it would be like with him in it, but he didn't.

Instead, I went out and down the hall. He wasn't in the bathroom or the kitchen either. His maid told me he was on the back step, but it was empty when I went out there. The step itself was a solid block of some strange stone, something taken from somewhere else to guard this passage into the home. There were stories every few years where people discovered their step was taken from the grave of this king or that saint, but that didn't interest me right now.

The rain had mostly stopped, but there was the faintest drizzle in the air. I could barely feel the drops, but cool water beaded up on my skin, weighing down the hems of my dress. From the magicked step, I could just barely make out the shape of Nick under the branches of the enormous black elm that took up most of his carefully groomed backyard.

I dashed across the yard just as the rain got worse, and when I arrived, my shoes were quite ruined. He looked at me with faint surprise. It wasn't as if he were surprised to see me, more as if he were surprised that anyone remembered him at all. He was in his shirtsleeves leaned against the monstrously coarse bark of the tree. The tree's leaves, broader than my outstretched hand, stitched a canopy over us, leaving us mostly dry.

A cigarette burned down unheeded between his fingers, so I pointed at it and he held it to my lips, letting me take a quick draw. It gave me an excuse, anyway, to cup my hands around his, steadying them, steadying him a little bit as well. When I let him go, he stubbed the cigarette out on the tree trunk and tucked it behind his ear.

"Come here," Nick said, pulling me into his arms, dragging me against his body.

I allowed it for a few moments, fascinated by the depth of his emotions, and then I gave him a hard shove back because I knew that a light one wouldn't do it.

"Don't," I said, deadly serious. "I'm not some little paper doll you can chew up."

Nick glared at me, and then nodded, abashed, sticking his hands deep into his pockets. I wondered where his jacket had gotten to. The rain gave the air a kind of English countryside chill.

"I feel like the morning edition someone left on a park bench, and it's begun to rain," Nick muttered, looking towards Gatsby's house. From this angle, it was the only thing to look at, a wonderland castle moored on the Sound for a season. When the weather turned, I thought, it would float away into the fall mists, the gray waves of the Atlantic slapping up against its pale stone walls.

"You're not," I said with confidence. "I like you too much for that."

"And it's only your opinion that matters?"

"It's the only opinion that matters to me," I said with half a smile.

I offered him my hand, and he took it, bringing it absently up to his lips for a kiss and then hanging on as if he had no other lifeline. He nodded at Gatsby's house.

"You know he raised it up out of the ground," he said. "There was a mansion there before, something small and sensible. One night this past spring, he drove here straight from the city. He had bought the land and the house from some bootlegger or other, pennies on the yard for the marshland, the terns, the foundation that would never dry out and the old ghosts of the sailors they marooned here. He looked around and said, *No, that won't do.*"

Nick's voice had a distant quality to it, telling me a story he had once been told. I had noticed before that he was good at telling other people's stories.

"So he stepped out of his car, and beckoned as if he were some great old king, something whose want was law, and it came, all of it, the mullioned windows, the marble floors, the glass blued by age and the books with the demons still sealed inside them. He didn't even have to ask, all he had to do was *want*, and there it was waiting for him. The history was his, the ghosts were his, and all of it waiting for the . . . the soul that would come in to make it perfect, make it shine."

"His soul," I guessed, but then I corrected myself. "No. Daisy's. It's for her."

Nick laughed a little, not looking at me.

"Of course. It was all only ever for her."

If he had said it bitterly or angrily, I would have had some defense against it. Instead there was a longing and sorrow there that I had not learned to guard against, and I reached up, taking his face between my palms and turning him back to me.

"Come here," I said, and I pulled him down for a kiss.

"You didn't want—"

"I changed my mind. I'm allowed to do that. You are too."

That messy entangling anger had gone out of him, leaving him sweeter and more pliable. I didn't mind the sadness; he wore it like a girl might wear a becoming if old-fashioned veil. It left him open in a way he hadn't been before, raw and pretty and intriguing.

He put his back against the tree and I leaned up on my toes to kiss him. He set his hands on my shoulders almost tentatively at first, but after a few moments, he clung to me. He was going to leave small finger-tip marks on my skin, and the thought made my heart flutter a little, made my breath come faster. The kiss went on until my lips felt bruised, and his hand reached for the hem of my dress, tugging it up so he could palm my bare skin above my stockings. He traced his fingers under the strap of my garters, plucking at them restlessly until I nipped at his chin.

"You can get a little more serious than that today," I told him, and with a slight groan he reached down to cup me between the legs, making me rock against him with a pleased sound. He buried his face in my hair, and I tugged his shirt open, nuzzling at the base of his throat.

I could feel his cock harden against my hip, and deliberately I pressed against it, making him swear softly. Something about the way he swore, foreign words, words I didn't have a hope of understanding, made me laugh.

"Poor Nick," I murmured with false sympathy. "Are you feeling quite overwhelmed, darling?"

"Every day of my life," he retorted, and to my surprise, he took me by the shoulders and pushed my back against the tree. For a moment, a spark of uncertainly singed me, making me wonder if despite all the precautions I had taken, despite all of Nick's fine recommendations, I had made a mistake after all.

Between deep kisses, he was still rocking up against me, and now my dress was flipped up to my hips. I did a quick check; we were out of sight of both Gatsby's mansion and Nick's own little house, and if that didn't satisfy propriety, I didn't know what did. He was stroking me with the confidence he had earned in the weeks after finding me on the street in front of the Bijoux, a sweet sure touch that I had shown him, his mouth laying a line of soft kisses down the side of my throat. I raked my fingers hard up his arms and his shoulders and then up over the back of his neck, making him hiss. He could always take at least a little bit of rough treatment, and while I suspected that I didn't give him the kind of rough he liked best, it still made his eyes close in pleasure. He pressed his face against my neck, his hands still moving as if they belonged to someone else.

"Oh I believe I love you," he said, and I laughed again at that. I liked to hear it, I liked to laugh at it, and it made me wonder what Daisy would say about it when I told her later. I liked my secrets, but there were some that were for the telling, and I dropped a fleeting kiss on his forehead.

"You hold that thought," I whispered. "You hold on to it for dear life, all right?"

He told me *yes* in a way that was half a dream and half a daze, and I leaned back against the tree as he worked at me, delighting in my own indolence and the way his body moved against mine. Once in a while, I reached out to palm the front of his trousers, but after the third or fourth time, he reached for my wrist, shaking his head.

"I won't thank you if you make a mess out of me," he said, and I was a little disappointed because I realized that was exactly what I wanted to do. I wanted to make a mess of him, to walk him back in front of Jay Gatsby all red-faced and shattered. In some strange and half-formed way, I realized, I wanted to do him that favor, of showing Gatsby that there was more to life than just him. Of course, what kind of favor would it be if Gatsby never saw, and what kind of favor would it be if it mended Nick not at all? I sighed.

"All right, but I won't always want to," I told him warningly.

"Why, Miss Baker, I would never presume."

Presuming actually wasn't one of his flaws, so I let it go, knocking my head back against the cool wet elm bark and letting it dig patterns into my back and into my palms where I reached back to grasp it. I felt pastoral, like some kind of wild nymph come to enchant a human man from his world. I wondered if Nick liked my looks as well as Gatsby's for all that they were of a different sort.

Then thoughts of pastoral nymphs and even Gatsby himself went straight out of my head as Nick's fingers quickened on me and in me. I could feel my body hitching like a car whose engine wouldn't turn over, that familiar tightening inside me that always took me at least a little by surprise.

While I still had the wit to do so, I tugged on his hair. He thought it was for fun at first, so I tugged harder, until he yelped.

"You might have said that you didn't care for—"

He paused when he looked down at my face, his eyes bright as the foil around a candy bar, his mouth a tempestuous red. There was my answer to if he thought I was as beautiful as Jay Gatsby, and it made me smile.

"Get down on your knees," I murmured, pushing down on his shoulders.

"*Why?*" The confusion in his voice was genuine, and I laughed. It was just a little mean, prep school girl to the boy who worked at the garage, and he flinched, biting his lip.

"*You* know."

After a moment he did, and he dropped as pretty as you please. I stepped out of my silk drawers, stuffing them into the back of one of my stockings to keep them neat. I hauled up my skirts with one hand and with the other, I took hold of him by the hair and dragged him forward.

"I don't . . . That is . . . I'm not sure how . . ."

He looked up at me, begging, and I stroked his cheek.

"Well, I'll tell you if you get it wrong, won't I?"

Eager. He was *so* damned eager. He might not have done it for someone with my precise looks between the legs before, but it's not all that different overall. Skin's skin, and he liked mine. His large hands curled around my thighs, and there was a kind of Middle Western, old religion fervor to how he devoured me. His people weren't that far from the tent revivals that spoke of angels like spinning chariot wheels in the sky and demons under every apple tree, and he chased my pleasure like it might be his very own salvation.

I didn't think I'd tip over. I might have done with his hand, but mouths were usually trickier for me, without the pressure I usually liked behind it. Then I remembered that I could do something about the pressure, or at least, I could with Nick, and

I took a fistful of his hair and dragged him against me hard. His hands tightened on my legs, palms pressing my garter clips into my skin, and oh I didn't care, oh it was good, so good, and he thought he loved me, and absolutely nothing else in that moment mattered but how good he made me feel.

In the middle of it, I turned my head and though the angle was all wrong, I could see into the orchard on Gatsby's property, and I saw myself there, watching with eyes that hadn't even fallen on Nick yet or on Gatsby himself for that matter. I tasted that fruit again, sweet and bright and lovely, and I started to laugh.

There's this moment, during good sex at least, where you forget how you're meant to look or what you think a properly self-contained creature should look like. My hair was full of bits of bark, one of my garters had given up entirely, and I didn't even like to think of what my paint was doing on my face, but none of it mattered at all when I could feel just the barest innocent threat of Nick's teeth against me.

I went over with my hand over my mouth, still not quite ready to give him more, but he groaned when he felt me shake, pressing against me even harder. He was so enthusiastic that I had to give him a hard shove backwards at the end, pushing and then dropping back against the tree because I would fall otherwise.

He rose unsteadily to his feet, and I saw with satisfaction how I had ruined him. His face was flushed and slick, eyes starry, and a grin that didn't know what to do with itself on his red, red lips.

"Just a minute . . . Just give me a minute and . . ."

"You don't *have* to—"

"Think I would if I *had* to?"

That shut him up, and he braced his hands on either side of my head against the tree as I reached down to unbutton his trousers and return the favor. My wrist ached, and I suspected he was holding back to make it last, but he finished with his face buried in the crook of my neck and I decided that fair was fair.

When he got his breath back, before I was quite ready to be

done with the satisfaction, Nick tried to put us both in order, buttoning up his trousers and pulling out a single sad handkerchief before staring at it in dismay as if wondering which disaster it could possibly help.

"No, come on," I said, dragging him down towards the water. "When you can't fix a thing, the best course of action can be to ruin it all so that no can see what truly happened."

Nick laughed, and I wondered if that was what love was, making someone forget the pain that gnawed at them and would not stop.

After the rain of the week before, the water was murky and gray, frigid like January. Nick grabbed me as if he expected me to be able to warm him. My dress floated around me like a swirl of green liqueur in vodka, I lost my drawers entirely, and Nick kissed me so hard I lost my breath as well.

"Why, you're affectionate," I murmured, ruffling his hair, and it occurred to me without much rancor that with me, he was permitted to be.

We hauled ourselves out of the surf, our shoes dangling from our fingers. A car filled with women dressed like bright buttery flowers chugged by, and we waved merrily at them before we crossed the road back to Nick's front door. We were at our best, I decided, when we were just the two of us on our own, but of course that changed once we crossed the threshold.

In the parlor, Daisy and Gatsby sat on either end of Nick's sofa like children on a seesaw, Daisy with her knees curled up and her face full of tears, a tremulous smile on her face. When she saw us, she leaped up in a showy flourish, dabbing furiously at her flushed cheeks with the pads of her fingers until all gracious, Gatsby offered her a handkerchief.

Gatsby—

What does it look like when a thousand-year hunger gets a taste of what it's craved? His eyes were pale before, but now there was something blackened and charred about them, sending up wisps of steam that I could almost feel but not see. He was still buttoned up to a nicety, but there was something stripped to him, as if we had come in from the water and caught him in the midst of shedding his skin like a snake. I took a step back, bumping right into Nick's chest, and from the way he held my hand, I could tell he saw it too. Daisy didn't react at all.

"Oh there you two dears are," she said, drying her face furiously. "We were just beginning to wonder where in the world you might have gotten to. Nick, your house is just the dearest thing, but there's not much space to lose oneself, is there?"

"Just your mind, your memory, and your dignity," Nick offered, and I smiled.

"Nick and I decided we were done doing things by half measures," I chirped. "The rain half-wet us, so I thought the sea should finish the job. We do look rather too awful, don't we?"

"Not at all," Gatsby said with friendly indifference. "But you can hardly stay like that all day. Come on."

"It's fine," Nick said hesitantly. "I mean, it's stopped raining . . ."

It had, the clouds rolling back to let some refugee sunshine through, and Gatsby grinned.

"So it is. Come on, we'll take my car."

I started to say how silly it was when we could simply go out the back and cut through his small orchard, but Daisy seized my hand.

"Oh, just give us a moment to powder up a little! We'll meet you on the lawn . . ."

She crammed us both into Nick's tiny little bathroom, closing the door behind us. The moment we were alone, she fell into my arms, shaking as if she had a fever.

"Daisy?"

"Oh God in Heaven, he loves me so much," she said, hiding her face in her hands.

"I don't think God has anything to do with it," I muttered, but she shook her head.

"There's just so much, and so deep, and oh Jordan, I don't think I could reach down to the bottom of it if I drowned."

I shivered, nervously running my hands up and down her arms. I had just been in the freezing ocean, but there was something even clammier and colder about her. He hadn't warmed her at all, him or his love.

"Don't do that, Daisy. Do you want to go? Should we just call Ferdie back, or ask Nick to drive us back to East Egg?"

Her eyes were wide and startled, and she looked at me with a delicate little kiss on her pursed mouth.

"Oh Jordan, but he loves me—"

"Daisy . . ."

She shook her head, as if all that it took to tip her one way or the other was me saying her name with disbelief.

"Oh Jordan, he loves me so much. I've never felt anything like that. There's nothing like it in all the world, being loved by someone like Jay Gatsby."

She said his name like some kind of incantation, a god if you could own a god.

"What are you going to do?"

I thought of the night of her bridal dinner. She straightened, pushing her shoulders back, and then went to splash some cold water on her face, scrubbing away the little touch of lipstick which was all she ever used.

"Why . . . we're going over to his house, darling."

CHAPTER FOURTEEN

And so we did. The entire time, I felt unreal, a little as if I were floating, a little like I was getting ready to fall. Daisy and I bundled into the back of Gatsby's car with Nick in the front, and we drove down Nick's drive and up Gatsby's, tumbling out in front of his gracious marble steps like so many puppies.

If I had thought about it at all, I would have guessed that Gatsby's house would have a haunted air to it during the day, when the only people who walked its gorgeous halls were servants, when the only people enjoying themselves might be the ghosts. For some reason, it had never occurred to me that Gatsby himself actually lived there. It was too big to live in, but now he proved me wrong as he led us in the doors, nodding an absent hello to his butler.

He showed us Daisy's suite, done up after the fashion of Marie Antoinette, and he pulled Nick through the door to his own, shutting it firmly behind them.

We explored her set of rooms, roving from her marble bathroom with solid gold fixtures and a mirror tinted a nostalgic copper, to the small sitting room with a silk robe edged with peacock feathers hanging off a hook waiting for her. In the bedroom was a four-poster bed draped with blue velvet and she lay back on it as I went to explore her generous cedar-paneled closet.

I expected something remarkable and gauche. I had visited the Park Avenue apartments of the expensive boys and girls who were lavishly entertained by their old men, and they kept their real clothes in trunks under the bed. The closets were marvels of marabou feathers, sequins, leather, and lace, everything from clothes that were two straps and a patch away from being illusory to what I was told was a full Elizabethan ball gown kitted out with corset and farthingale.

Instead, the first thing that met my eyes was a rack of dresses not unlike what Mrs. Fay would have back in Louisville, updated of course because New York was not Missouri, but all longer hems, high as hell necklines, and conservative lines. I saw camel and charcoal and navy, and I made a face, pushing them aside.

"Come on, *Jay*," I muttered. "Surely you can dream a bit grander, can't you?"

Behind that first rack was one of presentation gowns, fewer because the skirts were so thick and full. I guessed that they were for fantasies of White House visits and balls of the kind that only the older set ever seemed to have anymore. I knew that Gatsby had never consulted anyone for this wardrobe, because anyone clever would have told him that Daisy would never do off the rack for such a thing, even if that rack was enchanted and made to fit her to the very shadow.

Finally, at the back was a rack of dresses I could at least imagine Daisy wearing, both the lightly boned dresses in seemingly ephemeral blue silk to the more dashing things in orchid, fuchsia, and jonquil that would be pronounced fast.

"Can I borrow this one?" I asked wryly, coming out with a number in soft pink crossed with a geometric design of diamonds.

"Oh take whatever you like, my dear," she said, waving her hand grandly. "I'm sure I won't miss it."

"So generous of you."

The white drawers built into the far wall opened to reveal layers and layers of underwear, camisoles, stockings, jeweled garters, French knickers with real lace insets, all stacked neatly between pale sheets of perfumed tissue paper, all as tempting as marzipan on Christmas. My hair was a disaster, but the clothes suited me just fine, and soon enough I was in bed with Daisy, hands clasped together and counting the stars on the night-sky canopy over her bed.

"Are you happy?" I asked.

"Happiness must come later, don't you think?" she said in wonder. "When you want something so very much, and then you have it?"

I almost asked her if she was talking about herself or Gatsby, but then the door opened and Gatsby and Nick entered. Daisy stayed where she was while I propped myself up on one elbow to look at them.

Gatsby had the self-satisfied swagger of an overgrown tomcat, and he pulled Nick behind him by the elbow. Nick was taller and thinner than Gatsby, but he did surprisingly well in a dove-gray suit with the most discreet green stripe over a matching green shirt. The entire thing, I was certain, cost as much as Nick's rent for the summer did, and he wore it awkwardly, all angles and reticence.

They came to stand on either side of the bed, and I reached up to twine my arms around Nick's neck, pulling him down for a kiss. I guessed that we both still had a hint of the Sound on us, but we had been baptized with some better scents, lemony Emeraude by Coty for me, and the fantastically popular L'Ambre de Carthage for him. He hardly smelled like himself as he dipped down to brush his lips against mine.

"This is utterly mad," he whispered against my mouth, and I smiled.

"It's a dream," I said, kissing him back. "Why not enjoy it for a little while?"

We turned our heads and felt a little shabby at the fact that Gatsby and Daisy were barely touching at all. Instead, he was simply bent over her, ravishing her, worshiping her, and adoring her with just his eyes. Daisy herself looked like Sleeping Beauty awakened, a delicate flush on her cheeks and her lips slightly parted, if unkissed.

It should have felt as if we were intruding, but these two were

made for an audience. I could feel that Nick was quite taken with
the picture that they made; for my part, I only wondered if I
should clap.

Finally, it was Gatsby who broke the spell, standing back and
helping Daisy to her feet.

"Come on," he said. "Let me show you around the place."

There was a something Middle Western about the way he
said it, I thought as we followed him into the halls, like *the place*
might have been a hundred-acre spread of timber or perhaps some
prime riverland that would be good for leasing out to hunters
once the weather turned.

Nick briefly tried to excuse himself, but Gatsby and Daisy
wouldn't hear about it, and I wound my arm through his.

"Don't you dare leave me with just the two of them," I said
with a grin. "I do hate being a third wheel. With you along, we
rather complete the coupe, don't we?"

Daisy insisted on seeing Gatsby's room before we went farther
afield, and we wandered through a room that was only Spartan
compared to Daisy's, and if a room with its own mahogany bar
could be said to be in any way lesser. She cooed over a solid gold
mirror and comb while I inspected the drawers where pocket
watches and cuff links were stored like prize jewels. In one velvet tray, I found a pigeon blood ruby the size of my thumbnail,
and for some reason, it made Nick laugh. Where Daisy's were
gracious and sprawling, Gatsby's rooms went up, his beautiful
clothes located not in polished inlaid wardrobes but in open cab-
inets and racks a story above, accessed by a winding staircase that
uncurled into a brass walkway all the way around the room.

"I made Nick come up and choose something for himself,"
Gatsby said with a conspiratorial wink. "I couldn't get him to
choose something nicer than that old thing."

"I like it," Nick said with a shrug and a slight smile.

"No, no, old sport, you should have had the peach or the aqua,
certainly . . ."

Gatsby sprang up the delicate staircase to the mezzanine, drawing out shirts for me and Daisy to see.

"Look at this," he cried, shaking out a pale orange shirt with a winged collar. "Wouldn't this be splendid on our boy? It's from England, and before that, Egypt. Or this, they call it Nile Blue . . ."

Nick tried to laugh, Daisy clapped her hands for the colors, and Gatsby threw them down towards us, grabbing at linen shirts and cotton shirts in a mania, tossing them down to us by the handful. There was something here directed at Nick, but before I could figure it out, the shirts tumbling down towards us spun and stretched out wings, sleeves stretching into long and graceful necks.

As a dark blue shirt Gatsby had named faience from London spun past me, I caught a glimpse of a mother-of-pearl button eye before it swept up to the glass skylight above, followed in turn by the rosy plum from Paris and the lemonade yellow from Quebec.

We gaped as the shirts flew around our heads in a rush of crisp fabric, rising up towards the gray glass sky. I saw Daisy closed her eyes, but I watched as they gained the ceiling, and then, freedom just a shower of shattered glass away, they fell back defeated as shirts, coming back to the ground limp and disappointed.

Gatsby opened his hands like a stage magician, and Daisy clapped, her eyes filled with strange tears. It struck me that there was something in her that seemed to want to speak, to cry out perhaps in protest or in question, but she only smiled, smiled.

"*What* beautiful shirts they were!" she cried, but for a moment they had been birds.

We trailed after Gatsby, who was pointing out all his particular treasures to Daisy, like the rose window set at the top of the stairs, preserved from the wreckage of a cathedral in Mont-Louis and shipped all the way to the United States, or the statue of the Venus emerging from the mountain, missing only her right raised hand and flecked with bits of ancient paint.

The house had taken on more galleries and even grander aspirations since I had last been there. There was a hall made of glass where lush green plants wove together to scent the world with lemon, and bay and honey, and a hall roofed in what Gatsby told us was the longest night of the year in some town in Norway. We stood in that hall for several minutes, letting the Norwegian winter cool us down as shimmering green and violet lights danced above our heads. We could hear bells in that room, and the clacking of bone chimes hung up in lonely pine trees. I was pleased to leave it, though Daisy less so.

Daisy was an old hand at admiring the houses and lives of others, but I thought I heard a genuine delight in her voice. It was easy to be impressed by Gatsby, a man with rugs so intricate that they were known to send the twelve-year-old weavers blind and whose halls played a tender kind of music, not quite pipes and not quite violin, wherever we passed.

The thing he had not quite grasped yet, I thought, was that as the master of such a fine and notable place, he wasn't meant to be impressed with them himself, and of course he was. As he pointed out this frieze or that memorial urn, I could hear a sense of wonder in his voice, as if in showing Daisy, he was showing himself as well. Maybe he hadn't allowed himself to think that it was real until she was here to admire it.

He took us past a gallery I had spent some time in earlier that summer, a shallow hall full of marble statues of Gatsby's Greek ancestors, and as we went by, I saw a strange flush of movement, someone darting behind one of the wide granite bases and standing very still after that.

A guest, I thought, because servants would know better. *I wonder which one that is.*

I walked on a few steps, and then let go of Nick's arm. I was barefoot after leaving my shoes in Daisy's suite and utterly silent as I slipped back to the gallery and peeked past the edge of the doorway.

The guest I had seen had come from his hiding place was now looking around as if he were at the art museum. He was dressed like a workman, without a jacket in gray duck trousers, his braces hanging down around his thighs, a flat cap stuck into his waistband and his shirt sleeves rolled up. When he turned, I saw that he was eating a sandwich, that he was surprised to see me, and that he . . . looked like me.

I blinked, drawing back a little in surprise to see a face round like mine and dark like mine. I felt an immediate rush of recognition and warmth followed by an almost equal amount of repulsion and panic. When you're alone so much, realizing that you're not is terribly upsetting.

Gatsby's guest didn't seem to suffer from my little crisis, instead focusing on looking at me desperately and pressing a finger to his mouth.

"Jordan?" called Nick from the corner. "Come on, they're getting ahead of us."

I looked for another moment at the boy in the gallery, for some reason unable to tear myself away even as he grew increasingly frantic.

"Coming," I said finally. "I was only looking at the pretty things."

I turned and tripped along towards Nick, who squired me away after Gatsby and Daisy's disappearing shadows.

We were just examining a set of steel gates to the observatory (from some cloister filled with mad nuns, apparently) when his butler appeared like a jack-in-the-box.

"A call for you, sir."

Gatsby gave him a puzzled look that hardened into something sharp and deadly.

"Now?"

"*Yes*, sir."

Apparently, there were some calls that even Gatsby couldn't ignore. We trailed after him like so many lost kittens as he re-treated to his study, picking up the ivory and brass phone with an impatient gesture. Nick went to the window to give him some privacy, but Daisy and I ended up at his desk, her seated with her feet dangling at his leather chair, me more interested in the picture hanging next to the volumes of legal texts to one side.

While his voice lowered to something like the rumble of the mythical 21 train that ran from Manhattan to the city of Dis in Hell—*well, yes, I know the vote is coming, just listen, old man, it will be done, it will all be done*—I took the small picture off the wall to look at it more closely. It featured a healthy-looking barrel-chested man in his fifties or perhaps his well-preserved sixties, staring unsmiling at the camera in front of a sleek and knife-like yacht. It would have been utterly unremarkable save for two things. The first was it was the kind of dull picture that one kept around of one's relatives, and I had no reason to think that Gatsby had anything like that. The second was that I could see perched on the railing an unbelievably young Gatsby him-self, lean as a ray of sunshine, grinning and unrepentant as a boy playing hooky.

"That's Dan Cody," Nick said quietly, drifting over to me. "Gatsby rounded the Horn with him in 1907."

Before I could react to that bit of news (doing the math now, Gatsby would have been seventeen at the time), Gatsby hung up the phone with a muttered curse and came to take the picture out of my hands.

"Cody was a good man," he said with a slight smile at me. "Think of him every time someone at the house asks for that damned pisco from Chile. He was a Chicago man, through and through, and it's only Chicagoans that drink *that* stuff."

"And Chileans, possibly," I suggested, but no one was listening.

"Can we go back to Chicago, Jay?" asked Daisy, spinning lazily in his chair. "I did love it so. They're saying that they've found a way to send their winter downstate, so it'll always be sunny on Michigan Avenue . . ."

A brief frown passed over Gatsby's face, and I saw his eyes flicker around the room. Just as quickly he shrugged, because if he could raise a palace like this out of the muck of West Egg, then he could certainly do it next to Lake Michigan as well.

"Of course we can," Gatsby said, spreading out his hands. "Why stop there? We could go to Paris, Marrakesh, Johannesburg, perhaps even have Jordan show us around Ceylon."

The last was addressed to me with a broad wink, one that I acknowledged with an eyebrow raised in mock friendliness.

"Well, if you want to test my ability to find a drink in under twenty minutes, we certainly can, but for something really exotic, why don't we ask Nick? He could show us all the wonders of St. Paul."

"My great-grandmother was from Bangkok," Nick said suddenly, and I reached over to give his face a little squeeze.

"And such a family resemblance, don't you think?" I asked, and he ruffled my hair with a grin.

"Not in the least, dear. Her parents were missionaries from the order of Francis the Redeemer. She was born on the banks of the Gulf of Siam just as her mother and father disembarked from the ramps of their ship, the *Carmine*."

Closer then, in some ways, than mere geological coincidence, though Nick certainly didn't know that. I had never told him the sad and tragic story of Eliza Baker, or how I came to be a Louisville Baker myself. I suddenly wondered how he thought I'd come about at all.

Of course Daisy knew, and she had already grown bored with this conversation. She wandered from the study to the conservatory with the three of us in her wake like the tails of a lovely kite, and in the conservatory, quite to our surprise, we discovered a piano player.

Michel Klipspringer had fled Germany that year, not ahead

of any wartime retribution, but after his wife, famous stage ac-
tress Greta Manning, took up with some high-ranking warlock
or another. They crowned him with a pair of the most delicate
and dear antelope horns that stuck up insistently from his curly
brown hair. It turned out to be a mistake, as he ended up shooting them both, killing the warlock and maiming his wife. He
fled to Makhnovia, which ceased to exist when the Bolsheviks
pulled the plug, and then to Greece, and then to New York City.

I had seen him a few times that I had been to Gatsby's parties,
but admittedly I had never seen him in his striped undershirt
and drawers, scrambling up from a decidedly awkward position
on the floor. His clothes hung neatly over the edge of an open
cabinet door, and his heavy black concert shoes were pressed,
toe-first, to the wall.

"Oh," he said, recovering badly. "Just at my exercises, you know.
They are for—for my liver . . . I will get out of your way in . . ."

"Oh I don't care about that," said Gatsby. "Only play for us."

Klipspringer peered at us in a near-sighted fashion. With his
small horns, he looked startlingly fawn-like, tentative and sensitive.

"Ah, I'm all out of practice, you see. I told you I couldn't play.
I'm all out of prac—"

"Don't *talk* so much, old sport," Gatsby said sternly. "Play!"

He turned with every expectation of his orders being followed, squiring Daisy to the rear of the room to settle her on a
velvet chaise. He lit her cigarette before sitting down next to her,
and I took Nick's hand in mine as Klipspringer approached the
grand piano like it was some kind of slumbering beast.

He was a ridiculous sight as he sat at the keyboard in his underthings, but at the first touch of his fingers to the keys, a shivery silvery tremolo went through the air. He curled the melody
around his fingers, and I realized that he was playing something
he had only heard before.

Nick pulled me around so I was facing him, and we swayed

together in surprise. Elsewhere it was a bright kind of song, tinkled out on some small upright piano. Here, as the twilight finally came on and stretched our shadows over the tile, it was something else entirely.

> *Night or daytime, it's all playtime*
> *Ain't we got fun . . . ?*

Under Klipspringer's fingers, the jaunty little tune turned into something sad, something too wise and too bitter by half. As he played, Klipspringer closed his eyes, tears running down his cheeks. In the back of the room, Gatsby pushed away Daisy's hand holding the cigarette and hid his face in the crook of her neck.

Nick and I had come to a full stop, watching them. The air in the room was thick with summer and the fact that at Jay Gatsby's house, it wasn't too much to expect that summer, this summer, might go on forever.

Nick's arm was around my waist, and finally I turned towards him.

"Come on," I said quietly. "We're not wanted here, are we?"

Nick hesitated, and then one or the both of us must have made a noise because Gatsby looked up at us. He wasn't angry or sorry. Instead he was only confused. Wherever he was with Daisy, there were no names for other people. He had no idea who we were any longer.

Nick could see it too, and he nodded reluctantly. Hand in hand like fairytale children leaving a burning gingerbread house, we made our way out. We were in no particular hurry but both of us were done with the pleasures that Gatsby could provide for the moment. We couldn't find the front door, but we could find the servant's entrance. In the end, we climbed over the narrow hedge that separated Gatsby's property from Nick's. The rain had come back, solid and drenching, and we fled to the cover of

Nick's doorstep, catching our breath and peering back across the way at the garden we had left.

"Oh!" I said with some hilarity. "My clothes. My shoes. I've left them at Gatsby's."

We ended up sitting on his back step together, his jacket—Gatsby's jacket, just as my clothes were Daisy's clothes—slung over my shoulders, sharing a cigarette of harsh Turkish tobacco. Nick told me that he had gotten a taste for the stuff in the war, and I liked it better than I thought I would.

"You should come to France with me someday," he said. "Just you and me. I could show you Rouen and Le Havre."

"Paris or nothing," I said, but it wasn't a no.

CHAPTER FIFTEEN

Summer in New York goes by slowly until it goes by fast, and for the four weeks that took us out of July and into a sullen and ferociously fevered August, I could barely catch my breath. First there was Aunt Justine's difficulty, where we ended up with a few sleepless nights and a live-in nurse, and then there was the riot that took over Brooklyn and Harlem for a full weekend over the Manchester Act, which would bar the way for all unwanted unworthies from a long list of places, while starting the repatriation of those who had, as so many of Aunt Justine's friends put it so delicately, *overstayed their welcome*. Naturally it didn't specify whether it meant the Chinese, the Irish, the Mexicans, the damned, or the dead that occasionally returned with them, so it was a terrible mess.

Nick asked me if I was worried, and I took him dancing at the Preston when I hate dancing at the Preston because I wanted to answer him even less. I told him that the Manchester Act had nothing to do with me, that I couldn't even remember being from anywhere else, and his response—"Prove it"—made me so angry that I ran off the floor and went home with Jodie Washington. She kept me for a few days until her boyfriend came back from his European tour, and by then, I was ready to make up with Nick, so it mostly worked out.

We were becoming something of an item, written up when the gossip papers were having a slow day, which was pleasant. He was proving surprisingly resilient to the kind of pressures that had crashed me and Walter. Anyway, it helped that I had gotten myself kitted up with a cap through one of Aunt Justine's friends, and that was at least one catastrophe I didn't have to worry about any longer, though Nick, charming thing, told me he didn't worry too much about what we did as long as he was doing it with me. I even mostly believed him, though I was making no further headway on bringing him to the Cendrillon. I wondered if, after Gatsby, he had outgrown that sort of thing, but I doubted it. I had never known of anyone who did, though of ones who said they had, plenty.

It was a beautifully clear night halfway through August when the whole city seemed to pull up roots and head for Gatsby's palace. A ghostly little whisper suggested that we stay to enjoy the deserted clubs, but instead I followed Nick home with my new dress—white satin beaded with opalized beads in shivery blue—in the back seat along with some essentials. I had, willy-nilly, started to stay overnight at Nick's, braving the disapproving looks of his maid and the unreliable water of his bathtub. We were playing house, we both knew it, but it was a good game when played with someone who could be as calm and as sweet as Nick was.

Gatsby's mansion spilled light from every window, from every door, and that night, from every tree. Something at the heart of the trees on his property gleamed, and I saw more than one beautiful girl up in the branches, trying to grasp that sweet and lovely light with their hands. They came up empty, and while most gave up, a Black girl in a moiré silk dress remained up in the bare branches, her dress like a cocoon and her face stained with tears for seeing her desire so close and yet so untouchable.

By the water and in the tall grass were fireflies. At first, they made me think of the long slow nights of the Louisville summer, but when I looked closer, I could see that they were another species entirely. Instead of a sweet soft lime green, they glowed a deep red, and when I caught one in my hands, I saw a

brassy metallic sheen to the wings and pincers that clicked at me
threateningly before I let it go again.

Nick and I went arm in arm, and just inside the garden, we
met Daisy, who was with Tom of all people. She wore a blue
gown overlaid with a sheer fine net of crystal, and the crystals—
teardrops and brilliant—were echoed in the tiara perched so
sweetly on her head. Tom in black looked around aggressively,
and I felt Nick stiffen next to me. I wanted to tell him that I
didn't like Tom either, but that could certainly wait for later.

I hadn't really seen Daisy since that day at Nick's. I tried once
or twice, but she had made herself scarce, wrapping up in a kind
of silken solitude that never suited her unless there was a secret
someone there with her. She leaned over to give me a distracted
kind of kiss on both cheeks, but when she addressed Nick, her
voice was strained, and shaded behind the blue of her eyes was
a small and animal worry. She took his hand and folded a green
ticket into it with a tremulous smile as Tom looked on indulgently.

"Oh Nick, if you'd like to kiss me at any time tonight, simply
come give back, won't you? I'm handing them out tonight . . ."

I could see the green slips sticking from the clasp of her
purse, see the absolute ease with which Tom regarded that exchange, and then Gatsby was among us like a fox among the
chickens, a smile too wide and toothy on his face. The look he
gave Daisy was so fond that I almost thought he would give
away the game right there, but then he turned to Tom. He was
coldly, vividly triumphant, and he spread his hands out as if to
encompass the whole world that belonged to him.

"Welcome, welcome," he cried. "Come look around, there's
bound to be so many people you know . . ."

"I think it's quite marvelous," Daisy said faintly. I caught her
startled glance as if she were *only now* realizing that she had
brought her husband to her lover's house, and I gave her an ag-
gressive little shrug because there certainly wasn't anything I
could do with men like Gatsby or Tom.

"I was just thinking that I didn't know anyone at all," Tom drawled, determinedly unimpressed. The easy arm he kept over Daisy's shoulders looked like it got a little heavier. "I'm not so fond of parties where I don't know anyone . . ."

"Oh well, surely you know her," Gatsby said, pointing like a guide at the zoo.

We followed his arm to where Anna Farnsworth languished beneath the ghostly lights, the illumination giving her a flickering phosphor tint. She had just appeared in *The Girl on the Strand*, utterly scandalous. It was common tat around New York that an old wizard had made her from a whole garden's worth of peonies. He should have made her out of something more sturdy, because she was looking wilted under the August heat.

We didn't talk about that, of course, but Gatsby let on that the man standing over her and sprinkling her with seltzer water was her director. He led us deeper into the garden, pointing out that star or that politician. I hung back, letting them get ahead, and after a moment, Nick returned to me.

"All right?" he asked, and I plucked the green ticket out of his hand.

"Honestly," I said, a little tartly. "No one's giving out green tickets this summer."

They entitled the bearer to a kiss, a talk, or a secret from the giver, and Nick's hand had already become stained with the cheap ink of Daisy's name. I tore it to little bits and dropped the bits into a half-empty flute of champagne sitting on the edge of a concrete planter.

"Jealous, darling?" asked Nick with amusement, and I waved my hand dismissively.

"Of course, painfully," I told him. "Always. Anyway, that's a strange to-do between the three of them tonight, isn't it? I shan't want to stand too close to that."

It was true. There was something fraught in the air between all three of them, not just between Gatsby and Tom as might be guessed. I was worried about Daisy, but then none of my experience with her had anything in the world to do with stopping her.

Nick didn't seem to share my opinion, looking after them as they walked towards the dancers on the canvas floor.

"I don't know," he hedged. "Are you worried?"

"Only for my own good time," I said a little sharply, but I sighed when he looked back at me with some guilt.

"Go on if you are going," I said to him.

"I won't if you're cross . . ."

I put my fingers to the corners of my mouth, lifting them up.

"No, no cross here, darling," I said. "I shall entertain myself with these very entertaining people, and I shall come find you later. Though when I do find you next, I am sure that I will be perfectly demanding and in need of your attention."

Nick smiled with some relief, lifting my hand to his lips in a brief salute.

"You're a doll, Jordan Baker," he said.

"Rather *not*," I responded, but he was already gone.

I was a strange combination of bereft and relieved when he was gone. Even after all our time together, I hadn't quite resigned myself to being a couple yet, half of an equation when the male half could somehow continue as a whole without me. He was gone, I felt more myself, and to celebrate, I downed a surprisingly strong French 75 and took another with me for company as I wandered through the playground Gatsby had made of his home.

I hadn't been lying before. There's no better place to be alone than a large party, especially when almost everyone around you was trying to be the biggest and most gleaming version of themselves. Through the crowd, I could glimpse Gatsby introducing Tom and Daisy to another famous movie star while Nick looked on in consternation. No, certainly *not* my scene that very moment, so I moved on.

I was ready to be delighted by Gatsby's home, but there was something desperate about it. If hanging around in New York in the summer of 1922 taught me anything, it was how to nose out desperation, and Gatsby's party reeked of it. Everything was just a shade too bright, everyone just a little too brilliant to be borne. There were tumblers darting through the crowd, human statues in the garden that the people could direct in an enormous chess game, and the usual ubiquitous lights that danced over us like angelic halos, but it all felt so very tiresome to me.

Or maybe I'm the tiresome one, I thought with a grimace. It had been known to happen, and the summer was wearing on like a runaway car or at a snail's pace, depending.

I was just beginning to wonder if I should find a quiet ledge to play gargoyle when I came around a corner in the garden and nearly had my head taken off by a dragon.

Despite my earlier jaded thoughts, there was a moment when a rush of wind pulled my clothes awry, when I stared after a flash of light over gold scales, that I forgot everything except a startled wonder. For a moment, I thought some exotic bird had made its escape from the trees, but then I saw the dragon for itself, larger than a horse, long and slender as a lamp post.

It *was* a dragon, I knew that, even if it was like no dragon I ever saw in the fairytale books. The head recalled the wickedly blunt heads of the crocodiles that I had seen at the menagerie, while a pair of deer's horns sprouted from its brow. The tail was the vast majority of its length, corkscrewing and curling as the dragon seemed to swim through the air, cat-like paws reaching out, toes extended for purchase.

The golden dragon twisted around to dance over my head, and I clapped at the display of skill and delicacy. It was a marvelous thing, one more wonder to add to Gatsby's list, but then the dragon pointed its nose at the night sky above me and started twisting its way up, the tip of its tail weaving back and forth like a counterbalance.

I stood staring after it, craning my neck, and I saw the moment when it started to drop. First it was flying, then it was falling, and then it was doing some combination of the two and gaining speed as it did so.

The moment that I realized that it wasn't going to stop was the same moment when I realized that I couldn't do more than stumble back, likely landing on my rear. I had had cruel tricks like that played on me before, and I narrowed my eyes at the diving dragon. I wasn't going to be bullied, and that was why I did quite a silly thing, looking back.

The dragon could have been anything. It could have been a clockwork wonder taken from a German workshop after the war, and it could have left scars in my arm from jagged metalwork teeth. It could have been a slight and narrow aerialist in some kind of enchantment with more daring than sense. It could have been a dozen and one other things that would have utterly ruined my night, but in the end, it wasn't.

Instead it was *paper,* and I brought the blade of my hand up in an instinctive motion that let the dragon sheer in half from nose to tail tip, the ripping sound making goosebumps stand up on my skin and a prickle of something almost achingly familiar running up my spine.

I stood there in surprise as the two halves of the dragon, nothing but paper intricately cut and scrolled, drifted down to either side of me, and a delighted laugh rang out behind me.

"Rotten brat, that took two hours to make."

I turned to meet the speaker with my chin up and my shoulders back, nearly losing my poise with surprise when I recognized him.

He was the boy in the gallery the day Gatsby had shown us his treasure house. Now he was dressed in a black skullcap and a red brocade robe, covered all over with dragons, though, I saw after a moment, ones that were different from the one that had flown at me with such aggression. A long black beard, neatly combed, had been attached to his chin with spirit gum, and a pair of green spectacles obscured his eyes. I shouldn't have been able to recognize him at all, but I did, and I felt at once that sense of attraction and repulsion again.

"If it took so long to make, then you shouldn't have sicced it on me," I retorted.

He shrugged, unrepentant, folding his hands in his sleeves like a mandarin from the picture books.

"I can make another," he said. "I'm Khai."

I crossed my arms over my chest, looking him over as he looked me over.

"Jordan Baker," I responded. "Have you been here all month?"

"Something like that," he said. "The troupe performed here just a few days before you caught me. They were moving on to Philadelphia, and I don't get on in Philadelphia, so I decided to stay until they came back."

"Just found yourself a guest room, and pretended you had been invited?" I asked, and he gave me a curious look.

"What's it matter to you? You're one of Mrs. Chau's girls, aren't you? I heard she got some girls from Vietnam . . ."

A dull red heat came up on my face, and I felt as if my spine were turning to clear, cold ice.

"I'm not one of Mrs. Chau's girls at all," I bit out.

He gave me another look, up and down, speculative and curious. I realized that he thought my dress was a costume just as much as his own outfit was. He thought there was another world I lived in, like the one where he dressed in gray slacks, striped shirts, and braces. For a moment, I wondered what he imagined I wore in that other world, and I almost choked.

"Hey," he started, but I was turning away. I decided I was bored, and he was tiresome.

"Hey wait," he said, grabbing me by the arm. "Wait. I'm sorry."

"Good!"

"Here, let me make it up to you. You cắt giấy, right?"

I had no idea what the words meant, and they felt like rocks dropped in the middle of his otherwise perfect English. Still they made me choke a little. I couldn't have heard words like that since I started walking, and I wasn't *supposed* to hear them at Gatsby's party.

I stood as still and straight as a garden trellis and Khai must have taken that to mean that I cared what he had to say, because from his sleeves, he pulled out an elegant pair of shears and what looked like a thick piece of gold paper.

"All right, are you looking?"

He waited until I nodded, and he started to cut, the shears moving so quickly that they seemed to blur, throwing scraps of paper everywhere like a tiny blizzard. Something about the snick of the blades cutting through the thick card stock sent a chill up the back of my neck, made me want to hug myself for warmth even on the hot August night. I felt exposed, I realized. I had done what he was doing twice, once in my bedroom, once in Daisy's, and he was doing it for fun, in front of God and Gatsby's guests and everyone.

I started to tell him to stop, that I wasn't going to be impressed, but then the shears disappeared and he was plucking at the edge of the card stock. With a single flick of his fingers, there was a bright orange chrysanthemum blossom in his hand, flecked with gold as the paper had been. He spun it up in the air, and before it had reached the top of its arc, there was another one in his hand, red this time, and up it went as well. In a moment, I was standing in a shower of flowers, and despite my reluctance, I looked around in wonder at the shower of red, white, orange, and violet falling down around me, brushing against my arms, my cheeks, and my shoulders.

At the end, Khai held a pure white chrysanthemum edged in with gold around each narrow petal between his fingers and presented it to me. I took it without smiling, but I brought it up to my face anyway, curious. I was disappointed when there was no scent.

"Of course there's no smell," he told me. "It's only paper after all."

"It feels real, though," I said, plucking some of the petals and crushing them to a wet pulp between my fingers.

"Well, of course it's real," he said with a hopeful smile. "It's just real and made of paper."

I bit my lip. Somewhere in the back of my mind lived a paper lion and a paper Daisy, tottering on her high heels and grinning to make her babyish cheeks even rounder.

"But *how* real?" I asked, and he gave me a curious look.

He bent gracefully to pick up a yellow blossom.

"This real," he said, brushing the petals over my cheeks.

"This real," he said, splitting the blossom in half and letting a torn sheet of thin yellow tissue paper drift to the ground.

"Silly, really," I said, but he didn't seem to have the sense to be cut.

"Of course it is," he said with a grin. "Silly is all we can do at a place like this."

He spoke with a kind of scorn that made me catch a laugh in my mouth. People called Gatsby's parties brilliant, de rigueur, the most exciting thing since M. Bartholdi and M. Eiffel raised first an island out of New York Harbor and then a gorgeous woman clothed in copper from the island. People also called it the new return of Babylon, surely a sign of the rotten heart of the twenties, and excess that would make us all ashamed if we had anything like a sense of honor to shame.

I had never heard them called silly before, and Khai grinned to see me surprised.

"Look, Bai is going to have my head if I don't actually step up," he said. "Don't come to watch us right now."

"Why not?" I asked, piqued, because that was probably the best way he could have gotten me to come and see.

"Because like I said, this is silly. Here . . ."

He produced a card from his sleeve, tucking it under the strap of my dress like some kind of reverse pick-pocketing.

"Come see us Tuesday," he said. "I'll put you on the list."

"Well, I do like being put on lists," I said, and with a slight grin, he turned and made his way across the lawn towards a troupe of people in similar clothing. I must have missed them when they were at Gatsby's last. They were all Asian, all weaving around each other in the steps of some intricate dance, and then I saw them spread out an enormous sheet of paper between them, pale cream, and as it spun faster and faster, opening up into a lotus flower the size of a dining room table. The petals, the same cream as the paper, opened to reveal a slender girl no taller than a mailbox, and I turned away.

A while ago, I would have been as charmed as anyone, but after what Khai said, I could see it for what it was: cheap, showy, silly.

I ventured around to the pool, where Nick had swum a few times, but as far as he could tell, Gatsby, never. From his stories, I expected the pool to be an eerily silent place, but of course it wasn't.

The pool was enormous, clad in marble tile with a mosaic of a beautiful woman covering her face at the bottom. The water was the turquoise you imagined the Mediterranean must be, almost silky when you slid in. Some people had brought along bathing suits, but more simply dropped in in their clothes when the spirit of the evening moved them. I watched the fun for a while, and as I did, I saw that the people who dove under the surface took on the long and sinuous shapes of enormous swimming carp, gliding through the water as if they were flying through air. They flashed green and copper and vermilion as they swam by, turning their round gold eyes towards those above as if we were wonders or gods.

When they rose above the surface, they were human again, offered towels and drinks by a small army of pool attendants standing by. I couldn't tell if it was only a clever illusion or if something had changed their forms, and the swimmers themselves were unclear on the subject.

At the eleven o' clock dinner, I held myself aloof, sitting on the balustrade above the dining area with a cocktail in my hand, watching the kingdom below me with interest. It was the place where Gatsby had stood often enough, waiting for Daisy, hoping for Daisy. It was where he had stood when he saw me and Nick the first night, and I wondered what he felt now, dragged into the common tumult with the rest, because I could see him sitting at the table with Nick and with Daisy.

A swift look around for Tom found him at another table nearby, using his bulk and his boyish smile to impress a silly-looking young girl who I thought must be the daughter of the cultural attaché from France. I could almost hear Daisy call her pretty but common.

Even from where I sat, I could see that Daisy wasn't having a good time. She had put on that lolling, rolling manner of hers, the one that so many people simply assumed meant that she was drunk. Nick leaned close to try to snap her out of it, and I realized that at some point, Gatsby had disappeared.

"Another one of your mysterious phone calls," I muttered to myself, taking a scornful sip from my drink.

"Well, yes."

I choked, corpse reviver going down the wrong pipe, and Gatsby had to steady me with an arm around my waist so I wouldn't go toppling off the staircase.

"You startled me," I said, trying to brazen it out.

"You're in my spot," he responded good-naturedly.

"I don't mind that," I said, and then daring a little, "was I right? Was that another call with one of your *drugstores*?"

That was a story that I had heard more and more lately, that all of this glamour was paid for with headache pills, cheap glamours that were ever so much more dignified than paint, and boxes of school supplies. It wasn't true, but it gave people who wanted something to believe in something to believe in.

Gatsby looked at me steadily, long enough to make me uncomfortable.

"You don't like me," he said.

"Is there a reason I should?" I asked.

"Well, you're important to Daisy. We should get along, don't you think?"

I laughed because it felt like such a quaint thing to say. One would almost think that we were normal people.

"I get along with everyone," I said, and he decided to believe me. He came a little closer, close enough that I could smell his cologne, see the black nail on his left hand. Recklessly, I reached out to tweak his tie a little, straightening it. It surprised a laugh out of him. This close, I could see the tiny wrinkles at the corner of his eyes.

"I can be a very good friend to you too, just as I am to Nick," he murmured quietly. "Nick likes me so much. It's only Tom that doesn't. Tom and you."

"Maybe," I said deliberately, "it's because you like to fuck people who don't belong to you."

The smile froze on his face, jagged like slips of lake ice. I couldn't tell where my recklessness had come from, only that the corpse reviver was strong enough that I didn't regret it yet.

"I think you'll find that I *only* fuck people who belong to me," he said. "But think about it, won't you? I've a lot of friends, here and in DC. It could be that in a short while you could use some friends."

"Think about it yourself," I said with a smile. "They don't want you any more than they want me, or weren't you paying attention?"

There was something raw in his gaze right then, something trapped, something that was suddenly aware that its camouflage was not nearly as good as it had imagined it to be. I had stepped on some secret, obviously, but he had no idea which one, and no idea that I had no idea either. He forced a shrug and a smile.

"Fine. Be that way. Shall we keep it civil for Daisy's sake, or would you like to make your distaste public?"

"I don't think of you enough to care about any of that," I said. "And just because I don't like you is no reason we shouldn't be friends."

He shoved his hands in his pockets, ruining the line of his slacks, regarding me with his head tilted to one side.

"You know, I had thought you a Southern girl," he said. "Like Daisy, like so many others I've known."

I pointed at my face.

"That speaks well of you," I said. "No one thinks I'm a Southern girl."

"And they shouldn't. You're some East Coast thing, aren't you? Sharp and mean and cold. What a prize you are."

"Don't let on you like me like that," I said. "People will talk."

He grinned, boyish and easy.

"You think I don't mean it, don't you? You shouldn't. I think you're pretty wonderful, Jordan. Nick and Daisy sing your praises—"

"If you expect me to believe that either of them talk about me when they're with you, I have a bridge to sell you," I said. "It's a very East Coast thing, selling bridges."

"They do," he insisted. "Daisy told me about Fulbright's, you know. We're not going to have any secrets from each other. And Nick's going to marry you."

His outrageous words made me snap my mouth shut. I sat up straight on the stone balustrade, my ankles twisted together. Gatsby drifted a little closer, setting one hand on the stone beside my thigh.

"Listen," he said softly. "They adore you. I want to adore you too."

"There's nothing stopping you," I said, shoving down off the stone. It put me closer to him than ever, and this close, it was impossible to ignore my attraction to him, the way he could drink all the light out of the room and present it to you as if it was a special gift, his to give.

"You could make it easier for me," Gatsby said with mock exasperation concealing real exasperation.

"I could," I said. "I might. But you do come off awful strong, you know."

He laughed at that, shaking his head.

"That is certainly something I have heard before," he said.

He didn't touch me as I made my way around him. When I looked back, he was gone.

Whether he meant to or not, Gatsby got his revenge on me by keeping Nick until dawn. There had been some kind of scuffle with Daisy, more likely, with Tom, and when I was ready to leave, Nick came for me with a regretful kiss.

"Sorry, darling. Gatsby wants me to stay for a word after everyone's gone. Sounds like he's had a rotten night."

"And you're going to make it a little nicer?"

Nick scowled at that, and I reached out to stroke his arm.

"And why shouldn't you? You're sweet as sugar, and you always make things a little nicer for me . . ."

He could sometimes be jollied out of a bad mood if only I was a little sweet with him. The trouble was that I was so bad at being sweet on command.

"Would you like me to walk you back?" he asked, but I shook my head.

"Stay," I said. "Who knows if you can even get back into this sacred space after you have left it?"

"You could stay too," Nick suggested, and to my startled delight, he cupped a hand around the back of my thigh. "Plenty of open rooms . . ."

"You absolute monster," I said, pleased.

"If I am, you've made me one," he retorted. I let him kiss me for a little while, but then I stepped back with a sigh.

"Come back home as soon as you can," I said. "I shall languish and fall into a life-in-death faint without you."

"I'll wake you up," he promised me, and I made my way back to his humble little house.

Nick's house was small enough that you could see into all the rooms if you stood in the hall and all the doors were open, but there was something about it that gave me the creeps. I was too used to living with people on all sides, even if politesse and good manners prevented us from acknowledging it.

At Nick's place, you could be alone and lonely, and I went straight to his bedroom, firmly closing the rest of the house away. The moon—the real moon—was high in the sky, and I opened the drapes to let the silver light spill onto the bed. I toed my shoes off and hung my dress in the portion of the wardrobe that Nick insisted was mine. As I did so, the card that Khai had given me fluttered to the ground. I picked it up, rubbing my fingers over the characters I couldn't read and the address that I could.

I told myself that I could just throw it away. I didn't *have* to keep it. I didn't *have* to do anything. That comforted me enough that I was able to slide it into my purse, deferring my decision a little while. That helped.

I had brought pajamas along—slim, silk, and with my initials embroidered on the cuff—but the night was too stuffy for that. Instead I stripped to the skin and stretched out on Nick's mattress, hoping that he would be done with Gatsby soon. I wondered if he would bring back a touch of Gatsby with him, whether it was the scent of Gatsby's cologne or the taste of Gatsby's mouth on his own. I licked my lips restlessly, turning away from the moonlight, letting my eyes drift shut.

This summer is never going to end, I thought.

CHAPTER SIXTEEN

The next day, I said a cheerful goodbye to Nick, who had come back from Gatsby's thoughtful rather than half-wrecked. He offered me a lift into the city or over to East Egg, but I waved him off.

"I don't want you getting too used to my comings or goings, you know," I said. "Wouldn't that be boring?"

"I think having breakfast more than a few times a week isn't going to be considered the height of banality just yet," he said good-humoredly, but he let me go.

In truth, the calling card that Khai had slid me was burning a hole in my purse. I didn't recognize the address precisely, but I thought the neighborhood was rather close to the intersection of Elizabeth and Canal, and that meant Chinatown.

Unless the nightly fun wanted to roll over to Alexander's on White Street, I usually steered clear of Chinatown. It was a place that made me prickle uneasily, made me feel not poised and light on my feet, but anchored in a strange way by looks that I simultaneously wanted nothing to do with and that I also wanted to recognize me. My few accidental forays into Chinatown always left me irritated and insufferably arrogant for a while after I came out.

In truth, I felt less special in Chinatown, and that made me dislike it.

There was no question of whether I was going or not, however, so after a long nap in a proper bed, I got up, asked Lara to do me up a bit of fruit and cheese, and had a long soak in the bathtub. I was still tired. The heat seeped through the cracks of the apartment, coming in from outside to curl, feline and unwelcome, on every available surface.

When the cold water grew tepid, I came out to sit awhile with Aunt Justine, who had managed to prop herself up on a mountain of silk pillows and glare angrily at the paper.

"Really," she said, referring to the riots in Washington, DC, and Chicago, "if this many people will not stand for it, they must yield."

Buttering my toast, I glanced at her paper, where someone with a face not unlike mine and Khai's was being led into a police wagon. The riots had been going on for a few days now, and it was impossible to ignore, even at the kind of clubs that I liked to go to.

"I hope it all dies down soon," I said with a sigh, and Aunt Justine, in an uncharacteristically soft moment, reached over to lay her thin hand over mine. She wasn't maudlin enough to squeeze, but she let me feel its papery weight for a moment before withdrawing.

"*You're* safe, you know," she said quietly. "You're a Baker. No one would question that."

I decided not to let her know where I was going that night.

She directed me in filling out some paperwork for her for the Aid Society for Hunger Relief, and then around seven, the nurse we had hired, Pola, came in to clean up and to prepare Aunt Justine for bed. Aunt Justine allowed her work to be taken away with ill-grace, but we could all see that she was tiring.

"I cannot wait until I am recovered," she grumbled, and none of us mentioned the truth of it.

Around nine, I went to dress. I had a pumpkin-orange dress embroidered in faux gold beads in a starburst pattern, and I thought it would do; not too flashy and not too dull. I didn't think I could bear it if anyone in a place like Chinatown thought me dull.

The cab dropped me off in front of what looked like a restaurant that had closed up for the night, and I looked it over curiously. The menus taped to the plate glass were all written in characters I didn't understand, and when I tugged experimentally on the door, nothing happened. I thought that there might have been some people moving inside, but the heavy blinds kept me from seeing clearly.

I ended up looping around behind the restaurant to find a solid steel door, which was more familiar. I rapped briskly on the steel, and when the peephole slid open, I gave them my best grin.

"Hello, I got a card from—"

To my surprise, the door swung open, revealing a squarish Chinese woman in slacks and a long maroon tunic. I blinked at her in surprise, and she nodded impatiently for me to come in.

Oh, it's because I'm . . .

The thought was a foreign one, and bemused, I walked up the half-flight of steps to the restaurant level.

I suppose I was expecting something grand, with great gold idols and opium beds scattered throughout. I certainly didn't expect a restaurant ringed with red vinyl booths, and a dozen people sitting around a table picking at plates of demolished leftovers. They were my age and maybe a little older, the women in slacks just as the men were, and they passed a bottle from hand to hand, pouring each other shots in small teacups before passing it on.

One girl in a man's dress shirt with the sleeves rolled up noticed me first, and she elbowed the boy next to her, who was still wearing ferocious patrician eyebrows and a goaty beard over his undershirt and braces. Soon enough, they were all looking at me with various degrees of curiosity and hostility. I gave them back look for look, unsmiling, and I held up the card.

"Khai gave this to me," I said. "He said I should come."

I waited for whatever ax was going to fall onto my head, but then it was as if the table gave a collective shrug and people were squeaking their seats aside so I could drag over a chair from another table. I stared in fascination at the picked-over food in front of me, startlingly white buns, piles of stringy meat, and barely cooked vegetables gleaming with grease, thin white things that made me think of the tendons on the back of Aunt Justine's hand. I averted my gaze quickly, but the girl sitting next to me caught me staring.

"You want me to put a plate together for you?" she asked. "Are you hungry?"

"No," I said stiffly, but she was already moving, taking a plate and piling it up with something I couldn't even identify. Now everyone was watching me as she handed me a pair of chopsticks to eat with. I took them, and then glanced at the bottle.

"I wouldn't mind some of that," I said hopefully, and there was a quick glance that went around the table before the girl took the bottle decisively and poured me a slug into a teacup.

I was smart enough to know that they didn't think I was, and this was a game played all over the world. It was also a game I had played before, and I was willing to bet that I had done it with better alcohol than they ever had.

The liquid in my surprisingly dainty teacup had a yellowish tone and a slightly sluggish movement, almost syrupy. I had seen some of them sipping at their cups and others tossing it back as I came in. *I can already tell that I'm not going to like this,* I thought even as I lifted the cup to my lips and swallowed the contents.

The liquor hit the back of my tongue, burned its way down my throat, and scorched my chest before settling uneasily in my belly. I opened my mouth, dragonish, to suck back a mouthful of air to calm the fiery sting. I had had worse, but not often, and not recently. I shook my head hard, and the table burst into laughter, and in the case of one boy, applause.

"Here, here, have another," the girl said, and I was smart enough to get the bottle away from her even if my grasp felt a little shaky.

"No, darling, no, I saw you, let me . . ."

I fumbled for her cup, slopping more in than out. She lifted it to me in an ironic salute before taking a ladylike sip and pulling it away from her lips.

"Oh, is that the way I'm meant to do it?" I asked, mock-aghast. "I just don't know *anything* . . ."

It started what sounded like a familiar fight at the table, conducted half in English and half in something else, fast and fervent and intense. The girl next to me took another sip, giving me a smile that was entirely in her eyes. I couldn't tell if it was friendly or not.

"So Khai invited a girl who doesn't know anything."

"Well, I know that I don't know anything," I said, leaning in. "Maybe you could teach me . . ."

She narrowed her eyes at that, leaning back away from me in a way that made me sit up straighter. Of course this wasn't the Cendrillon, and it wasn't Peggy's either, the tiny little place under the Porter Bowling Alley which was mostly for girls and only served up pickled hard-boiled eggs from enormous jars of brine for refreshments. I had forgotten, so I lifted my chin and pretended I hadn't forgotten anything.

"What's someone like you come here to learn?" she asked.

"How about your name for a start?"

She hesitated as if even that was asking for the moon, and then she shrugged.

"Bai. What's yours?"

"Jordan Baker," I responded, and she gave me a confused look.

"No, your right name," she said, and I scooted back a little farther.

"It *is* my right name," I said coolly. "You can use it or you can pick out something better to call me."

She frowned as if trying to decide if she wanted to name me, and then the steel door burst open and a whole new group of people came in, led by Khai. They were half-in, half-out of what I now knew to be costumes for their act, and they were trailing bits of paper behind them, slivers of turquoise that slithered through the air like snakes, shreds of pink that blew into cherry blossoms as I looked, scraps of crimson that landed on one girl's long sleeve to smolder there before a helpful boy beat it to steam with the flat of his hand.

More importantly, they had two more bottles of alcohol, and despite how little I liked the stuff, I felt a jolt of relief.

The night got fuzzy after that. Bai insisted on filling my glass again, and so I filled hers in vengeance, and I know that someone laughed at us and someone else was trying to explain the history of the liquor to me, though I listened as well as I ever did, which was to say, not at all. I remembered throwing my arm around Bai's shoulder and having her shove me off quickly, and then I went and leaned against Khai, who liked it a little better though not as much as I wanted him to.

At some point, after everyone was red-faced and staggering a little, people started pulling out the most delicate scissors I had ever seen, spindly as storks with long narrow blades and deadly sharp tips.

"Here! Look, look," Khai said in a voice I remembered as being loud and brassy and far away. "I'll show you."

As I watched, sitting on the ground with my head tilted against the seat of an empty chair, he pulled out a sheet of green-blue paper, shimmering like mermaid's scales. As he cut, the paper opened up in his hands like a flower or a song, and from the heart of it roared a dragon, filigreed so that you could see the dim lamplight straight through, so that I could see Khai through the sinuous curves of its body.

He let it go, and it flew around the room, wide crocodile mouth opened in a roar.

"Can't let the king go alone," said another boy whose name I didn't catch, and he pulled out a sheet of sunny yellow paper, cutting quickly and producing a shadow puppet of a beautiful lady, though with only a cursory band across her breasts for modesty, I had no idea how much of a lady she could be. She was perfectly flat, and as we watched, clapping and stamping our feet, she pranced along the wall, her head always facing left or right and the angular movements of her arms and legs as much a joy as the dragon's curves had been.

With a gesture, Khai brought his dragon around to circle the female figure. The dragon's body waved like a banner, and after a few arching, slithering circles, it came down to wrap around the woman.

"They're fighting!" I said, and Bai, who was sitting on the ground next to me, her legs stretched out in front of her, made a scornful noise.

"That's the mountain goddess and the sea king," she slurred. "And if you think they're fighting . . ."

I blushed at her words, fortunate that it could be passed off to the ridiculous alcohol we were somehow still drinking. Now that I was looking for it, no, they were not fighting at all.

"They're the mother and father of Vietnam," Bai was saying. "Tonkin. Ha, Vietnam. It can still be Vietnam here. But the dragon and the goddess. Our mother and father."

Mine too? The voice came from somewhere inside me, and I firmly locked that voice back in the box.

"Why is the father of Vietnam a . . . a lizard?"

She reached out to backhand my upper arm too hard. I yelped and would have hit her back, but she was talking again.

"A dragon, a dragon, ghost girl," Bai said. "He was a dragon, and he fell in love with the mountain goddess. They had a hundred strong sons . . ."

"Sounds painful," I said, trying to sound flippant, but she gave me a look with eyes as dark as mine, and I had no experience reading them at all. I could have looked at her all night in a kind of narcissistic fascination, taking in how similar she was to me, where she differed. How I would look like her if I didn't get the faint hairs on my face carefully plucked every week. How much she would look like me if she dusted her eyelids with sparkling green powder.

"It was. She gave birth to them, and then . . . and then she didn't want to be married anymore. When she was in the sea with her husband, she missed her mountains, and when he was in the mountains with her, he missed the sea."

"Did they fight?"

"Of course not. They loved each other. They split up the family instead, half the sons going north into the highlands and half going to meet the sea. That's why Viet people are the best fishermen in the world and the best mountain climbers too."

I know that I made some kind of polite noise, and everything broke into fragments after that. Khai and another boy stripped to the waist to prove who was the better fighter when the answer was clearly neither of them. Another boy whose name I didn't catch accordion-folded a long strip of paper, made a few cuts, and then there were a half-dozen tiny elephants following each other around, fixed together long nose to whippy tails. Bai tried to tell me the story of the two elephant-riding sisters who took on all of China in Vietnam's pre-history, but I wasn't able to focus on her for more than a few minutes before my brain wandered away in desperation. I was not good at history, and it felt like everyone in the room was trying to give me some, whether it sat well on me or not.

I drank some more of that fiery liquor, and then I drank as a chaser a glass of plum wine, which was not nearly as sweet as I was hoping for. I thought I would be sick for a bit, and that was hilarious, so I stayed on the floor, laughing helplessly as Bai tried to put me in a chair.

At some point much later on that evening, she put a pair of scissors in my hand, and then a little while after that, I had a memory of her slapping me so hard that I landed on my rear on the floor. I had to think about whether I wanted to see a doctor or not. At the very least, a doctor would have given me a few doses of something pleasantly fizzy to get me through the night.

There were hands hauling me to my feet and a babble of voices raised in a clamor. Someone was saying that they had to talk to me. Someone, Bai most likely, wanted me gone. Someone else commented acidly on what kind of danger I posed to them, how it was something like me that was to blame for all the recent trouble.

"Oh I really am just a danger to myself instead of the individuals of my community," I sang out. "Before I can answer your question, though, you must tell me what I'm posing for. I won't do it for just anyone, you know. It has to be someone who can capture something new about me, something that no one here would have eyes to judge me for."

"Goddammit, Khai," someone else said, and I heard him sigh somewhere close to me.

"It's fine, it's fine, ah? I'll take care of it."

Then I was being lifted up with Khai's shoulder under my arm.

"I'm going to take you home now," he said patiently. "Tell me where you live."

"Oh, I'll just come home with you," I said, momentarily forgetting myself. I thought home was on 41 Willow Street, and I certainly didn't want to go there anymore. Too many dead people.

"You won't like that," he said, tilting his head away when I tried to press my face into his neck. "I'm sharing with Charlie and Wang. Tell me where you live."

This time I remembered I lived on Park Avenue, and out on the street, where I was able to take my breath and hail a cab, I took several gulps of fresh air, feeling a little better.

"I can get home on my own," I said, and he laughed a little at that.

"Doubt it."

I pouted, but I wasn't fond of late night city cabs without company, so I let him come with me all the way back to Park Avenue. On the ride home, I slumped against the window, letting the lights chase each other over my face.

"So who are you?" he asked finally.

"*Jor*dan Baker," I snapped. "I told Bai that already."

"And you're Vietnamese, right?"

"I'm from Louisville," I sniffed. "But . . . yes. Before that, from Tonkin. I came back with a missionary, Eliza Baker."

"She stole you?"

"She *rescued* me. From the village where she was missioning. The Chinese were right across the river, so she took me and ran all the way to where the carriage was waiting. She used an orange crate as my cradle on the ship back to New York."

It was family legend, trotted out every Christmas while I lived in Louisville. I had grown quite immune to it with the judge and Mrs. Baker because the story was really about Eliza rather than about me, but when I told it to Khai, it stuck a little. It felt a little strange, a little bit shameful, though that could have been the bad alcohol.

"Were your parents dead?"

"They must have been. Otherwise why would she have taken me?"

The answer came back in Eliza's sweet voice, worn thin and a little ragged from age in my mind.

You were my very favorite. Just the very best baby. I could not leave you, I could not bear it.

"She couldn't bear leaving me," I told Khai, deliberately ignoring the conclusions that we were both reaching.

I stared out the window.

"Was she good to you?" he asked, his voice determinedly neutral.

"She died when I was a little thing," I said absently. "She was frail, prone to illnesses of all sorts, you know. Her parents raised me."

They had, where I hadn't raised myself. I could feel that that wasn't enough for Khai, so I groped around for something else in the dim toy box that held my earliest memories.

"She . . . she said I was born in the pig year."

"You told Bai you were twenty-one."

"Yes?"

"I'm the year of the pig, and I'm twenty-three."

My head spun. I remembered Eliza doing a silly little song for me, her hands on her head to mimic a pig's ears. I could remember her telling me I was born in the year of the pig, which was part of the Tonkinese religion, like the golden statues they worshiped and the food they set out for their ancestors. If she was telling me the truth and Khai was, I was two years older than I thought I was, the same age as Daisy.

"Oh God," I said with a wet little giggle, "I've gotten so *old*."

Khai was silent as if he didn't know what to make of that.

"We're going to be in town for another month," he said finally. "If you want to try that again—"

"Not really, no."

"—I'm staying at St. Curtis Hostel. Maybe if we kept the alcohol out of it."

"No," I said again, more strongly this time. "That was the only thing that made it bearable."

"You almost made a person out of trash," he said. "Baijiu wasn't going to make *that* bearable."

We had gotten back to Park Avenue. Khai's eyes widened as he handed me out of the car.

"I live here with my aunt," I said, before he could say something about me being one of Mrs. Chau's girls again. They had been all over the papers lately because of the one they had caught with that married judge. She'd turned up dead with vines growing out of her mouth and the rest went into hiding.

"Right," he said, as if he doubted me, and I stood up straight.

"Thank you for seeing me home," I said. "Paul won't want to see you through the doors."

"Paul . . ."

"The doorman."

I reached in my purse and pulled out three crisp dollar bills, folding his hand over them neatly.

"There you go. That'll get you back to Chinatown, and pay for the alcohol I've drunk so very much of."

He glared at me.

"You know that's too much."

"You *mustn't* give it back, I'll be ever so—"

"What *are* you? Of course I'm not going to give it back."

He pocketed it, shaking his head.

"I'm here for another month," he repeated. "If you want to come, then come."

"You're so welcoming," I said stonily.

He let me get the last word, which was good because I was likely going to fight for it. He gave me another dark look and got into the cab, the front seat this time. I turned before I could see him drive off and went home.

That night, I dreamed about sitting on a sticky tile floor, laughing crazily as I gathered up menus and receipts, cutting them, crushing them in my hands as I shaped the pieces into a soldier's form, a gun in his hand and death in his eyes.

CHAPTER SEVENTEEN

Then everything sort of stopped.

It was sticky, sickly August, the worst time to be trying to do anything. Aunt Justine had me throw all the windows of our apartment open, no matter what her nurse said, and I swung my bare legs out onto the ledge, leaning over my thighs to look down at the street below.

Nick had made himself scarce again, and I wondered a little at that. The party at Gatsby's had lurched to a stop, or so said Margaret Dancy, who had gone over there with the Wellhurst crowd. They found the gate chained and the windows dark, and no matter how they shook the iron bars, it would not open for them. Just as they had left, Margaret said, a tall man in a sharp black suit had driven up. They'd watched as he stood at the gate for several long minutes, and then, without any expression, got back in his car and drove away again.

One lazy afternoon at Ripley's, Margaret guessed that the man himself had gone abroad.

"Heat's too hot even for him," she said with a significant look down.

I doubted that. As far as I knew, Daisy still kept house in West Egg, though Tom, who was being noised a bit in the gossip pages for stepping out with some mysterious redhead friend, not so much. I couldn't imagine Gatsby willingly leaving Daisy after having found her again. It just didn't make sense.

The demons themselves were little seen in Manhattan lately.

The Manchester Act was moving forward. The Democrats were pushing for a vote by the end of August, and even as little as I tried to care, it was everywhere. I wished Nick were around, variously because I wanted a snuggle or a distraction or a dance, but he was vaguer than ever. I told myself I didn't care.

Daisy finally called up on Thursday, telling me to come out to West Egg. She and I disappeared from each other's lives like this enough that it wasn't suspicious, but I held back a little.

"There's ever so much to do in the city right now . . ."

It wasn't a lie. There was plenty to do; I just wasn't doing it. She laughed a little, the sound cool in my ear.

"Oh, but isn't that terrible, darling? There's nothing to do here, and I would love to do it with you."

"And what about the talented Mr. Gatsby?"

"Jay is for the afternoons," she said primly. "I'm not permitted to intrude on his evening hours."

On the other end of the line, I narrowed my eyes. That didn't sound right to me, and even if I was trying hard not to think about the Manchester Act, it was hard to ignore the people who were pulling up stakes, setting out for parts east, west, and down. I figured if Gatsby were too busy to keep Daisy entertained, the only thing he could be busy with was feathering a little nest for her somewhere in Paris or Rome or Morocco.

"The truth is, Jordan, I miss you," she said, lowering her voice to a conspiratorial tone. "Isn't it just too awful? I really do delightfully and deliriously miss you. I've been so very lonely, and it's been ever so long since you came out."

"Being lonely is not the same as missing me," I said dryly, though the wind and the water did sound just the faintest bit appealing.

"Oh but it is, dear," she said coaxingly. "Let me bribe you. I know that Nick has been haunting his sad little shack like a ghost lately rather than taking you out as you deserve. If you come out,

I'll bring him over, just for you, wrapped up in string and pushed into whatever linen closet you like . . ."

I laughed at that, shaking my head because Daisy was talking faster now. If I let her, she'd start to promise me every star she could pluck down from the sky as if I were a boy whose attention she wanted. I wasn't, though, and I gave in gracefully.

"All right, Daisy. And if I want Nick in a linen closet, I can lure him there myself. You *do* keep some of Gatsby's cologne around, don't you?"

"You awful thing. Come soon, darling."

Aunt Justine insisted that I take the car ("after all, dear, it's not as if I am going to get to use it for a while") and I went out to West Egg with a goodly supply of dresses and shoes so that I would not have to borrow.

The house was unbearably hot when I showed up close to sunset, so I went to find Daisy in the garden, dozing on a long low couch under a sunshade, her feet bare and her eyes gazing towards the sea. I came to sit on the couch opposite hers, taking a sip from her untouched highball before choking a little.

"Demoniac before dark?" I asked, and she offered me a hazy smile. Now that I looked, I could see a lassitude to her limbs, something unfocused in the way her fingers ran along the edge of the cushion under her head.

"Oh, but it's from Warsaw," she said. "Better than what we've been getting from Berlin. It's ever so good, and Jay brings it over special for me."

I cautiously took another sip. It *was* better than the kind coming from Berlin. Of course with the trouble in Vienna, the Viennese demoniac had disappeared, but Warsaw made up for it. I let it sit on my tongue before swallowing it. It was good, hot enough to make the day seem cool. I stretched on the couch and reached over to take Daisy's hand.

She was flattened by the heat, her dark hair curling lank

against her damp cheek, the edge of her white chiffon skirt fluttering like the flag of a defeated city. My eyes half-closed and
shining under the lids, I thought I could see what kind of monster she was.

Daisy Buchanan was, underneath her dress waving surrender
and her face like a flower, a rather handsome and lazy monster.
She wasn't something that stalked her prey for miles through the
underbrush. Instead she would lie so still that something unwary
might think she was dead, and when they came for her skin, for
the reputation of killing her, for her virtue or her wealth, then
she would be upon them.

Don't get too close to Daisy Fay, a voice told me. *Only disaster,
my girl.*

Didn't I know that already? Hadn't I risked my reputation in
Fulbright's for her? Hadn't I made a girl out of trash and let Daisy
murder her?

I remembered more of the night in Chinatown now. The demoniac helped, and apparently the kind from Warsaw was especially merciless. In the hazy vision that wasn't truly vision, I saw
faces like mine far above where I slumped on the filthy tile floor.
They were the members of the paper cutting troupe that was performing all over New York that month. At the same time, I saw
them with animal heads, cats, oxen, dogs and snakes, and Khai I
could see had the face of a pig, just as I did.

No, I don't want that, I told them, but Bai, who had the fat-
cheeked and comical face of a rat, shook her head.

Should have thought of that before you did what you did.

There was a pair of shears in her hand. Unlike the ones they
had given me that night, they were heavy as gardening shears,
the blades dark and rusty. They didn't have to be sharp as long as
Bai was strong enough, and I knew she was.

She took my hand, the shears opened, and the blades squeezed
shut over my littlest finger, bouncing a few times to let me feel
how blunt they were. The next pass, she would take my pinkie off

at the second knuckle, but then there was a heavy tread on the stone path leading to the sunshade.

I was faintly surprised to see Tom making his way towards us. He looked hot and uncomfortable, his hat tucked under one arm, his face shiny with sweat and his hair faintly sodden.

"Hello there, Jordan," he said, and instead of greeting Daisy as well, he bent down to kiss her lightly on the forehead.

For a moment, I expected her to rise up and devour him, but instead she sat still, eyes half-shut and mouth unsmiling. Tom smiled at her, and I realized that he had no idea what she was thinking of him, the slow animosity that rolled off of her like a wave over a sandbar, the narrow-eyed malice that would make any young girl in Louisville nervous.

"Good to see you at home today," he said. "I came back from the city early hoping to see you."

"So you've seen me," she said sulkily.

Tom narrowed his eyes and, at the last moment, remembered I was there. Sometimes, having a witness around was enough to remind him he was a good man with a foolishly temperamental wife, and even if Daisy didn't agree, I liked it better than the other options.

"I was thinking we could go to eat at the Bay Harbor tonight," he said. "Fresh scallops, something cool for all this heat, don't you think?"

Daisy's expression went from sullen to positively mutinous, and I shifted a little.

"Oh, let's not," I said indolently, though fresh cold scallops sounded good. "Let's just stay in and watch the shadows travel across the lawn. It's just about the only thing I can stand to do when it's this hot. And Tom, of course you're going to have to fan us to keep us cool, that would be a perfect job for you since you're so fresh from the city, don't you think?"

Tom smiled at me peaceably, since after all, I wasn't the one he was married to.

"I'm no woman's coolie," he said affably. "But why don't you let me call someone from the house? I bet I can find someone slacking who wouldn't mind the work . . ."

"Don't be ridiculous, the pair of you," Daisy broke in. She was in a slightly better humor, even if she twisted easily away from Tom's hand when it came to rest on her shoulder. She had a cat-like way of doing it, something that you couldn't take offense at. Touching Daisy was largely a privilege, even, and sometimes especially, to those closest to her.

"Let's call for food tonight," she said. "We could have the chef from Bay Harbor come up, and then we would never ever have to leave the house ever again. Wouldn't that be grand?"

Tom eyed her suspiciously as if unsure whether he should take her seriously.

"Of course, Daisy, whatever you like best."

"Of course," she echoed, slightly acid.

Later that night, in my bed with the windows open and a stray sea wind blowing over us, Daisy's eyes were unfocused but gleaming.

"I've called for him," she said. "Nick, I mean."

"Well, good," I responded. "I've been wondering what he's up to."

I hadn't had the inclination or the determination to go chasing after him in the wake of Chinatown. I was a little disappointed that he hadn't come chasing after me. If Daisy brought us together again, that would soothe all the necessities of pride. I had missed him.

"And he's bringing Jay, of course."

I turned my head to look at her. She stretched out flat on her back, eyes staring at the ceiling. If I looked hard, I imagined I could still see the fingerprints we had left on the plaster when we'd used a Greek charm to float up close to the ceiling earlier in the season.

"Why are you doing that?" I asked, vaguely alarmed.

"Oh Jordan, may I tell you a secret?"

I nodded, and she pressed a little closer, her dark hair settling spider-like over her pale cheek.

"I'm leaving with Jay," she whispered. "We're going away, far away."

"Greece?" I asked; it was popular for that kind of thing.

She looked dreamy.

"First Greece," she said. "And then London, and then Oslo, and then France. And then I think I should like to settle in Philadelphia. I know all his family are dead, but it is where he's from. I could love a place if Jay came from there, I think . . ."

I couldn't help the way her fantasy tugged at me. The world was a book for the two of them. They would let the wind flip the pages, Daisy would put down one delicate finger, and away they would go.

"And you must come with us, Jordan," she said. "Gatsby wants Nick along, and so of course you should come too. It'll be splendid, we can have a double wedding on top of the Eiffel Tower, or maybe in front of the sphinx in Egypt."

One moment I was gently envious of Daisy's daydreams, and the next I was struck with a wave of opposition. I wanted to see all of those places, maybe with Daisy, maybe alone, but for some reason, I didn't want to see them as myself with them, or even with Nick.

"Sorry," I said lightly. "I have to stay with Aunt Justine. I'm taking over some of her causes after her unpleasantness earlier this year."

"Oh, but darling, of course you can't! And what will happen when Nick meets some pretty little China doll in a Shanghai port and gets his head turned all around?"

"Well, I would say if he can't tell the difference between us then he's welcome to her."

"Don't be cross, Jordan, you know that I cannot stand it if you are cross. Let's say this instead. I'll give you tickets to wherever we are traveling, special ones that get you where you need to go no matter where you start from."

"Gull tickets?" I asked in surprise. They weren't magic but money, offered by the enormously prestigious Paul Wright Gull travel agency. They were edged in real gilt with enough enchantments piled on that they could never be duplicated, and no matter where you were, city street, cow byre, moor or castle, if you could get your Gull to a ticketing booth, it would take you on.

"Yes," Daisy said with a sly smile. "You'll forgive me for a book of Gull tickets, won't you?"

I rolled over onto my side, away from her.

"I'd consider it, anyway," I said, but for the first time, the idea of getting out of New York appealed to me. I was tired of the heat and the summer, I thought, but maybe I was only tired of who I was in the heat.

CHAPTER EIGHTEEN

The next morning, we all woke up late, the heat of the day beading sweat and damp on every surface and rolling a haze through the air that made everything look oddly flat and faraway.

Tom was the only one who could dress first thing. Daisy and I draped ourselves over the cold marble stairs of the foyer in nothing more than our long silk robes, and I pressed my cheek against the marble and made a face at Pammy when her nurse brought her by. Daisy's daughter, I thought, had been replaced with a rag doll in the heat, so very limply did she slouch over the nurse's arm. Then I realized with a bit of a start how long it had been since I'd seen Pammy in the skin. Changelings were growing less common as time went on, the fairy magic draining out of the east and flowing west, but there were a few cases every few years of it happening, usually in the good families as well.

I was just thinking about suggesting we go to check when Tom nudged us both with an officious booted foot.

"Come on, girls," he said with a patience I liked less than his bombast. "Time to go get changed. Nick and that damned drug store mogul are coming over soon."

Daisy took a lazy swipe at him like a bored cat, but she helped me to my feet.

"Oh very well," she said, making a face. "If the great Napoleon tells us we must."

"He was only a little man," Tom said indignantly. "I'm just the opposite."

"Of course you are, dear," Daisy said with such poisonous sweetness that I thought she must surely have given the game away. Tom seemed all smiles however, and it came to me that he only ever really took offense when she wasn't needling him. When she was only herself and moody or strange or angry for herself.

With reluctance, we rose from our place on the marble stairs. I noticed that we had left a heat-imprint of our bodies there with our sweat and the oil of our skin and the oil of our perfumes. I hoped that those impressions would last in the marble, some kind of permanent snow angel that Daisy and I could leave behind to haunt the house long after we were both gone.

We decided on matching white. Daisy thought of brides, I thought of Iphigenia, the virgin sacrifice on the shores of Aulis, and then was roundly mocked for it. We found, willy-nilly, the pot of lip color that Daisy had discovered above the wardrobe that day. It had made its way back to her. I had my own color, something plum and pretty from Macy's, but I paused when Daisy held the little pot out to me between her finger and thumb, her other fingers fanned out like a peacock's tail.

"Wear this for good luck," she said warmly. "It's what you were wearing when you met Nick for the first time."

I let her smooth the color over my lips, but it didn't feel like good luck. It felt like a bookend, in that we had started something that day in June and today we were capping it off. I shook the thought off. It was far too Protestant for words, and I was an irreligious modern girl after all. No gods or idols for me.

We waited for Gatsby and Nick in a dim and cavernous room, curled together on a marvelous round couch as if we were boneless Siamese cats. When the butler showed them in, we looked up in unison, making Nick smile as he came to kneel down next to me.

"You're a lovely thing, Jordan," he murmured, kissing my fingertips.

"Not that you've been around to see," I teased.

Gatsby was looking around with such curiosity you had to assume he had come through the whole house that way. I could almost hear things being dropped on the great scales that served for his mind, the house Daisy shared with Tom against the one she would share with him, the windows against his windows, the finery of Tom's servants versus his own.

We all four looked up at the strident shriek of the telephone, and from the next room, we heard Tom's voice, loud even when it was trying to be discreet, conciliatory in a way he never had to be with his own wife.

Nick had learned something at least because he didn't ask who it was. Daisy, on the other hand, had crossed some kind of Rubicon of her own, and glanced disdainfully through the wall at where Tom stood.

"That's Tom with his girlfriend," she said. "Isn't she a doll?"

I glanced at Gatsby, who had acquired a vicious sort of look. For a moment, I thought he might storm into the hallway and challenge Tom to a duel or something equally ridiculous. Daisy had gotten a hold of his hand, however, and was hanging on. Indiscreet, perhaps, careless definitely, but she did like to keep what was hers close by.

Nick was saying something in defense of Tom, and then the man himself came in, bringing Nick to his feet. Gatsby took his hand from Daisy's more slowly.

"Ah, at last, at last," said Daisy, her tone as relaxed as an overcooked noodle. "Tom, do see about mixing us a drink, won't you?"

"I brought something to pass around," said Gatsby, offering a dark and dusty bottle. With no label, I guessed it must be some more of that powerful demoniac from Warsaw, but Tom turned away and was gone from the room so brusquely it stayed in his hand. Gatsby shrugged and set it on the floor by the fireplace. Later that night, I would find it and be grateful, but right then, I was more concerned with the fact that Daisy had risen, going to push Gatsby back down on the divan by the window. I caught a glimpse of his startled face, the surprised O of his mouth, and then she was straddling his lap, her dress in meringue ruffles around him.

"Oh how I do love you," Daisy purred, sliding her fingers through his short hair before she kissed him. I had never seen her kiss anyone like that before. It was languid, entirely for her, and as pretty as it was, as much as I liked Gatsby's shock at her aggression, I liked my own shock a little less. I was meant to be Daisy's best friend, and I didn't know this version of her. This version of her felt like a gun primed to fire.

"There's a lady present," I said from the couch, hoping she would knock it off before Tom came down on her like a thunder bolt, but she only looked over her shoulder at me, batting her eyes.

"Then you must kiss Nick as well, mustn't you?"

"Vulgar," I said, affecting both disinterest and disdain, and Nick squeezed my hand a little, mouthing *thank you* at me when Daisy returned to Gatsby's mouth. He had a horror of performance and was typically at his best when he thought no one looked or cared.

I rolled my eyes at Nick to show him how very silly I found them both, and he rewarded me with a dim smile.

Daisy nearly toppled off of Gatsby's thighs when there was a swift knock at the door. Tom never knocked, and after touching a clean piece of tissue paper to her eyes and her lips, she stood up and away.

"Come in," she said.

To my surprise, it was Pammy and her nurse, and as Daisy cooed with delight in a language that she shared only with her daughter, I glanced at Gatsby.

He was frozen in place, quietly absorbed and fascinated, and a little horrified as well. I wondered with some cynicism where Pammy fit in with all of Daisy's plans for Europe and the Mediterranean.

Oh God, what if she wants me to look after her?

The thought was sudden and sobering, unlikely, but not as unlikely as all that. Daisy might as easily ask an old school chum to look after her daughter as she would to take a cat she had adopted for a short while.

"Here's my darling, my darling, my love and my life," Daisy said, taking Pammy's hand and encouraging her in a bashful pirouette.

Pammy's eyes were full of Daisy, but when her mother pushed her towards us, she went easily enough. She called me Aunt Jordan and kissed me dutifully on the cheek, and she curtsied prettily for Nick and for Gatsby. Nick treated her with the grave courtesy that makes some adults so very popular with children, and Gatsby seemed oddly shy of her, darting glances between her small face and Daisy's almost askance.

"Doesn't she look an awful lot like me?" Daisy asked. "She's all of me and none of Tom, isn't that nice?"

She had the nurse take Pammy away again, the delicate child and the woman in white narrowly dodging Tom, who had reappeared with a tray of gin rickeys and a newly suspicious look. He handed me my drink without glancing at me, so I took the opportunity to look at him, taking in the clench of his jaw and the way his brows lowered like the horns of a bull considering a charge.

In the middle of Daisy saying something about the earth falling into the sun, he interrupted her.

"Say," he said, looking at Gatsby, "why don't you come out onto the veranda with me. Let me show you a thing."

I couldn't have been the only one who noticed the subtle darkening of Gatsby's eyes, the way his shoulders came up like those of a young prizefighter. The genteel courtesy rippled and for a moment, I saw the willing brawler underneath.

"Why, of course, old sport. Nothing would please me better."

The gin had gotten to me, I decided, freezing the inside of my head. For a moment, I was utterly sure that one of them would kill the other, and then we would be in some kind of wretched murder mystery, trying to decide how to cover up the crime and falling into paroxysms of paranoia as we offed each other one by one.

They rose almost in unison, and Nick rose a half-beat later, a serious look on his face, and followed them out.

They tromped out to the veranda like hunters going off into the marsh, and I took Daisy's drink away from her, setting it on the table. She wasn't drunk, she had barely started when my glass was already drained, but it was hard to remember that when she looked at me with such a fuzzy expression.

"Why hello, Jordan," she said, and I resisted the urge to shake her.

"Daisy, you are going to get someone killed."

"No, darling, not *me*," she said. "We'll be well away before anything happens."

"You and me?"

She blinked.

"Me and Jay. You and Nick. It will be fine, I promise."

She leaned to kiss me, I guessed, on the cheek, but instead she slipped or I did, because she was kissing me on the lips. We both tasted of gin and lime, and my lipstick was fainter, ghostly on her mouth. The kiss sent a shock through me because it didn't seem to shock her at all. She winked at me, pressing her thumb against my lower lip as if to wipe the kiss away.

"Shh, it'll be fine."

The maids hung the dining room with swathes of dark blue silk, barricading us from the sun as the infrequent gusts of wind billowed the makeshift curtains like sails. Lunch was a plate of cold meat and more gin, and we picked at the platter in a depressed way. Nick had given me a significant glance upon coming back in with Gatsby and Tom; I would have to get that story out of him later.

The talk wound back and forth like a dazed mouse caught in a box trap; if I had to hear Tom talk about turning a garage into a stable one more time, I might save Gatsby the trouble and simply stab him myself.

Daisy, seated between Tom and Gatsby, seemed to turn thinner and tighter, and when she jumped up, it was like a steel guitar string had been plucked too hard.

"Well, what in the world are we going to do with ourselves this afternoon?" she cried. "What are we going to do with ourselves tomorrow, and then for the next thirty years?"

"You're being morbid," I said, because I mistrusted that look in her eye. "We don't have to do anything. We can just wait for fall. Life starts over again in fall."

Daisy shook her head, her eyes filled with tears. It made me think of the night she wanted to see a lion. They were real tears at the moment. They were real tears *in* the moment.

"But it's so *hot*," Daisy said. "I can't take much more of this. Let's all go to town!"

Nick and I stared at her, too stunned by the heat and the awkwardness to do much more than watch her politely. While Gatsby probably would have liked nothing better than to make it snow for her, Tom was monopolizing him with talk of horses that Gatsby obviously didn't have and didn't care about.

"Who wants to go to town?" Daisy said, raising her voice insistently, and when Gatsby looked up at her, she stopped.

I had always thought that Daisy was like the rest of us Louisville girls, liars every one for the right cause, though of course you would never convince any of us of what one right cause that should be. Now I could see that she was no kind of liar at all, as her hand came out to touch Gatsby's face right in front of her husband.

"Oh," she said in faltering tones. "Oh but you look so cool . . ."

At the last moment, she pulled back. That feeling of disaster that had hung over us all day finally disappeared, because the disaster had come.

And Gatsby, who turned out to be nothing more than the son of a dirt farmer and his half-Chippewa wife, who had constructed a palace so profoundly beautiful that we need never look for the truth, simply forgot to lie with any part of his body in that moment. In that moment, they were alone together in the dining room, in the mansion, in the state, in the country, in the world, and the rest of us were left to beat our fists on the wall outside.

"You always look so cool," she said, and then the spell was broken.

"All right, then," Tom said, pushing away from the table. "Let's go to town. That's what you want, right, Daisy?"

Gatsby's eyes narrowed at Tom's tone, but Daisy turned conciliatory, looping her hand through Tom's arm.

"Oh but we've not even had cigarettes yet, surely we should let everyone—"

"You've all been smoking through lunch," said Tom the athlete. "Let's go."

I dragged Daisy up to her bedroom ("Oh, just a little touch-up and hats, of course!"), and I soaked a cold cloth for her in the bathroom. She took it, dabbing at her eyes and her red face.

"I don't know what's happening," she said vaguely, more doubtful than she had been before.

"I don't know either," I said, "but Daisy, *make a decision*. You can't have them both, you know. You can't live in East Egg for Tom and your parents, and row across the Sound to Gatsby's as soon as the sun sets."

"But of course I can," she said as if scandalized. "You just don't know, Jordan. It's not just double lives. It's triple, quads and quints . . ."

She wasn't drunk. That was the horror of it.

I was tempted to make our excuses, but then she dropped the clammy cloth on the floor and rushed past me, dragging down her boxes of clothes and hats from her closet. Coats and capes scattered over the floor, and she handed me one round little metallic gold cap while taking the other for herself.

"Come on," she said. There was a heat to her that put the day to shame, as if she were burning up with fever from within. "Oh Jordan, come on!"

Nick, Tom, and Gatsby waited for us patiently in the drive, Tom being tiresome about the cars, Gatsby running out of patience, and Nick looking subtly panicked. I wanted to tell him it was just people behaving badly, that what would be cause for years and years of stiff necks and pointed spurns in St. Paul would likely be forgotten in a season. Tom was still going on; for some reason, he wanted to drive Gatsby's car to town.

"Well, you take my coupe and let me drive your car."

"I don't think there's much gas," Gatsby said, and Tom's face grew hard even as he smiled.

"Plenty of gas," said Tom. "And if it runs out I can stop at a drugstore. You can buy anything at a drugstore nowadays, *can't* you?"

There was an uncomfortable shuffling silence. I fingered the gold cap in my hand, wondering if it would be better for all concerned if I faked a fainting spell and had to be carried inside. Disasters had been averted with less.

"Well, golly, that's fine," Daisy said with a laugh that was almost natural. "Jay and I can take Tom's coupe, and Tom, you, Nick, and Jordan, meet us in the city. That will be fine."

Everything that happened afterward wasn't worth it to see the look on Tom's face, but everything that had happened up until that point definitely was. His jaw dropped, he turned even redder, and if he had had a cigar, I was sure he would have bitten it right in half.

Before he was quite over it Gatsby helped Daisy into the coupe, dashing as a cavalier earning his lady's favor, and she glanced back at us as they roared off, giving me and Nick a wink and a jaunty wave.

Then of course Tom had no choice but to pile Nick and me into Gatsby's cream-colored Rolls, Nick next to him and me stretched out in the back, and set off for the city eating their dust.

It's all very well for Daisy, I thought with irritation. She got to drive in with Gatsby. Nick and I were stuck with Tom's growling that swung between righteous fury and a self-pitying whine. I tuned it out until we got to Willets Point in Queens, the ash yard. It was entirely uninteresting, of course, except for the Wilson Gas Station that I knew from Nick driving me back and forth.

"Say, shouldn't we stop for gas?" I asked, sitting up.

"We've got enough to get us to town," Tom said dismissively.

"Oh stop, for goodness' sake," I exclaimed. "I'm not going to walk in this heat if you run out."

Tom groaned, but pulled over. As Nick helped me out, Tom engaged in a surprisingly spirited banter with the crabbed owner, Wilson himself. The man had always pointedly ignored me when I showed up with Nick, so I did him the same favor now, looking around at the tall piles of ash pushed up against the high wooden fences. There was no wind to blow the ash around, but the ash heaps loomed ominously, threatening to bury us all if we so much as took a step out of place.

There was a small store inside the gas station, but no one to mind the till. I picked up a pack of violet-flavored gum, leaving a penny on the counter, and I came back out popping it loudly. Wilson had finally got the gas going, and he was exclaiming to Tom about money woes and infidelity while Tom only grew more and more red.

"Like they have anything in common besides having two legs, two arms, and barely a brain between them," I scoffed to Nick, who still looked slightly sick.

"Oh poor darling," I murmured. "This is going to be an absolute disaster. What do you say we have a few drinks and then vanish to my place? We can get just as drunk and be just as sweaty on Park Avenue as we can wherever Gatsby and Daisy want to go."

Nick shook his head.

"No, I want to stay. I want you to stay too."

"Fine, fine," I sighed. "I do spoil you."

He smiled a little at that, and by then Tom, shaking over some slight or another, was wrapping things up with the odious Wilson. Wilson gave me a perfunctory look of dislike as Nick handed me back into the car.

As I climbed in, I happened to catch a glimpse of a red-haired woman at the window above the shop. I only saw her for a moment before Nick shut the door, but she was furious, anger making two deep and abyssal holes out of her eyes, her lips peeled back over teeth that were shockingly white. She looked half-mad, and it shook me for a moment as we drove off.

We passed under the eyes of the same hideous billboard advertising some defunct optometrist's office, a pair of eyes that gazed at us with avuncular malice as we left the ashes behind. I always felt an obscure kind of relief when Nick and I passed under its gaze, as if we had escaped some kind of calamity or other in Queens, and I was happy to leave the gas station and the madwoman in the attic behind us.

Tom grew insufferable as we got closer to Astoria, alternately speeding and tapping on the brakes to curse the speed of the other drivers around us. He almost ran us off the road coming up too fast on a corner, and even Nick barked at him to keep him from hitting a pair of veiled women dressed in black. The women shook their fists at us as we sped by, and I shrugged and waved as we passed.

We came up around Perry Street to find the blue coupe snug on the shoulder, and Daisy stood up to wave us over.

"Oh there you are," she laughed, her cheeks flushed and her hair a mess after the ride with the top down. "We were afraid we'd *lost* you."

"Fat chance," Tom said shortly. "We're in the city like you wanted, Daisy, what do you want to do now?"

"Let's take in a movie," I suggested. "The theaters are always cool and quiet."

And we wouldn't have to talk, and maybe that would mean we would survive the afternoon without someone getting a fat lip or a black eye. At this point, I couldn't even figure out who was going to be the most likely victim.

Daisy shook her head, patting down her dark hair with birdlike flutters of her hands. She was pretty, if common, like this, and Gatsby almost reached up to smooth her hair back before he remembered himself.

"No, no, *you* go to the theater," she said. "Jay and I will ride around and meet you afterward. You'll find us on the street corners like buskers or streetwalkers, so very shameful . . ."

"Absolutely not," I said to forestall Tom's explosion. I was wondering if she was hoping to provoke him into one, but if so, she should have told the rest of us so that we could be good witnesses or, better yet, have stayed home. "No, come on. The city's empty, and it's all ours, let's not waste it . . ."

A truck honked at us in strident offense as it narrowly missed Gatsby's cream monstrosity coming around a corner. Tom looked as if the insult was personal.

"Well, we can't stay *here*. Follow us over to the Plaza, at least we can talk above the muck and the noise there . . ."

It was one of those untidy and inelegant affairs, where everyone has some vague idea of what to do, but no real ability to force the issue, and half the people have secret opinions and the other half, in this case, Nick and Gatsby, were too easily swayed by one person or the other to decide.

We ended up at the Plaza where Daisy's idea of renting five rooms for the five bathtubs actually seemed enticing for a bit, and then we ended up renting one of the grand suites on the seventeenth floor.

I never liked the Plaza all that much, though many of the people I ran about with did. The staff was always a little too stiff about me, a little too curious about who I was there to see, though of course the garden was charming and more at ease. Today at least, the man behind the desk was giving us all a certain look as we rolled in and demanded a place, as Daisy put it, to cool down and to make love. I wasn't sure if it was Tom's frigid Puritan looks or Gatsby's wink that got us through, but the elevator attendant was nothing but cordial as we tumbled in and tumbled out, tipping him extravagantly.

The suite's sitting room was broad and tall, but even when we threw open every window, we couldn't cool it down.

"We should send for an ax," Daisy said so decisively that I thought she might actually do it. "Bam, bam, two more windows in just like that, and it might cool down in here, God . . ."

Unbidden, I remembered her in her slip in the garden on a night almost as hot as this one. I remembered a shovel in her hands, and I shook my head. I didn't want to think about that right now.

"No, send for ice instead, then we can make up some drinks," I offered from the low divan by the window. I shamelessly took it up all on my own, leaving Nick to sit on the ground beside me, occasionally reaching for my hand to kiss it. His eyes kept darting between Gatsby and Tom, as if waiting for a fistfight to break out. I would have said it was too hot for such nonsense, but I had seen stupider things.

"Drinks," Daisy said dreamily, drifting to the mirror to fix her flat hair. "Drinks would make this ever so much more bearable. The mint juleps were the only thing that helped at my wedding, Jordan, don't you remember? Why, a June wedding in Louisville . . ."

From my angle, I could see just a sliver of her reflection in the mirror. To my heat-dazed eyes, her reflection seemed to glance at me, rounder and younger than Daisy was herself. She glared at me and then went back to studiously replicating Daisy's pursed lips and useless attempts to put her hair back in order as I looked away. We hadn't even *had* any of the demoniac.

Tom pulled out a bottle of whiskey I hadn't seen him bring from the car, and he started pouring a measure into each of the gold-rimmed glass tumblers that the hotel provided for us.

"Let it go, Daisy," Tom growled. "Don't you know that the heat only gets worse when you *talk* about it?"

"Let's talk about something else, then," Nick said suddenly, reminding us all that he was there. It was his peculiar gift again, that he could fall flat out of existence when he was quiet and watching, because he was always watching.

"Oh, just leave her alone," Gatsby said from his chair, watching Tom with a glittering look in his eye, "and all that after being the one to insist we come to town."

Tom splashed some of the whiskey over the rim of the last glass, turning towards Gatsby like a wounded bull.

"What's the matter with you, anyway," he said. "Don't think I don't see what you're doing, *old sport* . . ."

"Well, if you know, then certainly tell me all about it," said Gatsby with interest, but Daisy made an exhausted huffing sound.

"Oh don't be so *tiresome*," she said. "Tom, if you're going to be so positively wretched, I will leave right out that door. Just send for some ice for the whiskey, if you please. Be useful."

Tom grudgingly turned away from Gatsby, denied his proper prey, I thought, but as he spoke on the phone, I saw his face in profile. He looked confused and devastated, like the old bear whose kingdom has been taken over by a bunch of democratic sparrows.

He does love her, I thought in surprise, and at that point, I suppose I thought that it counted for something even when it stood up alone, without kindness or consideration or mercy or intelligence to back it up.

After Tom hung up the phone, the peculiar silence that falls over a group of people already ill at ease covered us, bringing the tinny opening strains of the "Wedding March" floating up from the ballroom under our feet.

"Oh!" Daisy cried. "A wedding!"

"Imagine getting married on a day like this," I mumbled, but then she was thrusting a handful of dripping rosebuds from the vase on the table into my hands before she pushed me at Nick. She snatched up the telephone book from where it had fallen on the ground, standing before us with a great production of mock solemnity.

"And I now pronounce you man and wife," she intoned. "You may kiss your bride!"

Nick turned to me with a shy halfway grin, and I gave him a loud and smacking kiss on the lips over Gatsby's laugh and Tom's faint protests.

"Be gentle with me, darling," I told him.

"Always."

There was absolutely no telling what stupid thing I was going to say next when Daisy shoved the phone book at me. My heart sank when I saw her grab Gatsby's hand, and I acted without thinking.

"All right then, Jay and Nick, it's your turn," I cried, ignoring Daisy's hurt gaze. To make sure I wasn't misunderstood, I gave Gatsby my roses and wound Nick's arm through his.

"But it's—it's bigamy," Nick said, taking a stab at humor despite the startled fear in his eyes.

"Don't worry, I shan't tell if you make sure to keep me in mink and diamonds."

"I'll take care of that," Gatsby said playfully. "You won't want for anything so long as we can share, Mrs. Carraway."

Actually, it turned out I hated the sound of *Mrs. Carraway*, but I was more than happy to keep Tom only fuming rather than explosive. I married Gatsby and Nick with great pomp and circumstance, and while Nick refused to kiss, he took the phone book from my hands, and pushed me towards Daisy.

"Now, you two!"

That was awkward, but Daisy had picked up one of the tumblers of whiskey, and sipping steadily, she gave in to the fun, forgetting the idea of trying to marry Gatsby in front of her actual husband. When Nick pronounced us wife and wife, she leaned over, splashing a few teaspoons of whiskey on my dress, and bent me back in a showy Broadway kiss. She bent me so far back that we lost our balance. We would have gone down in a tangle of limbs and laughter if Gatsby hadn't been there in a flash, getting us both back on our feet. He would never have bothered with me if it was not for Daisy, but he did it all the same, and I thought maybe I could grow to like him a little more, that he was not such a terrible person with whom to share.

Then the ice came, and I started to think that we would get through the terrible day without any actual trouble. I was just starting to relax, my ankle pressed against Nick's where he had finally managed to claim a spot next to me, when Tom spoke again, glancing at Gatsby out of the corner of his eye.

"What *is* it with you and with Nick, anyway?" he asked meaningfully. "Are you friends from the war, or something like that?"

"Afraid I didn't have the honor," Gatsby replied. "We were strangers until he came to one of my parties this summer."

Gatsby refused to care about the menace in Tom's voice, but Nick stiffened next to me. I frowned, putting fingers chilled from my glass against the back of his neck, and he relaxed a little, though not all the way.

"Those parties," Tom said, shaking his head with theatrical disgust. "I suppose you've got to make your house into a pigsty in order to have any friends—in the modern world. Nowadays people begin by sneering at family life and family institutions, and next they'll throw everything overboard and have intermarriage between Black and white."

"Well, no one's Black here," I snapped. "Really, Tom."

Tom spared me an irritated look.

"There's nothing for you to get so hot over, Jordan. You know I wasn't speaking about you."

"In this heat, you needn't bother speaking at all," I started, but he was already blundering ahead, lurching to his feet, and glaring at us all in turn as if we had all in our own way challenged him and his American family values. I realized that leaving aside the issue of his marriage, if it was Gatsby, Nick, and me, we did.

"What I want to know," he continued, gesturing emphatically with his almost empty tumbler, "is how long a man is expected to tolerate this kind of perversity in his own house. They may say it's all in good fun, there's no harm to it, but they never think about the way it *erodes* the values on which we built this country."

"We?" Gatsby asked, and Tom gave him a startled look, as if not expecting him to admit to his own perversity so quickly. Tom hadn't yet twigged to the fact that there were in fact several kinds of institutions attacking his precious country stretched out in the suite.

"Tom, stop," Daisy said. "You're embarrassing yourself."

There was something tense in her voice, and she was turned towards the mirror again, stroking her hair with agitation. It occurred to me that she could see our reflections in the glass. I wondered if the versions of us in the glass were doing much better than we were.

"No, you are," Tom shot back. "You think you can get away with so much more just because you're a woman? You and your little China doll . . ."

My hand tightened on the glass in my hand. The whiskey was mostly gone so I could likely throw it and storm out without much guilt, but Nick's hand tightened on mine, his face pale. In that, he matched Daisy, whose face peeking over her shoulder was as colorless as a mourning lily. They never looked more alike than when they were afraid, and I wanted to scold them both for paying Tom any heed.

"Oh we're all being so very silly," Daisy said mechanically. "Do let's go home, won't we?"

"No," Gatsby said, in the manner of a man who has not been

listened to enough in the last quarter hour. "No, Tom. Daisy's not going home with you. She loves me, only me."

His mistake, I thought in a distant kind of way, was watching Tom in that moment and not Daisy. Daisy looked untethered to the world, as if she might suddenly take a step and go flying, tumbling through the air like a piece of dandelion fluff. She gazed between Gatsby and Tom, and she looked unsure, her footing wrong. The light in the suite dimmed as clouds scuttled across the sun.

"Oh yes?" Tom said, scanning Gatsby from top to bottom. "And why don't you tell me where you'll take her to live? Do you have rooms at that damned perverts' club, or is it a little pied-à-terre in Hell? What about a tipi in—"

"Oh my goodness, look at the *time*!" I burst out in my gayest voice. I thought that I should just get out of the room, taking whoever wanted to come with me, but this was beyond salvaging. "I'm so sorry, but my aunt Justine—"

"Her aunt Justine," Nick agreed. "She's expecting. Us. Can't disappoint her . . ."

"*You're* not going anywhere, old sport," Gatsby said seriously to Nick.

"Oh no, don't go," Daisy said to me, her mouth drooping down excessively at the corners and a distant thunder rumbling somewhere over the bluffs. "Stay, stay, we can still have such a lovely time together."

I tried to exchange a speaking glance with Nick—these people have all gone mad, and I am afraid that madness is *catching*—but he wouldn't meet my eyes. Tom gave him a scornful look, shaking his head, before he continued.

"So you think you're taking my wife," he said, his voice flat and inviting.

"Your wife doesn't love you," said Gatsby, climbing to his feet. "She's never loved you. She loves me."

He said those words with a kind of set-in-stone belief. It was true, or he would make it true by believing in it hard enough.

"She never loved you, do you hear?" he continued. "She only married you because I was poor, and she was tired of waiting for me. It was a terrible mistake, but in her heart she never loved anyone except me!"

We all flinched from the theatrical sound of his voice. It was too much for people like us, too genuine and passionate. Some love could survive being put on show like that, but almost every kind of love that I knew would wither through it, curl up from shame and exposure and die.

"Jay . . ." Daisy said, faltering. "Let's go home . . ."

Tom turned to her, incredulous.

"With him? You're going to go home with him? Give up me and Pammy and Chicago and Louisville?"

"Five years," Gatsby continued, as if he had planned this out so well that he couldn't bear to deviate from the script. "We've loved each other for five years now, and you never knew—"

For the first time, Tom seemed genuinely appalled. He looked at Daisy in shock.

"You've been seeing him for *five* years?"

Before Daisy could answer, Gatsby cut the air with his hand, shaking his head.

"No, old sport, it was in our hearts. We met, we fell in love with a kind of passion you could never understand, and then fate split us apart. She never loved you, not for a moment."

It was like a romance out of the pulps, but he wasn't a dime store hero, and Daisy was certainly no one's pure and pale lady.

"Jay," she said, her voice warning, but Tom was shaking his head, rubbing his hands over his face as if he could rid himself of this confusion that way. We could all feel the shifting pressure in the room, water drenching the air and making it rest heavy in our lungs.

"She loves me," Tom said, his voice cold. "Of course she does, and I love her. We don't love perfect, and I like my little sprees. I make a fool of myself sometimes, but she always takes me back.

We've got Pammy, and the property in Lake Shore Drive, and the big house in West Egg. We've got her people in Louisville, and mine in Chicago. What have you got, Mr. Drug Store, Mr. Damnation?"

"The rest of the world," Gatsby said extravagantly, but Daisy was biting her lip, looking back and forth between them, as if suddenly realizing what was at stake and what she might lose. Daisy wasn't used to losing, not at all, and I could feel the wind changing course around us, whipping first into one window and then into another.

"Oh, we should just go home," she said faintly, but I doubted she could say then where that home might be.

Then Gatsby turned.

"Tell him," Gatsby insisted. "Tell him you never loved him. Tell him it was all a lie."

"Yes, Daisy," Tom said, his voice a little quieter, a little more beguiling. "Tell him that you never loved me at Kapiolani, the day I carried you down from the Punch Bowl to keep your shoes dry . . ."

I held my breath because *something* was going to die in that room. I might have wanted to leave before, but now I couldn't take my eyes away.

I saw the moment when Daisy broke, when it all became too much for her. Gatsby was beautiful, but there was a history he would never have, a kind of homey and dignified pleasure he would never provide. He might take her dancing every night under the moon, but there would always be a sting of dirt and scandal to it, and as a Louisville Fay, she could never abide by it. When she broke, it was real, even if she allowed it to happen.

She shook her head, her hands pressed to her eyes. Gatsby went to her, and Tom let him, something that told me the game was nearly over. The sun came back out, the wind died down, and any hope for the storm died without a whimper.

"Daisy," Gatsby said softly, holding her by the shoulders, his fingers digging into her pale arms before he remembered himself. "Tell him . . ."

"I can't," she cried helplessly. "I can't. If you can love more than one person at once, then why can't I?"

"I only love you," Gatsby insisted in confusion, and without looking I laid my hand on Nick's arm. I didn't think he had been such a fool, but I would have believed it.

"You see I've been doing some of my own investigations," Tom said after a tactful pause. "You didn't just sell your soul for some drug stores and way off the dirt farm, did you? No, you let Meyer Wolfsheim broker you some kind of deal. You traded up, *old sport*, until you got to someone grand, and then . . ."

Tom turned to me and Nick, frozen on the divan and by then entirely a captive audience.

"And what do you think they wanted from him?"

"I'm sure you'll tell us," I said acidly, and he nodded as if to say thank you. Jesus *Christ*.

"You kept the party going for Hell and for New York. You opened the doorway to all the fun, and you turned an old-world tipple into big business, got it running like blood throughout the East and the Midwest. You became the linchpin holding Hell to Earth, and how they all loved you for it."

It was more than that, I realized, thinking over the nights I had spent at Gatsby's. His house bridged the gap, and it was safe. It was safe for all of us, for me to kiss who I liked, for Nick to kiss Gatsby, for Gatsby to love Daisy, and for Hell to play its games.

"And then," Tom said with satisfaction, "the party stopped." It had, because of Daisy—who didn't care for his parties—and I wondered with a pang of contagious panic how that must have looked, what would happen when you didn't hold up your end of a bargain with Hell.

Daisy cried out, pushing at Gatsby in a panic. When she stepped back, we could all see a red handprint high up on her arm, the fingers distinct and visible. It was blistered a little, like she had spent too much time in the sun, but even for that he might have been forgiven. Just before he let her go, however, just before he realized what he had done and started to apologize, I saw the look on his face, cold and sick and furious. He had sold his soul, and in exchange for the power to be a man worthy of Daisy Fay, he had created a way station for Hell, a little piece of the infernal in West Egg where the demoniac never stopped flowing and where no one ever noticed if someone disappeared and came back strange and hollow, or never came back at all. Hell was as expansionist as France or England—and Jay Gatsby, with his singular focus and ability to harness the power of human desire, was the perfect envoy to gain them a foothold in the world above.

He had never asked them for Daisy. He had instead built and baited for her a gorgeous gold and velvet trap, as much like Hell as Hell was like itself, and I knew that Daisy had seen it too.

After that, it was just about over, and it was time for us all to limp back to West Egg.

With a kind of brutal sangfroid that I almost had to admire, Tom sent Daisy along with Gatsby in Gatsby's own cream Rolls, which the papers afterward called the death car, and Tom, Nick, and I bundled across the bench seat of the coupe. The sun was down all the way, and the black road unrolled in front of us like a mourning ribbon.

CHAPTER NINETEEN

I fell asleep with my head on Nick's shoulder, and I dreamed of strange things. I was a little girl standing on the deck of a ship as it pulled away from the mainland. It was not a memory, for I was younger when Eliza Baker took me from Tonkin, but there was something rather more than less real about the plumes of gunpowder smoke in the distance and the rush of people on the quay, some carrying their most precious things and others carrying guns.

The air was full of paper scraps, falling down from the tropical sky like snow, and I stretched out my hand, curious when they didn't melt like snowflakes.

"Against all the old laws, we made soldiers out of paper," I said wisely to myself, "but look what became of them."

A bomb went off on the quay, shaking the world and setting off the siren, I opened my eyes and found a world fractured by chaos. I sat up just as we passed beyond the sightless, spectacled eyes of T. J. Eckleburg, and I saw that rather than being wide and wise, they were now closed and refused to look any further. We pulled to a complete stop in Willets Point, and Tom was craning his neck up and around to see what was the matter.

"Some kind of trouble?" asked Nick, who had been sleeping as well, and Tom nodded excitely.

"Accident of some kind," he said. "Good for Wilson, I guess."

"How very vulturish," I said, sitting up and rubbing my eyes, but no one paid me any mind.

"Let's keep driving," Nick said, but Tom wasn't paying any attention to him either, swinging the coupe off the road to where a cluster of cars were nosed into the ash yard. There was a tired police officer taking names, and an ambulance as well, but there was urgency to the scene. After a moment, we realized that the long low wail was not the siren, but the sound of someone's pain trying to squeeze out their mouth.

"Oh G—o—o—d, oh God," came the wail, and I jumped because I hadn't heard that kind of religious suffering since I left the South.

"Tom, let's go," I said sharply, but he was already stumbling forward. His face looked pale, pale enough that Nick and I fell into line without further questions, and then we stood in the garage's open door, taking in the scene in front of us like solemn children told to learn a lesson.

Stretched on the workbench was a woman wrapped in blankets, only her red hair visible at one end and her small bare white feet at the other. Someone had tied her big toes together with string, a tradition in the East to keep a corpse from walking. The man who stood at her head was the garage station owner who had spoken with Tom earlier that day, and in the shadows behind us were his neighbors, come to see the carnage.

"She landed in the ditch left of the road, she must have flown like a bird."

"Struck her so hard her shoes came right off, flew who knows where."

"Which ones?" asked another voice, and still another answered, "The copper ones with the silk bows. Crying shame, they were expensive too."

Tom made a gruff and startled sound at that, taking a step forward towards the workbench. His face was pale, his eyes were too dark, and a thick sweat had broken out on his brow.

"What in the world is happening?" I asked, bewildered, and it was Nick, of all people, who answered me.

"What happens when a man's girlfriend is struck dead in the road," Nick said. "She might have had the courtesy to wait until we had passed by, don't you think?"

Despite his surprisingly cruel words, Nick was as pale as Tom, staring at the woman on the workbench as if at any moment she might stand up and try something against his virtue. You saw her wild, red, and wholly artificial hair first, as I think she meant you to, but her face was as round, soft, and white as a powder puff, the mouth small and dainty. Her face was still in good shape (open casket is possible, if desired, I could hear sensible Aunt Justine say in my head), and that meant that the rest of her must be pulverized.

I looked up to find Tom muttering incessantly into the bereaved husband's ear, his hand fallen like an anvil on Wilson's shoulder, repeating the same thing over and over again.

"That car that ran her down, it wasn't mine, it was a loan for the day," he insisted. "I was in the coupe, we came out from the city just now . . . do you hear me, we came up from the city just now."

"He looks guilty," I muttered, and Nick pulled me away.

"We all do," he said, sounding a little stricken.

"Not me," I said.

I got him into the back seat, holding him close. I asked him once if he needed to throw up, and he shook his head.

"I saw worse things at war," he said indignantly.

"But not," I said with a sigh, "in New York. Once I saw a girl hit by a car trying to cross Broadway, you know. She was hit so hard she was knocked out of her shoes and her hat. Her friend who was with her ran to fetch her hat and then tried to set it on her head as if she were alive again."

It seemed to take hours, but Tom came back out, stumbling a little bit, his thick frame hitting the car and making it shudder. Clumsily, he climbed into the driver's seat, ignoring Nick's tentative offer to take the wheel on the way back to East Egg.

Instead, Tom only stared at the road blankly for a few moments, and then he hit the accelerator so hard the coupe lurched back before surging forward. We got a half mile down the road before I realized he was weeping.

"The God damned coward!" he whimpered. "He didn't even stop his car."

No, he didn't, the thought came to me.

Gatsby would have known how to fix this, and he would have, I realized. It might have been with polite threats, it might have been with hundred dollar bills handed out like benedictions, but . . . he would have fixed this.

I felt my stomach sink as if it had been sewn shut with stones inside, and as we sped down the road, Tom's breathing thick with tears, Nick's head lolling back on the seat like he was a dead man, I thought we had come to the final disaster of the night.

We got back to the house in East Egg to find that all of the lights had been turned on, flooding the place with illumination as if for a great party. Despite the lights, however, it was eerily silent. Instinctively, I looked over towards Gatsby's place across the Sound. It was dark as it had been for weeks. Margaret Dancy had said that the party was well and truly over, and for the first time, I really thought I might believe her.

Tom halted the coupe in front of the porch, gazing up at the house lit up like a beacon.

"Daisy's come home," he said, and if he had said it with any degree of satisfaction, I might have struck him. He frowned back at Nick.

"Sorry, I should have thought to drop you off in West Egg . . ."

Nick shook his head as he handed me out of the car.

"No, no worries at all . . ."

"I'll have a cab sent for you," Tom said, handing the keys of the coupe off to an indifferent footman. "Til then, why don't you and Jordan get inside? You're likely both starving, and they should be able to do you up something."

"Oh, I don't know if I will ever eat again," I started to say, but Nick shook his head at Tom's retreating back.

"No, thank you, but I won't say no to that cab."

We both watched Tom ascend the porch stairs, his chin up as if he had some kind of noble purpose. When the gracious double doors closed behind him, I reached for Nick's hand.

"Come on," I said, being as gentle as I knew how. "Even if we're not hungry, we can poke at their plates as if we were."

"No."

"Oh come on, the Buchanans have just the most lovely plates," I said, trying to tease, but he turned to me with a look that stopped just short of being fury.

"I said no, can't you understand?" he cried.

I might have taken it better if he had been sorry immediately, stumbled all over himself with an apology for the terrible thing we had seen and for the conclusions we were all drawing. Instead he glared at me, and I glared right back.

"Of course I understand," I said coldly. "Good night, Nick."

I went in the front doors. I had some idea of going to the kitchen and getting some kind of food for my poor empty belly, but the moment I was in the house, I wanted right out of it again. Going through the sitting room, I picked up the dusty bottle of demoniac that Gatsby had so thoughtfully left, and I took the stairs two at a time. Tom and Daisy were in the middle of what sounded like a council of war in her sitting room, and though I pressed my ear hard against their door, I could not make out more than a few scattered words. I heard *Spain*. I heard *Shanghai*.

I thought of Chicago and how they had left so quickly. I had thought for a long time that it was some issue of Tom's, some little Pilar Velazquez or some Mrs. Wilson. Now I was beginning to wonder.

Try as I might, I could not make out more than one word in a dozen, and I was just about ready to give it up for a bad job when I heard Daisy take a sharp breath of surprise. It sounded like she had seen a mouse or found some unpleasant news waiting for her in the paper. Then there was a soft clatter of something falling onto the carpeted floor, and I drew back as I realized what was happening.

They would be at it for a while. Tom had little to trade on back during his football game except for his animal endurance, and that hadn't changed. I decided to give them some time for the occasion, and that perhaps everything would be a bit more sane when I got back.

As I passed through the dining room, Providence offered me a corkscrew on the table, and some imp of the perverse convinced me to use it on the bottle clutched in my hand. If I were in good company, someone would surely have protested my rough handling. The cork came to pieces as I roughly yanked it out and dropped the gritty pieces on the floor. I didn't care, and I took a hurried sip from the bottle, compounding my sins by swallowing fast. It hit my throat like a controlled prairie fire, too hot and almost out of control, and it burned all the way to my belly.

I opened my eyes to see an old woman with disheveled hair streaming down over the shoulders of her antique gown glaring at me from the window of the dining room. The moonlight shone through her like silver arrows, and she started to raise her finger to point at me. I ducked out of the dining room double quick because whatever ghost or phantom that might have been, I certainly didn't want any part of it.

Impulsively, I took another sip of the demoniac, and then another and another until I bounced myself outside. I came down the broad steps, staggering to the side yard, and half in the bushes and half out of them, I was startled to see Gatsby and Nick.

Gatsby looked like a plucked rooster, shoulders hanging and eyes cast up to Heaven—no, only to Daisy's window, and if I didn't remember what kind of thing he was, I could hate her for making someone look at her like that. I could almost hear the chorus, his only sin was loving her too much, and at the same time, I could hear the rejoinder in my own voice: his sin was in only loving her and nothing else.

Nick put his hand on Gatsby's shoulder, murmuring something soft and urgent to him. I was suddenly as sick of him as he apparently was of me, and taking another pull from the bottle in my hand, I circled around them, giving them both a wide berth that neither of them noticed or cared about.

I briefly interrupted a huddle of horses in the paddock closer to the house, and as I walked through the tall grass, they came to investigate me, whuffing at me with their velvety noses, their flanks shining silver and gold in the risen moon. The demoniac gave them great purplish eyes, big and dark like the deepest wells in the country around Louisville. You could lose almost anything in those eyes, and it felt as if the horses were inviting me to do just that, to drop my secrets into their eyes, to open the locked gate and to let them run away.

"No," I said, shaking the bottle at them and sending a few drops sizzling into the grass. "*No*. Haven't you heard, darlings, I don't have any secrets. None at all. That's for better than the likes of me."

"You're a fool if you think you've no secrets worth sending away," said a roan foal.

Before I could ask it what it meant, it fled across the paddock, taking most of the herd with it. I could see strange sparkling things kicked up as they ran, and imagined it was the glory of the Triple Crowns and Derbies in their future, flying up behind them before they met their ends with their long legs shattered on the field and a bullet between their eyes.

I made my way across the meadow to the garage which hadn't been turned into a stable just yet. The door had a heavy-duty lock on it, but neither Daisy nor Tom could be bothered when they wanted to go for a quick drive so I found it unlocked as usual, and the keys to the cars kept there were halfway hidden in a turquoise pot high on a shelf at the back. I was shorter than Daisy or Tom, and I had to reach all the way up to hook my finger through the rim of the pot, pulling it down with my fingertips to shatter on the concrete floor with a terrible smash. The earthenware fragments went everywhere, and I had to pick out the keys I wanted from the dust and the shards. The keys to the coupe were missing, but I pulled out the keys to Daisy's little blue roadster, a glittering platinum D hanging off the key chain to let the whole world know to whom the roadster belonged.

I took Daisy's car out onto the road, roaring west as soon as I was clear of the drive. I took another bolt of the demoniac for luck, and I turned towards Willets Point and the ash yard.

CHAPTER TWENTY

It was all over except for the shouting by the time I made it to Willets Point, and in truth, the shouting was just a long thin wail that came from the garage, the door still open and the thin light from a hurricane lamp spilling out. Every time George Wilson paused for breath, I could hear a lifetime of chewing tobacco in his throat. I parked the car crooked on the verge close to the gas station, behind the edge of the building so it would be out of sight.

While I was driving, the moon had risen, and I lifted the demoniac, almost half gone by now, to its pocked and imperfect face.

I wonder what the moon will look like in Tonkin. No, no, it's Vietnam, I remembered. Bai had been quite down on me calling it Tonkin, and now I was mostly doing it to spite her memory in my head. The Manchester Act was going to pass, I realized in my haze, and Louisville or not, Baker or not, I had better decide what it might do to me and what I would do about it.

I hated the thought of leaving New York, not for a holiday or a retreat but because I had to, and I drank down another measure of the demoniac in protest. The taste had mellowed now, or I had managed to burn away the part of me that cared. I thought it was getting less effective the more I drank, but then a pair of men stumbled by, arm in arm, and I saw their skeletons underneath their clothes and their skin, grinning faces knocking together affectionately as they passed a bottle of something cheap back and forth between them.

Or not so very weak after all, I thought, and I got out of the car.

The moment I stepped out of the car, I was in some dark land, separate as Park Avenue was separate from Chinatown. The few city blocks of Willets Point was its own kingdom entire. With a solemn face, I wandered through the tall ash palaces where the towers and the wings were always drifting away, only to be replaced by the burning of New York itself.

Oh, I thought in sudden revelation, *this is where New York goes when it is tired, when it is done.*

I expected to see ghosts of all sorts, of gin baby socialites, of gangsters and bellhops and countermen and maids and grand dames and ambassadors, but I never did.

"C'mon, jelly bean," said a Black man with a trumpet case walking by. He had a brilliant maroon suit with a narrow black pinstripe, and the ash blew away from him as if too shy to touch the hem of his sleeve. "You know better than that. New York's ghosts are a discerning lot; there's no way they would stay here to play in the ash."

I nodded because he was right, and I waved to him when a black car with a driver whose face I could not see pulled over to let him in.

I walked through the palaces of ash, and more than once I had to hide because the men who lived there were a restless lot. Bearing the heads of pigs and dogs, like those cursed by Circe for crimes against her, they came out of their houses and crept into the windows of their neighbors, but their wives, I saw, roamed not at all. I giggled as a man with a parrot head somehow got turned around and climbed into his own window, making his wife shriek in anger and distaste, and I moved on.

The stars were fainter here than they were in West Egg, but I tilted my head back and drank to them anyway, letting the demoniac give them voices to tell me their secrets. Stars didn't talk like people did, and I couldn't listen with my ears, but when I closed my eyes, they appeared to throw moving pictures across the darkness.

The stars showed me a neat town of wood houses, not grass-sided huts like I had always pictured. A woman with her hair cropped like mine, her face round like mine, shook her head at Eliza Baker, shook it again and again before turning away, and I saw Eliza with a packet of money in her hand and a confused look on her face.

I was meant to love her, you know, I told the stars solemnly.

Oh? Which?

It was confusing to me, so I asked for something else, and after some thought, the stars offered me this:

Nick's great-grandmother died just as the war was starting. She was a tiny little lady, and age had put camouflaging wrinkles on her face, turned her sleek black hair white, and given her such a stoop that no one was much able to look at her straight on anymore. In her old-fashioned dresses and her small and elegant apartment in Milwaukee, almost no one in St. Paul remembered that she was foreign.

I remembered what Nick had said, that she was born as her missionary parents came off the *Carmine* on the Gulf of Siam. I wondered if I *had* seen some kind of family resemblance in his face after all, whether his dark hair was more like mine than Daisy's, whether there was something kept hidden somewhere in his easy handsome features. I didn't think so. I only considered the thought because of what I knew now, and then when his grandmother held up a pair of scissors in her hand, looking straight at me with a solemn look, I realized I knew something else too, and maybe had for a long time.

No wonder I like you so, I thought, and then I put it straight out of my mind.

"Can't you show me something important?" I asked the stars. "Drinking this much demoniac may just kill me, and I would like it to be a bit grander than old family secrets . . ."

The stars considered and then the ground in front of me lit up, the starlight catching on every bottle cap, scrap of metal, and lost bolt. Curious, I followed their winding path through the palaces of ash, and I came at last to the billboard west of Willets Point.

T. J. Eckleburg disdained the glorious city of ash below his eyes. They were closed tight, and while a sensible part of me told me that I only misremembered, that they had always been closed, I knew that that was not true.

I took another sip from the demoniac, thinking that it was rather shabby of Gatsby to give us one only partially filled. Surely I hadn't drunk enough for it to feel so light in my hand. I glared up at the billboard, frustrated with its silence, and frustration opened up into a childish fury.

"Well, come on," I said loudly. "Speak. You see so much, what's the point of you if you don't speak?"

The eyes stayed closed, but then I realized that I was trying to get water out of a stone.

"No mouth," I said to the stars. "I can fix that."

Off to the side there was a skinny ladder, and after I discarded my flimsy slippery shoes, I used it to climb up to the narrow walkway ledge that stretched from end to end across the billboard. I paced back and forth in front of it for a moment, but no further inspiration came until I looked down at the bottle in my hand.

Well, there's not a great deal more, I thought, and I drank the rest, ending on fumes like gasoline and honey, vanilla and gin. For a moment, I tottered on the ledge, clever enough not to look down though not to have avoided putting myself in this position in the first place. When I got my legs back underneath me, my stockinged toes digging into the grating of the walkway, I bent over and smashed the bottle against the steel.

There was an almighty crash as shards of glass fell to the grass below, gleaming like stars in the streetlamps, and I found a large shard from the shoulder of the bottle, about half as wide as my palm.

"All right," I said as authoritatively as I could. "You're going to talk to me, aren't you?"

I walked from one end of the billboard to another, the shard of glass digging into the paper glued to the wood backing. The paper split as if it was longing to do so, showing the wood underneath. Over the years, the glue had gone and the paper curled away, above and below. When I was done, it looked a bit like the lips of a drunk, lolling open and foolish. It was an ugly and careless job, and for a moment, I wished that Khai were there to show me how to do it properly. He would probably laugh at me for how badly I was doing, and I wanted him to close his capable hand over mine and teach me the way that I should have been taught.

Hey, where are you, anyway? I thought indignantly. *I want to see you, I have to talk to you.*

I sent the thought out of my mind, because I had always had to teach myself. I shook my head, continued.

When I was done, I dropped the shard of glass and clapped my hands.

"Talk," I said, and then more insistently, *"Talk."*

I felt it this time, my first bit of paper magic done only for myself. Daisy wasn't there to want it to look a certain way or to need me to be a certain thing. Instead it was just me under a plain Willets Point moon, drunk on something I wasn't sure people should be drinking at all, watching as a pair of painted paper eyes slowly, oh so slowly opened and loose paper lips started to flap.

What should I talk about? I am only paper.

I glared at Eckleburg's coyness, crossing my arms over my chest.

"You're paper with eyes," I said. "You're paper that sees, aren't you?"

My eyes are closed, and I have no tongue.

The eyes tried to close, but I clapped my hands hard right in front of where a nose should be.

"Your eyes are plenty open enough for me, and I gave you a mouth so you can talk. What did you see? Tonight? What happened?"

The eyes blinked almost coquettishly, and then the paper lips spread to speak.

I saw a car, too fast. I saw a woman who needed to leave, and I saw her go flying. I saw the car stop, and then I saw eyes.

"Eyes. Wait. Wait . . . you saw eyes."

I saw eyes, mistress, and then I saw no more.

T. J. Eckleburg lowered its lashes but I didn't think it was being coy this time. I was suddenly possessed of an intense sleepiness as well, a feeling of weight on every limb of my body. I knew that I had to get down before I fell down, and with my luck, I might fall straight into the glass I had shattered all over the ground below.

"I . . . I have to go . . ."

I will sleep, mistress, and I will see no more. I am through.

As I watched, the eyes closed and the paper started to peel back from my cut, slowly at first, then faster. Soon enough, the old paper was peeling away from the billboard entirely, the top half staying to promote the optician, the lower falling off to reveal an advertisement for the Bonney Brothers' Traveling Circus, featuring daring acrobats, the finest freaks, and the death-defying lion tamers.

I stroked the paper lion's face as I went past, and somewhere, whether it came from the paper or from some deep place inside me, I heard a soft growl.

By the time I hit the ground, I was exhausted. I could barely move, and it took all the strength I had to make it back to Daisy's roadster. I knew that the state I was in, I would never make it back to East Egg, so I simply crawled into the back, getting the white seat filthy with ash, with everything I had picked up on my sojourn through Willets Point. I thought briefly about smearing everything I had learned all over the leather upholstery, but I couldn't figure out how to do that, so instead, I fell asleep.

CHAPTER TWENTY-ONE

I could ignore the soft tapping sound on the glass, rolling over and pressing my face to the leather under my face, but the harder rapping that rattled the window finally convinced me to look up. My eyes burned like two eggs left too long on the skillet, and when I yanked the door handle, I spilled halfway out of the car. I would have hit the filthy ground face-first if strong arms hadn't pulled me back up.

"There you are," Khai said, and then I rewarded him by almost throwing up on him. He stepped back just in time, and crouched beside me as I heaved in the car's shadow.

At first he tried to stroke my shoulders and say encouraging things, but after a while, he simply stood back and let me empty out what felt like the entire contents of my stomach on the ground. It seemed to take forever, and then I was down to dry heaves, and then I was finally able to stand up.

It was just a little before dawn, and the heat had diminished in the night, leaving the day a little more bearable. I looked at the lightening sky until I felt more human, and then I turned to Khai.

He was in his shirt sleeves with dark rings under his eyes, and he looked at me with a mixture of curiosity and dismay.

"Couldn't stay away, could you?" I asked with a wink. I looked ghastly, but sometimes I could brazen it right out.

"You came looking for me," Khai said shortly. "Last night."

"I . . . did?"

"Through a dream about green parrots that run a Shanghai

bar. I heard you, and I saw that damned billboard that you mutilated. I remembered it coming back and forth to Gatsby's parties. You said you wanted me, and then I woke up."

"How very rude of me . . ." I murmured, but Khai glared at me. I had cost him some serious sleep.

"Stop it! Can't you just stop it? What do you want? Just tell me!"

People were stirring in the garage and, dead wife or no, I hardly wanted to have a run-in with George Wilson in my state. He wouldn't care for me or Khai, so I found the keys to the roadster thrown carelessly on the passenger's seat and thrust them at Khai.

"Here," I said. "Drive."

It wasn't until we passed under the ruined billboard of T. J. Eckleburg that I realized we were going to New York rather than back to East Egg. I started to protest, but then I shook my head. I wanted to go home.

"Oh!" I said. "Just so you know, I think this car is stolen."

Khai shot me a dark look as he edged the car forward on the crowded motorway. Somewhere in this mess would be Nick, making his way to work if he hadn't cried off after the night he had had.

"I don't have the money for a bribe," Khai warned me. "It'll have to be you."

We sat in silence for a moment, and I almost fell asleep before he spoke again.

"We're leaving on Friday," he said. "Bai found us a berth aboard the *Princess Titania,* and we're out."

I felt very strangely hurt.

"So soon? You told me . . ."

"They vote on the Manchester Act today, and they're going to pass it," Khai said. "Bai's parents still remember when the exclusion acts rolled through. She lost almost all of her uncles. She wants us gone."

I let that sink in. The Manchester Act was something that Aunt Justine's friends discussed over dinner, it wasn't even mentioned in the smart set that I ran with normally. Sitting in a stolen car with Khai, however, it felt more real than it ever had.

"I guess you could go anywhere you like, right?" asked Khai, trying to be encouraging. "You could go to Paris or London . . ."

"I suppose I hadn't thought about it," I said stiffly, and he laughed a little, shaking his head.

"Lucky," he said, without much rancor. "Well, if you want to come find us, we're going to be in Shanghai. Probably trying to stand up to acts that have been cutting paper since before someone came up with paper, but in Shanghai nonetheless."

"I may very well," I said, and then because I couldn't fathom the idea of being forced from my home, "my aunt Justine has perhaps been looking for a change of climate. Shanghai would be a change."

He parked the car on Park Avenue, handing over the keys in exchange for the three dollars that he didn't raise an eyebrow at this time. We probably both looked like we were ready for the trash bin. The morning foot traffic split around us, glaring, and I wondered if it had as much to do for what we looked like as it did for the fact we were in their way. I was more vulnerable with him, I realized. Alone I was a charming oddity. With him, I became a foreign conspiracy. Was that why I had never spent much time in Chinatown?

"A change," Khai echoed.

"Yes. A change."

He shrugged.

"However or whyever you come, just come," he said. I thought perhaps he wanted to say something stronger, but we were very little to one another. It would have been oddly shaming for both of us.

He tried a smile.

"Me and Bai will teach you about proper paper cutting, not

the butchery you were doing last night," he said, and then before I could tell him no, he walked away. It was, I thought, rather smart. If I didn't say no, there was a chance I could find my way around my own pride and come looking for him in Shanghai after all.

I was shaking by the time I locked the apartment door behind me. I kept my head down so I wouldn't see myself in the mirror by the door, and I staggered to my room that felt like I hadn't slept in it in years. I stripped down and fell into bed, leaving my white sheets smudgy with the ash that clung to my hands, my hair, the soles of my feet, and even my belly.

I wonder what the world will be like when I wake up, I thought blearily.

I woke up at noon. The Manchester Act had passed.

Jay Gatsby was dead.

CHAPTER TWENTY-TWO

It was George Wilson who shot him, of course, and Tom at the bottom of it, though I didn't know it for some while. It was Tom who told him who must have been driving the car that night, Tom who directed him to Gatsby's home where the smashed-up Rolls was all the proof Wilson needed.

I wanted to make Tom a lowering presence, the hand holding the gun that was Wilson, but I couldn't give him that much. Tom was only shoveling the blame away from himself, and the scales tipped over, this time against Gatsby and all of his promise and all of his potential.

George Wilson came to the mansion in East Egg, and the iron gates did not stop him, and the paths of the gardens did not confuse him. He found Gatsby in the pool where I had once watched people turn into gorgeous ornamental carp as they slipped into the water, and as the newspaper said the next morning, he shot Gatsby twice in the head before moving off to shoot himself behind the boxwood bushes.

Before I knew all of that, I saw the gleeful headline that the Manchester Act had passed, sitting alone at the breakfast table because Aunt Justine was sleeping almost fifteen hours out of every twenty-four. I ate my toast, I read the article carefully, and then I called Nick.

"I want to see you," I said immediately, and I heard him go still on the other end of the line.

"I'm at work," he said, the most Middle Western of excuses, and I decided to forgive it.

"I was thinking of doing some traveling," I said, my voice falsely gay. "I was thinking, oh, wouldn't it be fine to go somewhere now that the weather's not so horrid?"

"Traveling?"

"Yes," I said eagerly. "Montreal or Buenos Aires, or maybe even Paris . . . or Shanghai. You could show me around Paris, couldn't you, darling?"

"Great *God*, Jordan!" Nick exclaimed and my cheeks went hot red.

I imagined both of us touching the broken edges of our relationship, trying to decide what could be mended and what might need to be jettisoned entire.

"You know, you weren't so very nice to me last night," I said finally.

Nick snorted.

"Because that's what the world is about. People being *nice* to you."

I gritted my teeth until I thought they would crack. He was obviously new at this sort of thing, because otherwise he would have hung up on that.

"It's better than a world where they're cruel and you stay anyway," I said. "Keeping the line open for him, are you?"

I hung up, and because it was all rather too much, I went back to bed.

Two eyes, T. J. Eckleburg had told me, and in my shallow dreams, they opened and shut for me.

I had a busy week. Aunt Justine had another setback, and ridiculously enough, I had a match in Hempstead, where I performed abysmally. Nan Harper came back from Greece, and I had to break up with her, and then Aunt Justine wanted to speak to me about Shanghai.

"It'll be an adventure for you," she said from the bed at Bellevue, and I scowled.

"I don't *care* for the idea of running away."

"My dear one, you are rich. You don't run away. You go on retreat. You holiday. You take the waters, and when things are better, you return if you wish to do so."

When she tired, which never took long, I kissed her on the cheek to say goodbye and returned to the Park Avenue apartment to pick up Daisy's car.

The drive out to East Egg had never taken longer. I held my breath passing the ash yard, and I noticed that T. J. Eckleburg's billboard was worn quite away, great flaps of paper hanging almost down to the ground like broken wings.

As I drove east, I could tell that summer's back was broken. That terrible day at the Plaza snapped to yield autumn, and though there was no hint of gold or crimson in the leaves, the air seemed clearer and colder, the sky hinting towards gray and the white that would come after.

I couldn't see Gatsby's mansion from the road of course, but it was too easy to imagine it as I passed West Egg. Would it be worse to find it pristine as if nothing had happened or to see it falling down into a ruin? I couldn't say for sure, and I debated it with myself all the way to Daisy's door.

I found the house in a turmoil of servants and groundsmen, people in uniform rustling back and forth with tarps and with boxes and crates large enough to ship me all the way over the sea. Most of the furniture had been covered up with white sheets, and instead of looking ghostly, it gave everything a strange air of anticipation, as if the whole place was just waiting for some lucky new owner to whip it all back in delight at her good fortune.

I finally found Daisy seated on the wicker swing on the veranda, where, to my surprise, she was dandling Pammy in her arms. The tiny girl looked exalted to be so close to Daisy, a terrified look on her face as if she was afraid she might ruin it. Behind them both was Pammy's nurse, watching warily, eyes flickering from her charge to Daisy and back again.

"I've brought your car back," I said by way of greeting.

"Oh, have you? Thanks so, darling."

She handed Pammy to her relieved nurse, and when the two of them were gone, Daisy nodded after them.

"They tied me down so tight to deliver her," she said flatly. "I didn't know why my wrists and legs were so bruised until I started having the dreams."

I dropped the keys onto the small table that held an untouched glass of lemonade and a small enamel box for pills.

"You told me that before," I said. "Daisy, what happened?"

She looked at me so blankly that for a moment, I thought that she must be drugged. There was a perfect lack of understanding on her face as if she needed to sort out the events from the previous week from what she had had for breakfast, what parties she had been to, and whether the gardener had taken care of the roses.

Daisy shook her head, standing to walk down the stairs to the lawn.

"Oh Jordan, don't bother me with that, not today when I have such a headache."

I followed her down the steps, feeling an unaccustomed anger rise up in me. Above us, as if responding to my anger, the sky went a growling gray and the water reflected it back sullenly.

"I rather think we've been friends long enough that you can spare me some time even if your head does ache!" I said. "Daisy, what *happened*?"

"It doesn't matter, does it? Of course it doesn't, it's all in the past, and Tom says—"

"You don't care what Tom says, and I will know you for the worst kind of liar if you start saying you do now," I said. "*Tell* me."

She shook her head, not as if she wanted to say no to me, but more as if she was trying to clear the cobwebs that had fogged up her memories of that night. In front of us, the Sound rose up in delicate white foam blooms, the water choppier than it had been.

"Oh, darling, why are you being so cruel to me? It was an accident, of course it was an accident."

"Yours," I said, and she shook my hand off to stalk down towards the water.

"Of course mine," she said, staring out over the water towards Gatsby's mansion. Even from this distance, there was something hollow about it, something defeated and caved in. "It's always mine, isn't it?"

Two eyes, T. J. Eckleburg had said, and then it had seen no more. Daisy couldn't do that kind of thing, but I had a feeling that Gatsby could have.

"What else?" I asked, and Daisy wrung her hands.

"Jordan, you must stop this at once, I cannot bear this kind of questioning, not now . . ."

I saw the tears in her eyes, real as they always were, but I didn't care about them today. I clenched my fists, shuddering as a cold wind cut both of us from the east.

"Daisy," I said sharply. "Stop looking at that damned haunted house, and talk to me."

"Oh, why should I!" she said with a flash of temper, turning to look at me. "What does it matter now? Jay's dead and gone, it's over, why can't you just let it be over?"

"It's not over to me yet. Daisy, just tell me."

She glared at me, and I cast around for more than just orders.

"No one's going to believe anything I say even if I did say anything," I said finally. "Aunt Justine's probably sending me off to Shanghai to see the sights. Come on, Daisy."

She turned from me, stumbling to sit on the lawn facing the mansion again, her thin legs cast like pick-up sticks in front of her. She shook her head, and then she nodded. The sky went a flat aluminum gray with sullen purple highlights, a warning of danger.

"She ran out so fast," she said, her voice soft and dull. The sky rumbled thunder after her words. "She seemed certain we would stop. She shook the whole car when it hit her. I felt it all the way through my arms. The only reason I didn't hit the steering wheel is because Jay threw his arm across and stopped me."

"She flew," I said, remembering what I had been told.

"Yes. Straight forward. In our headlights like a showgirl doing a tumble."

I swallowed, stopping myself from stopping her. Why did I think I wanted to hear this? What in the world did I think would be improved?

"And then what happened?"

"Oh Jordan, you won't *like* me if I keep going."

I realized I didn't like her now. Maybe I hadn't for a while. The love might take a little longer to die out, but I could work on that. I waited. Daisy abhorred a silence.

"Jay. . . . did something. Made sure that no one saw. He stood up in the car, closed his eyes, and the world went quiet around us. It was frightening. I never saw him do anything like that before, never saw *anyone* do anything like that."

I thought then that it must have been his infernal powers coming into play. Later, when I learned about his half-Chippewa mother, and when I learned that her other half was Black and not white, I came to a different conclusion. The native nations had taken in plenty of escaped slaves after the Civil War, and the old spells to help the hunters helped them now even when they were the hunted. Two eyes, closed.

"And you, Daisy?"

"Oh Jordan, she was right in the road in front of us. Jay was chanting, and doing that crazy stuff, and I knew . . ."

"You *knew*, Daisy . . ."

She shook her head, and the wind caught at the trees, making them sway back and forth like an overly dramatic Greek chorus.

"What was I supposed to do, Jordan? We couldn't drive around her! So I pulled her off the road, that's all."

She must have flown like a bird, I heard in my head. Something deep and dark yawned open in me; I was sick.

"Daisy . . ."

"She was making the most terrible noises," Daisy said, shaking her head so that her hair fluffed out like a chick's feathers. "She was saying something, or at least, she was trying to say something. Jordan, she sounded like she was trying to *curse* me, and the blood . . ."

My heart was beating too fast, I had broken into a cold sweat. She flew. She landed. She cried out. She cursed. When had she died? I knew now it wasn't on the road.

"Her mouth was moving, open and shut, open and shut . . . it was frightful," Daisy said, covering her face. "I still see it sometimes when I close my eyes."

"Good!" I exploded. "Good! I'm glad!"

She was on her feet, slapping me hard on the face just as a crack of lightning struck off the headland. We stared at each other, in shock, and as the sky opened up to drop a torrent of cold autumn rain on our heads, I reached up to touch the ringing flesh. It felt oddly good, real in a way that nothing had been since we'd gone to the city for the day.

"Oh darling, I'm so sorry," she said, her fingers brushing over mine as she touched my cheek. The rain slicked her hair straight to her head, dripped off the delicate point of her chin. "I'm so sorry. This has been terrible for you, hasn't it?"

It had, and for a moment, I swayed towards her.

"Come with us," she said, her voice warm in spite of the rain. "Come *with* us. Why go to dirty old Shanghai when you can come to Barcelona with me and Tom? Barcelona's a delight, and we can come back in October, just in time for the best part of fall, won't that be grand?"

I jerked back from her soft touch, my heart pounding, because there had been a chance, not a large one, maybe, but one nonetheless, where I might have gone with her, if only she hadn't forgotten that I might not get to come back.

"Stop," I choked. "Stop, stop, I'm not in love with you, you can't treat me like this."

She looked at me stunned.

"Of course you are," she said, and the thread between us snapped, stinging me hard as I stared at her. The rain flowing down my face suddenly felt warmer, almost like blood.

Of course I am, I thought, but I wasn't Jay Gatsby. Love wasn't enough for me, and Daisy had proved it would never be enough for her.

I turned on my heel and ran for the house.

She called my name twice, faltering, and then she stopped.

I walked through the house, trailing water over the parquet floors, out the front door, and then I kept walking. I had picked wretched shoes for this, dark forest green suede to match my green dress, so I took them off and let them swing from my hooked fingers.

I sloshed through the soft grass by the side of the road, and every time a car came up from behind me, I thought it might be Daisy sending for me, or even Daisy herself in her blue roadster.

If she stops me before I make it to the main road, I might forgive her, I thought, and it horrified me.

She didn't, however, and instead the car that stopped for me came from the opposite direction.

It was Nick, dressed in a good suit I hadn't seen before, his eyes red and hollow.

"Oh it's you," I said as he pulled up in front of me.

"Come on," Nick said, and when I got a stubborn look on my face, "please. Please, Jordan."

He opened the door for me, and we drove back to West Egg as I slipped my shoes back on.

CHAPTER TWENTY-THREE

We took the main road in, and Gatsby's palace loomed up in front of us. From across the Sound, it looked like a ruin, a reminder of the wages of sin. Now, coming up on it before we veered to Nick's house, it looked . . . normal. Just a building, though a beautiful one. It still gleamed as if at any moment it might burst like fireworks on a hot July night, as if it still had some kind of potential for glamour and for beauty. It likely still did, for it had survived Jay Gatsby, and now anything was possible. We all had.

For one horrid moment, I thought that Nick would take us to the mansion for some reason. I let out a held breath when we pulled into his own weedy drive.

"His funeral was today," he said when he saw my relief. "His father is staying there now."

"How was it?" I asked, and his mouth tightened.

"A pauper's affair," Nick said. "I've seen mass graves given better."

"Is that why you were in East Egg? To see if you could shame Daisy into going?"

He blinked at me in confusion. He hadn't been thinking of Daisy at all.

"No. I . . . I couldn't stay there, and I couldn't stay here. It was too much. I wanted you."

"He never liked me all that much," I said coldly. "I don't think he always liked you either."

Nick flinched from me as if I had struck him. I suppose I had.

He gave me his hand out of the car. We ended up walking slowly through the rain to his door, as if neither of us wanted to remember the last time we had dashed from the water to his doorstep. We were different people now. We didn't run through the rain together.

"You've forgotten a few dresses here," Nick said. "You should change, you're soaked."

I felt a kind of bitter twist in my heart as I looked at him. I hadn't forgotten them at all, and instead of being dresses I could spare, I rather liked them. He stood still dripping in the doorway as I changed into a pale orange dress of figured silk, too fancy for such a dull rainy day, but I hardly cared.

When I turned back towards him, he was watching me with a gaze that was nothing so much as exhausted.

"Did you really love him so much?" I asked.

He hesitated, and I saw the terrible moment when he realized he had nothing left to give me but the truth. He stared at the floor between us as if it held the answers.

"I still do. I'm not going to stop. It was like no matter what I did, no matter who I met or slept with in France or this summer, it was just him, it was *always* him . . . Maybe it always will be him."

I felt as if I had been spun around several times and then encouraged to drink a champagne glass full of what turned out to be top-shelf whiskey. My mouth tasted like smoke.

"Who you slept with this summer?"

"That boy from Amherst, Grayson Lydell, Evelyn Bard. None of them could even . . . no one else compared."

"How could they?" I asked, faint and appalled.

You must always be precise when commanding imps, Mrs. Crenshaw said in my memory. *Never say wealth when you can say the precise number of dollars, never say eliminate when you can say murder.*

And apparently, never say *women* when you should have been asking about *people.* No wonder the singed thing had snickered so upon telling me about the girl from Jersey City.

Nick finally looked up, and noticed my surprise. A red blush swept up his face, not embarrassed but exposed.

"I thought you knew," he said.

"And you wouldn't have told me if I didn't."

"No. God, you always seemed to know so much."

"Not everything," I had to admit. I suddenly felt very young and very lonely.

I sat on his bed, wiping my eyes. Outside, Daisy's storm had slowed to a kind of soft patter. I imagined tears pouring ceaselessly down her face as she sat at the dinner table. I shut the thought away because I did not want to think about Daisy Buchanan again.

Nick stripped off his jacket and came to sit sodden and sad on the bed beside me. *Two broken hearts,* I thought with a kind of strange pleasure at it.

He touched my chin to make me look around, and he kissed me. This time, I was searching for it, and I could taste something pulpy and dry in his kiss, something I knew. A lion, a paper girl, and now a paper soldier. I would have laughed if it wouldn't have hurt his feelings.

"Tell me the first thing you remember," I said softly, and he kissed me again, open and gentle and searching. "That you really remember, I mean."

"I remember muster at Fort McCoy in Wisconsin," he said between kisses. "I remember hearing my name, my rank, and my service number."

"And that was you, Nicholas Carraway, forever and ever."

"Lieutenant Nicholas Carraway, five-two-seven-one-one-five."

He felt good kissing me. I wondered again if I had always known, but then the question came back—always known what?

I pushed him back on the bed, straddling his hips as I bent down to kiss his throat. He watched me, docile not just because of the tingle in my fingers or the strange and new hunger I had for him, but because he had been made to be so. I wondered if the original Nick Carraway had been like this. I decided not, and that I probably wouldn't have cared for him at all. I heard in passing that that tragedy that had kept the St. Paul Carraways from Daisy's wedding was a car accident, and now I knew who the mysterious casualty was. What a blow it had been for his parents when he died just as the war was ending, all that work by their shameful foreign secret gone to waste.

No wonder they had sent this one east, this one made of paper, this one with a heart that he ripped to pieces and threw like trash in front of the worst people. This one was mine.

"I like you best," I told him, and he smiled at me, halfway happy.

"No, you don't," he said. "You like Daisy best."

"Not anymore."

It would be true in a while. I would *make* it true. I would tear her straight out of my heart if I had to, and fill the hole she left behind with paper flowers.

"Besides," I said, "you never liked me best either."

"Oh, I love you," Nick said regretfully as my hands tightened on his shirt. "It's just that my love only goes so far."

I laughed at him, and then I reached for the small penknife on his shabby nightstand, kept terribly keen through countless night watches of idle sharpening. His breath went soft and long, so long it seemed he stopped breathing entirely, and his eyes fluttered closed as I cut a long line from the base of his throat down to his belly.

Eyelashes wasted on a boy, I thought as I had years ago earlier this summer, and his hands fell lightly on my thighs, the fingers twitching slightly with a papery dry rhythm. He opened like a song; it occurred to me that I must have a talent for this. That pleased me, and it was strange to find any kind of pleasure on a day like that one.

I pulled out his heart so easily that I could see why he had been so free with it. His great-grandmother, out of some sentimentality, had cut it from a map of Minnesota and carefully glued to it a picture of the Carraway clan, two-dozen stern-faced

Lutherans at some church picnic or another. I looked closely, squinting under the soft light from Nick's lamp until I thought I found the ancestress herself, off to one side, hair as white as poplar bark, and a stern expression on her crabbed face. I traced her face, feeling an odd kinship with her. She had at least had the courage to choose a picture she was in rather than erasing herself entirely.

When I flipped it over, I saw a page from his yearbook at Yale, perhaps just pasted there to give him a little more sturdiness and strength, perhaps to give him some personality. It was the page featuring Yale's football team, and I picked out Tom from the lineup of similar, serious, slab-faced men. What a mess.

Over all of this, inscribed with what looked like heavy grease pencil, were names, names written large and crude and without understanding of what such a thing would mean. Largest of course was Gatsby's—not Jay, but Gatsby—and there were a few other men's names scrawled there as well, men I thought he must have known in the war.

I was touched to see that my own name was written neatly and with care paid towards the shaping of the letters. He had written it more deliberately, perhaps with more purpose and with more duty and fear involved than with the others, but I didn't blame him for that. It was still there.

"Poor love," I said, looking down at him. His head was turned to one side, his lips slightly parted. He was lovely. I had always thought so.

I folded up his heart and slipped it into my purse, and from my purse I drew out my planner, which only let me see two weeks in advance. I used the penknife to cut one of the pages into a pretty heart shape, like the Valentines I had refused to cut in school. I looked at it, toyed with writing my name on it and taking up all the space so that it could not be taken up with any other, but I didn't.

Instead, I only pressed a lipstick kiss to one edge, because I've never been so keen on being forgotten, and slid it back into his chest. A moment later, he shifted into a true sleep, and I climbed off of him, giving him another kiss on his forehead.

I put my shoes back on, and I found his car keys on the nail where he had left them.

I took one last look at his house, and when the door closed behind me, I heard the lock snap into place. The rain had stopped, leaving the sky a leaden gray, and I forced myself not to look across the Sound, where Daisy waited to be packed away like the good china and the delicate furniture.

I took Nick's car and drove west towards the city. The sun set below the edge of the world, and the shadows came out, longer and sharper than they had been during the summer. I wished I had a few sips of demoniac to hurry things along, but it was past summer now, so certain things would be easier.

I pulled over at Willets Point and bought a candy bar from the general store. I nibbled it hungrily, because I hadn't had anything since the start of the day, as I walked along the edge of the road. The rubber marks from the coupe's tires were still visible, faint and dim, on the road, but then the sun sunk a little lower and they disappeared as well.

I didn't have to wait long.

One moment I was alone on the slick grassy verge, and the next, Myrtle Wilson rose up out of the ditch beside me. Her pale face was perfect, her hair gleamed like a stoplight, her small feet were bare, and unless she left, she would be the Willets Point ghost for a generation or more. I was leaving. I didn't see why she had to stay.

She started for me, a dire look in her eyes, but I shook my head.

"You want Daisy, and you want Tom, one or the other," I said firmly. I sounded like Aunt Justine. "They're going to Barcelona. You could meet them there."

She looked at me, flat-eyed, pale, and dead. I reached into my purse and gingerly gave her a twenty-dollar bill. It wasn't much, but it would get her started.

As I drove away, I saw her in the rearview window, gazing towards oncoming traffic, and thumb crooked for a lift.

As the city grew up around me, as the noise and the brutal indifference of it took shape, it hit me all at once that I would be leaving it soon, and for the first time, I had no idea when I would be back. The thought was like a broad hand slapped across my chest, but the pain after that sunk in almost comfortable, like something I could live with until I learned to banish it entirely.

Shanghai first, I thought, because after all, I had been invited, and then Vietnam. It was, I could already tell, going to be a journey full of awkward pauses, terrible humiliations, and so many places where I couldn't be anyone but myself, but I thought I would survive it well enough. It was full dark by the time I made it to the city proper, and I stopped at a small drug store just as the weedy-looking young man was getting ready to close. I smiled and flirted until he opened back up for me, and as I made my way through the aisles for home goods, I wondered slightly giddily if this might have been one of Gatsby's, where there might be anything under the cashier's counter from demoniac to guns to other destructions no less seductive.

I overpaid for my purchase, and in the car again, I unwrapped it with care. Under the sodium streetlamp, I held a gleaming pair of delicate embroidery scissors. I admired them for a moment, their utter sharpness, their ladylike prettiness, and then I clicked them open in my hands.

I brought the blade to the pad of my left ring finger, and before I even felt more than a slight pressure, a dark drop of blood welled up from the cut. It was darker than I was used to seeing, and it ran molasses-slow down to my palm. I considered it for a moment, and then I lapped it up, tasting the copper, and under that the heat of something else.

I couldn't tell if I was dreaming or not, awake or not, but I caught a glimpse of something shining and gray just beyond my eyes.

I was on Gatsby's pier in West Egg, and if I turned I would see the green light from Daisy's dock. Instead, I stared at Gatsby's beautiful house, which hadn't fallen to pieces like everything else he touched. It stood, locked up and lonely, but I could see it wouldn't always be that way.

The sky spun over my head, sun to stars, slowly at first and then faster. The grass grew, the roof fell in, people came to gawk and stare at the site of such a tragedy. Some children threw rocks through the windows; a pack of teenagers, the girls with their hair tied back and the boys in workman's dungarees, forced the door and then ran out shrieking.

The sky spun and the stars shifted. The west side of the house fell down. The lawn grew even wilder, and sometimes deer and things that looked like deer picked their way across the grass, as sweet and dainty as the starlets that had once stumbled from the doors. A pair of men with still faces and long hands came to stare up at the broken windows, and they stood there, as still as I was on the pier, for seven turnings of the sky and were gone. The house was on fire. Burned. It was rafters and beams and char, and there was nothing gold in the black.

The sky spun. Someone came to cut the grass. Men came to measure the property, followed by an important-looking woman in trousers with her hair cut on a geometric angle, not that much unlike mine. They measured, they argued, and houses sprouted up, first one, then two, and then more, small and sleek and odd.

The sky went still, and far above, I could see foreign stars, stars that moved, stars that winked at me, stars that shot across the sky like comets. Under the wrack and wreck of what had come before, the sky was new, and I reached for it with a yearning eager hand.

ACKNOWLEDGMENTS

When I mentioned the idea that would eventually become *The Chosen and the Beautiful* to my agent, Diana Fox, she immediately said, "Stop writing that novel you're working on and write this!" The novel that I paused is still sitting at the halfway point, but that's not a terrible price for holding this book in my hands today, so thank you, Diana!

Ruoxi Chen at Tordotcom Publishing continues to be the sensitive and thoughtful editor that every writer hopes for, and she has championed this book from the beginning—I can't thank her enough for this.

Everyone at Tordotcom Publishing has been so incredibly supportive. Thank you so much to Lauren Anesta, Mordicai Knode, Yvonne Ye, Amanda Melfi, Eileen Lawrence, Stephanie Sirabian, Makenna Sidle, Becky Yeager, Lauren Hougen, Greg Collins, Angie Rao, Irene Gallo, Alexis Saarela, Isa Caban, Michael Dudding, Samantha Friedlander, and Sam Dauer for all your care and hard work!

Thank you as well to Christine Foltzer for her artistic acumen and to Greg Ruth, who is responsible for my amazing cover. I had a good idea what Jordan looked like before I saw the cover, but when I saw it, I knew.

Thank you to Cris Chingwa, Victoria Coy, Leah Kolman, Amy Lepke, and Meredy Shipp, because you guys are honestly just lovely.

And for Shane Hochstetler, Carolyn Mulroney, and Grace Palmer, I love you guys. You know that, right? I hope you do.

I talk a lot about the selling of souls in *The Chosen and the Beautiful*. I've never thought it would be such a bad thing to do, depending on who you're selling to.

BOOK CLUB KIT

THE
CHOSEN
AND THE
BEAUTIFUL

NGHI VO

READER'S GUIDE

The questions, discussion topics, and reading list that follow are intended to enhance your reading group's discussion of *The Chosen and the Beautiful*, Nghi Vo's dark and magical retelling of *The Great Gatsby*.

1. The novel opens with a wind that blows Jordan and Daisy around "like a pair of young women in white dresses who had no cares to weigh them down." Are they truly a pair of young women with no cares? Is that how they think of themselves? Does Jordan have a reason to want to be seen like that?

2. While *The Great Gatsby* is written from Nick Carraway's perspective, *The Chosen and the Beautiful* is written from Jordan Baker's point of view. Why do you think the author chose Jordan over Nick, or even Daisy? How is the world that Jordan sees different from that of the other characters?

3. Jordan very much considers herself a modern girl, but easily half of the book is taken up with the past, especially her and Daisy's shared years in Louisville. How does knowing Jordan and Daisy's past contribute to how you understand them in the present?

4. There are many stories told about Jay Gatsby during the course of the novel. How do these stories work for Gatsby and against him? How do they influence his relationships with the people around him? Which ones do you believe, and why?

5. Despite appearing to be a heterosexual relationship on the surface, Jordan's relationship with Nick is a relationship between a queer woman and a queer man. What do you think makes this relationship different from one where both people are straight? How does their sexuality play into how they relate to each other, and how does it force them to interact with the world they live in?

6. Jordan's relationship with Daisy is one of the most important in the book, if not the most important. How would you define Jordan's relationship with Daisy Buchanan? How do you think Jordan defines it? How does Jordan's changing relationship with Daisy affect the course of her life?

7. At the end of Jordan's romance with Nick, she realizes a surprising truth about who he is. Does this alter how you viewed Nick's actions during the novel?

8. While Daisy Buchanan's marriage is obviously abusive, the abuse is passed off as a normalized thing, hardly worthy of comment. How does Tom Buchanan's abuse of his wife impact your reading of Daisy's affair with Gatsby and then her choice to stay with Tom? Does Jordan's lack of engagement with said abuse affect how you see her character?

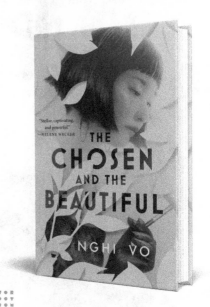

9. The paper cutting troupe represents a world where Jordan both belongs and yet is still a foreigner. How do Jordan's interactions with the group reveal her feelings about her race and her sexuality? What steps is Jordan going to have to take to be as fluent in that space as she is at Gatsby's parties?

10. One reason we continue to read *The Great Gatsby* is because so many of the themes it explores are universal and continue to be relevant in our world today. While both Fitzgerald and Vo write about issues such as money, class, ambition, identity, and how the past inescapably informs the present, what aspects of these issues does Vo address in her version of the story that Fitzgerald leaves comparatively unexamined in his?

11. Even in a world drowned in magic, nothing compares with Gatsby's parties. If you found yourself on the grounds of Gatsby's mansion in the summer of 1922, what would you want to see, and what would you be doing? What's the most magical party you've ever been to?

12. The novel covers one eventful summer in the lives of the characters. For those who survive to the end of it, where do you think they go from there? What is Jordan going to be like in her thirties, during the Depression, or her forties, during the Second World War?

13. Almost a hundred years separate us from Fitzgerald's time—and Gatsby's—but sometimes it feels as if very little has changed. What similarities do you see between the 1920s and the 2020s? Do you relate to the struggles and challenges faced by Jordan and the people she cares about? How does Gatsby's American dream persist in our current society?

ADDITIONAL SUGGESTED READING:

F. Scott Fitzgerald, *The Great Gatsby*

Maureen Corrigan, *So We Read On: How "The Great Gatsby" Came to Be and Why It Endures*

K. J. Charles, the Will Darling Adventures

Evelyn Waugh, *Vile Bodies*

Silvia Moreno-Garcia, *Mexican Gothic*

Wendy Rouse, *The Children of Chinatown: Growing Up Chinese American in San Francisco, 1850–1920*

Carlyle Van Thompson, *The Tragic Black Buck: Racial Masquerading in the American Literary Imagination*

Lillian Faderman, *Odd Girls and Twilight Lovers: A History of Lesbian Life in Twentieth-Century America*

Kate Beaton, "Great Gatsbys," *Hark! A Vagrant*

NGHI VO

Vo is available for virtual meetings with book clubs and for school and library visits! Please email nghivo.com/contact for her availability and rates.

Author photograph © 2021 by CJ Foeckler
Guide by Nghi Vo

ASIAN AMERICANS IN THE JAZZ AGE

While Jordan Baker's position as a glamorous outsider shapes her life in *The Chosen and the Beautiful,* Asian Americans have been a part of America's history for hundreds of years. However, most of the other Asian Americans in the book would have had a lot more in common with the Toy sisters in Louisville or the paper cutting troupe Jordan encounters at Gatsby's mansion than with Jordan's own privileged existence, and it's their experience that parallels that of Asian Americans living in our own reality.

Following World War I, American nationalism and anti-Asian sentiment was on the rise. The Chinese Exclusion Act of 1882 saw the end of the United States' free immigration policy, and the Asian Exclusion Act, included as part of the Immigration Act of 1924, essentially ended Chinese immigration to the United States and put severe limits on the number of other Asian immigrants allowed into the country. These laws indicated the public acceptance of racism against Asians. In *The Chosen and the Beautiful,* the passing of the fictional Manchester Act is based on those real pieces of legislation and their heartbreaking and terrifying effect on the Asian American community at the time.

At the same time that Asians were the subject of exclusion and persecution both in the courts and in the streets, the United States was developing a fascination with the "Orient," an exoticized picture of Asia. Mahjong entered the United States during the twenties and gained immense popularity, while chop suey restaurants developed a new cachet as trendy places to see and be seen. But while Asian goods and cultural exports were welcome, the presence of Asian people was still always questioned.

The 1920s also saw the flourishing of Asian Americans in entertainment, such as the vaudevillian and actor Lee Tung Foo, also known as Frank Lee, and the glamorous Anna May Wong, born Wong Liu Tsong, who rose to stardom in 1924 with a supporting role in *The Thief of Bagdad*. Both Lee and Wong built careers out of playing Asian stereotypes, the only roles that were available to them, but they simultaneously paved the way for the vibrant and widely recognized Asian American performing arts community that would come after them.

Other Asian American artists made careers out of subverting expectations, as in the case of the Chung Hwa Four, a barbershop quartet comprising four Chinese American singers. Organized in San Francisco, the quartet, made up of Lee Tung Li, Leong Hui Kim, Don Tin Yaw, and Chan Suey Ting—also known as Henry Lee, Hugh Liang, Edgar Don Sang, and Chan Shu Yin— became one of the most notable acts of the decade. They were known for their trick of inviting an audience to sing along in Chinese before joking, "Gee, maybe you don't like Chinese songs. We'll sing something American." The Chung Hwa Four lasted fourteen years on the vaudeville circuit, no mean feat in light of the fact they were considered a novelty act in a cutthroat business.

THE CHOSEN AND THE BEAUTIFUL
NGHI VO

Khai, Bai, and the rest of the paper cutting troupe draw their genesis from the work of performers like Lee, Wong, and the Chung Hwa Four, who were starting what would come to be known as the chop suey circuit. During the Roaring Twenties, the nightclub scene—where performers could earn the most money and acclaim—was starkly segregated. While Black and Asian artists might be allowed to perform, they could not mingle, and the first truly desegregated nightclub didn't open its doors until 1938. The efforts of marginalized performers in the 1920s would bear fruit in the decades to come, fruit that some of them would live to see and to eat.

Like Khai, Bai, and some of the other performers in their troupe, Jordan is Vietnamese; she states that she was born in Tonkin, which refers to the French protectorate of northern Vietnam. While there were fewer Vietnamese in the United States in the twenties than there were Asians from other regions, there were still some! The presence of the Vietnamese in the United States is widely believed to have begun with the waves of refugees in the late 1970s, but the truth is rarely so simple. During the period between the First and Second World Wars, Vietnamese people did enter the country, and the ones who did so were usually either very wealthy tourists or poor workers. Due to French colonialism, wealthy Vietnamese were often educated in Paris and then proceeded to tour the Western world, with New York, San Francisco, and New Orleans being frequent ports of call.

Less fortunate were the Vietnamese workers who found employment on French steamships, which would take them to Paris and from there on to any number of foreign ports. Some of those workers, occasionally incorrectly assumed to be Chinese or Japanese, found their way to the United States. The welcome they received ranged from warm to ice-cold, but their stories form part of the rich tapestry that is part and parcel of the Asian experience in the United States.

Much like Anna May Wong, who left the United States to find acclaim abroad, Jordan ends *The Chosen and the Beautiful* by leaving an America that has proved hostile to her. At the same time, however, she claims her place in a deeply American narrative and as a deeply American young woman.

FURTHER READING:

Krystyn R. Moon, *Yellowface: Creating the Chinese in American Popular Music and Performance, 1850s–1920s*

Charles Keith, "The First Vietnamese in America," *Sojourn: Journal of Social Issues in Southeast Asia*, vol. 34, no. 1 (March 2019), pp. 48–75. jstor.org/stable/26594524

Doug Blair, "The 1920 Anti-Japanese Crusade and Congressional Hearings," depts.washington.edu/civilr/Japanese_restriction.htm

Yuna Chung, "Forbidden City – Chop Suey Circuit," blogs.cornell.edu/asianammedia/2018/12/04/forbidden-city/

Adrian De Leon, "The long history of racism against Asian Americans in the U.S.," pbs.org/newshour/nation/the-long-history-of-racism-against-asian-americans-in-the-u-s

Kerri Lee Alexander, "Anna May Wong (1905–1961)," womenshistory.org/education-resources/biographies/anna-may-wong

COCKTAIL MENU

THE CORPSE REVIVER

"I COULDN'T
TELL WHERE MY
RECKLESSNESS HAD
COME FROM, ONLY
THAT THE CORPSE
REVIVER WAS
STRONG ENOUGH
THAT I DIDN'T
REGRET IT YET."

THE CHOSEN AND THE
BEAUTIFUL
p. 179

The corpse reviver is what Jordan drinks the most in *The Chosen and the Beautiful*. The name didn't originally refer to a specific cocktail, but rather a category of named drinks that were drunk as hangover cures because they could revive even the dead (not literally, although it has been tried). The version Jordan would have been drinking would be closest to what is known today as Corpse Reviver #2:

> ¾ ounce gin (Plymouth or London dry)
> ¾ ounce Cointreau
> ¾ ounce Lillet Blanc or Cocchi Americano
> ¾ ounce lemon juice
> A dash of absinthe

Shake with ice and strain into a chilled cocktail glass. Alternately, you can rinse the glass with absinthe or pastis before pouring rather than adding the dash of absinthe afterward.

THE MINT JULEP

"DRINKS WOULD
MAKE THIS EVER
SO MUCH MORE
BEARABLE. THE
MINT JULEPS WERE
THE ONLY THING
THAT HELPED AT
MY WEDDING,
JORDAN, DON'T
YOU REMEMBER?"

THE CHOSEN AND THE
BEAUTIFUL
p. 215

The mint julep needs no introduction, but for Louisville girls like Daisy and Jordan, this iconic drink would have been synonymous with their Southern roots. Traditionally served in silver or pewter cups over ice, it was an upper-class beverage that first became popular in the late eighteenth century and has been beloved ever since. The mint julep is also one of the easiest and most popular mocktails to make.

> 12 fresh mint leaves
> ⅓ ounce simple syrup (or 1 tsp–1 tbsp of sugar
> dissolved 2:1 in water, according to taste)
> 2½ ounces bourbon whiskey
> Crushed ice

Shake all ingredients with ice and strain into a chilled half glass or cup of crushed ice, stir, add more crushed ice to fill the glass or cup, and garnish with a sprig of fresh mint. Alternately, many recipes specify to muddle the mint by placing it in the bottom of the cup or glass with the sugar or simple syrup before adding the bourbon and ice.

Nonalcoholic version: Substitute sparkling water or ginger ale for bourbon and add lemon juice or syrup to taste; can also be made using fresh lemonade instead of bourbon.

GINGER WATER

A delicious and refreshing nonalcoholic drink, ginger water is made by adding ginger juice to seltzer or sparkling water along with some kind of sweetener such as sugar or honey, and optional extras like lemon or mint.

THE GIN RICKEY

No list of Prohibition-era drinks would be complete without a gin cocktail of some kind, in this case the gin rickey, which everyone imbibes before the tense dinner with Gatsby at Tom and Daisy's East Egg mansion. Named after Colonel Joseph "Joe" Kyle Rickey, a Democratic lobbyist, the first Rickey was created in the 1880s after a bartender at Shoomaker's Saloon in Washington, DC, saw him squeeze lime into his whiskey before adding soda. The recipe is extremely simple:

> Gin
> Freshly squeezed lime juice
> Club soda or seltzer water

Mix to taste and serve in a highball or other tall glass over ice, garnished with lime. Some people choose to add sugar or simple syrup, but the classic version is only the three ingredients above. For a nonalcoholic version, simply leave out the gin. You can also try a flavored tonic water, such as Fever-Tree's elderflower, to make the mocktail more interesting!

> "ONE THING I LIKED ABOUT MIRIAM, SHE WAS NEVER ONE TO LET GRASS GROW UNDER HER FEET. SHE WAS AROUND GATSBY IN A HEARTBEAT, AND SHE EVEN MADE IT LOOK NATURAL. SHE PLUCKED THE GINGER WATER FROM MY HAND AS SHE WENT BY, GAVE ME A SIGNIFICANT LOOK, AND THEN WAS GONE."
>
> *THE CHOSEN AND THE BEAUTIFUL*
> p. 96

> "TOM CAME BACK, PRECEDING FOUR GIN RICKEYS THAT CLICKED FULL OF ICE. GATSBY TOOK UP HIS DRINK. 'THEY CERTAINLY LOOK COOL,' HE SAID, WITH VISIBLE TENSION. WE DRANK IN LONG, GREEDY SWALLOWS."
>
> *THE GREAT GATSBY*
> p. 117

TO THE CHOSEN AND THE BEAUTIFU...

Jay Gatsby
Invites You to a N...
of Revelry and...

The First of June, 1922
Five Minutes to Midnight

West Egg, New York

BE WICKED
BE WITTY
BE BRIGHT

Dinner, drinks, and dancing
until summer's end

THE HISTORY OF PAPER CUTTING

The history of paper cutting actually predates the invention of paper. Paper was invented in China sometime during the Eastern Han dynasty, around 100 CE, by a palace official in the court of Emperor He known as Cai Lun. While paper cutting was first officially documented by the sixth century, the shapes and themes that characterize the art hearken back to decorative cuttings made using thin leather, fabric, silver foil, and even leaves.

In *The Chosen and the Beautiful,* paper cutting magic appears as a marker of Jordan Baker's lost homeland, something at once beautiful and frightening that ties her to a heritage she has never known. For Jordan, in a world drowning in wonder, the art of paper cutting is a link to her past. In our own world, the history of paper cutting likewise leads us to a rich tradition of folk art and storytelling.

Today, paper cutting is recognized as a fine art, but the cheapness and wide availability of paper has made it one that can be refined and enjoyed by people at all levels of society, and many different styles of paper cutting can be found throughout the world. In China, paper cutting is known as jianzhi. Historically it has been divided into the northern style and the southern style: where paper cutting in the north prioritizes smooth evocative lines, paper cutting in the south is more elaborate, concentrating on very detailed creations using very delicate lines.

Most of the earliest Chinese paper cutting artists were illiterate. Instead of adorning their walls with calligraphy or fine paintings, they decorated their living spaces with attractive paper cuttings produced from the materials they had on hand. Many of the designs were comparatively simple, but others were pieces of great beauty, featuring flowers, animals, and intricate geometric shapes.

Although there were some artists who sold their work professionally, paper cutting was also considered a craft suitable for anyone who could hold a sharp knife or a pair of scissors. It uses the same skills and many of the same tools as fabric cutwork and counted-thread embroidery, and women looking to decorate their homes gravitated towards the graceful forms shaped from colorful paper. These works could be displayed year round, but they were very popular around the Lunar New Year, when paper cuttings would be pasted in fresh paper windows to welcome a new beginning.

While China claims the invention of modern paper, paper cutting as an art is a global phenomenon. The secret of papermaking emerged in Europe during the thirteenth century, and today there are many paper cutting traditions of note. In Germany, there is scherenschnitte, where paper may be folded and then cut to produce art with repeating geometric motifs. The folded snowflake that so many children learn to cut is an example of German scherenschnitte. Paper cutting is also considered a Jewish folk art dating back to the Middle Ages, where paper cutting designs were used to adorn marriage contracts and as holiday decorations. In Japan, paper cutting developed very quickly after the introduction of paper. Japanese paper cutting, known as kirie or kirigami, covers many different styles and produced related art forms, like kamikiri, a performance where an artist cuts paper while taking suggestions from the audience.

Far from being a thing of the past, paper cutting is an art that has moved with the times. No longer restricted to knives and scissors alone, modern paper cutting artists make use of everything from stamps, stencils, and die cutters to holographic paper, multiple layers of exceedingly thin, fine paper, and globally sourced designs. Where once paper cuttings were simply pasted to windows, today they may be framed, mounted, and folded as pieces of 3D art or added to products ranging from furniture to electronic devices.

On the following pages, you will find instructions for how to get started making your own paper cutting art, along with several designs to print or trace!

To learn more about the art of paper cutting and its place in our shared world, consider a visit to the **China Paper Cutting Museum** in Yangzhou, China, the **Guild of American Papercutters National Museum** in Somerset, Pennsylvania, United States, or the **Musuem of Paper** in Amalfi, Italy!

FURTHER READING:

"Resources for Papercutting," the Guild of American Papercutters, papercutters.org/about-papercutting-2/

"35 Creative Uses for Papercutting," *All About Papercutting,* allaboutpapercutting.com/resources/

Eastern-style origami dragons, Origami.me, origami.me/eastern-dragons/

Links, Béatrice Coron. beatricecoron.com/links.html

HOW TO CUT PAPER

Khai, Bai, and the rest of the paper cutting troupe make paper cutting look easy, and while it takes years to learn to make the intricate paper cuttings that they have mastered, there's nothing stopping you from making simpler designs for your own home!

GATHER YOUR TOOLS

While you can cut paper designs with nothing more than a stable surface and a craft knife, there are some other tools that can help you get a clearer, cleaner end result. A cutting mat and masking or artist's tape will make things much easier for you.

CHOOSING YOUR PAPER

You can make paper cuttings with nearly any paper. Your local craft store will have plenty of decorative papers to choose from or you can look around your house for spare paper that might work for this purpose. Remember that it is easier to cut thin paper than thick paper, but thin paper is easier to tear. Printer paper is actually a bad choice for this art, as it blunts your craft knife very quickly.

PICKING A DESIGN

You can freehand a sketch on the back of your decorative paper or you can use a stencil to create your desired design. There are also kits that come with designs printed onto the decorated paper, and you can simply cut them out directly. Remember that when applying a design to the back of the paper that it should be reversed so that it is correct when the paper cutting is turned over to the right side.

SECURE YOUR WORK

Tape your work to a cutting mat using masking or artist's tape. If you are working with a stencil, put your decorative paper down first, and then place the stencil on top of it, securing them with tape. This prevents the paper from slipping and allows you to make cuts with confidence. Some people like to cut from the back of a piece of paper, while others like to cut from the front—in general, the side of the paper facing down as you cut will have a neater look.

CUT, CUT, CUT

Using your craft knife, start by cutting out the smallest pieces of the design first. As the larger pieces are removed, the paper becomes less stable, and the smaller pieces will be harder to do. Work from the center of the design out to the edges. As you get to the larger pieces of the design, turn your work so that you are still making controlled cuts. Remove the pieces as you go so you can see your progress. If you accidentally cut through an element of the design, you can always repair it with a tiny sliver of tape applied afterwards from the back.

FINISHING UP

When your design is cut out completely, remove it from the mat. At this point, you can frame it with another decorative piece of paper behind it, tape it to a window, or glue it to something that needs to be a little prettier!

THE CHOSEN AND THE BEAUTIFUL
NGHI VO

FALLING FLOWERS

GOLDFISH

PEACH
Symbol of Immortality, Marriage, Springtime

ABOUT THE AUTHOR

CJ Foeckler

NGHI VO is the author of the novels *Siren Queen* and *The Chosen and the Beautiful*, as well as the acclaimed novellas *When the Tiger Came Down the Mountain* and *The Empress of Salt and Fortune*, a Locus and Ignyte Award finalist, and the winner of the Crawford Award and the Hugo Award. Born in Illinois, she now lives on the shores of Lake Michigan. She believes in the ritual of lipstick, the power of stories, and the right to change your mind.

nghivo.com
Twitter: @NghiVoWriting
Goodreads: Nghi Vo

CPSIA information can be obtained
at www.ICGtesting.com
Printed in the USA
LVHW110427080422
715631LV00003B/141